DE

by

SAM HASTINGS

CHIMERA

Destroying Angel published by
Chimera Publishing Ltd
PO Box 152
Waterlooville
Hants
PO8 9FS

Printed and bound in Great Britain by
Cox & Wyman Ltd, Reading.

DESTROYING ANGEL

Sam Hastings

This novel is fiction – in real life practice safe sex

Berner put one of his hands on the back of Susan's head and twisted a handful of hair into his fist. His cock was rock-solid in her mouth, a hard rod of flesh on which he was pulling her face slowly up and down, controlling her as he fucked her mouth. He pulled clear, then put the tip of his cock against her lips. She pursed them obligingly, letting him penetrate her mouth and slide it in until it was squashed to the very back of her throat and she started to gag.

'That's good,' he sighed, once more starting the same action.

Chapter One

Susan MacQuillan squeezed the sponge over Paulette's chest, washing away the lather of bubble bath foam and leaving her flatmate's big dark breasts completely visible. Each breast was a full handful of glossy flesh the colour of dark chocolate, firm and tipped with yet darker nipples. Susan felt tempted to touch, perhaps stroking a nipple to test Paulette's reaction, but hesitated, unsure if such an action would count as service.

'Service' was the two women's agreement to take turns in acting as each other's maid between six and nine each evening. The idea was to provide the luxury of being waited on without having to incur the expense. It had been working well for several weeks, Susan's only difficulty being the strong sexual need that the intimate contact with Paulette always provoked.

'So why so tired?' Susan asked, partially to keep her mind off her friend's glorious breasts and partially out of genuine curiosity.

Paulette, a freelance journalist who covered London's social scene, normally took her work in her stride. Today had been different. It should have been Paulette's turn to be maid, but she had arrived back at the flat an hour later than usual, clearly flustered and begging Susan to swap days. Susan, whose work as a private investigator left her with gaps between periods of frantic activity, had taken sympathy on her flatmate and agreed. She also preferred to serve Paulette than the other way around, taking what she recognised as a distinctly masochistic pleasure in pretending to be the black girl's servant.

Susan had run the bath and poured a glass of wine while

Paulette undressed, only letting her curiosity get the better of her when her passion for Paulette threatened to do so instead.

'Would you do me a favour?' Paulette asked.

'Sure,' Susan replied, surprised at the response to her question and wondering if the favour might just possibly include soaping Paulette's chest for her.

'I think I've got a really good story,' Paulette continued, 'maybe even more than that, but I need some information from the police.'

'I'll try,' Susan said doubtfully. 'I can't promise anything though, it's been over two years since I resigned.'

'You've still got contacts,' Paulette answered.

'Some,' Susan admitted, 'but I didn't get on that well with my colleagues; that's part of the reason I left. Anyway, what's the story?'

'It's complicated,' Paulette began, lying back in the bath until only her head and the swell of her breasts were clear of the water and bubbles. 'Massage my neck, could you? Yes, that's nice... a bit harder... perfect...'

'Carry on,' Susan urged as her hands worked on the muscles of Paulette's neck beneath the water.

'There was this guy called Alan Sowerby, a freelance like me but pretty well established,' Paulette continued. 'He used to specialise in food, wine, restaurants; that sort of thing. I met him a couple of times but we didn't get on; he was really pompous. Use your nails a bit... Yes, thanks Susan, that's so nice.'

Susan changed the rhythm of her fingers, sliding her nails gently across the skin of Paulette's shoulders, then repeating the action more firmly. Paulette sighed, leaning forward so that Susan could get at more of her back. Susan continued to stroke, trying to ignore the warm wet feeling between her legs.

'So,' Paulette continued, 'I was quite surprised when I went into the Pipe of Port for lunch and the owner asked

6

if I could give Sowerby's briefcase back to him. It seems the guy remembered us talking and thought I was a friend of Sowerby's. I said I would because I'd been invited to a brandy tasting in the afternoon, and Sowerby was sure to be there.

'Of course I couldn't resist having a look inside, so I went and sat in Hyde Park and had a good rummage. Naughty, I know, but I've always been too nosy for my own good. Anyway, most of it was just long-winded notes for his work, but there was one bit that caught my attention. He'd tasted some wines at a restaurant and had decided that they weren't what they said on the label. Apparently, they were so poor in comparison with what they were supposed to be, he was certain they were fakes. That's lovely thanks, I feel much more relaxed. Could you get me another glass?'

Susan went to fill Paulette's glass, her mind hardly on her friend's story, but instead wondering if she could lay some hint to Paulette that she would be more than willing to have sex with her. It would have to be something subtle, and something that she could pull back from if Paulette didn't respond. As she watched the pale liquid splash into the glass, it occurred to Susan that by playfully extending her role as maid, she might just get what she wanted.

As Susan came back into the bathroom, Paulette turned onto her front, propping herself up on one arm. Her bottom showed above the suds, a chubby brown peach just begging for kisses. Susan knelt down by the bath and passed her friend the glass, hoping that her position gave the signals it was intended to.

'So,' Paulette resumed her story, 'when I got to the tasting, Sowerby wasn't there. But I did recognise a friend of his and asked if he was coming. The friend looked really shocked and told me that Sowerby had died of food poisoning only a couple of weeks ago!'

'Oh no!' Susan put in.

'I felt really embarrassed,' Paulette continued, 'and I felt I'd look really bad carrying his briefcase around when I'd hardly known him, so I didn't give it to him...' Paulette stopped talking, instead toying nervously with the stem of her glass. 'This is going to sound really bad,' she said after a while. 'You'll probably think I'm a real bitch.'

'No,' Susan assured her, 'tell me.'

'It's just...' Paulette began, 'well... you see, it's like this. If I was the one who discovered a really big wine scandal, then my reputation would be made, and Sowerby had been on to something that he obviously thought was major... Anyway, that's why I didn't hand over the briefcase. Am I a bitch?'

'Not really,' Susan said, more intent on soothing Paulette than worrying about the ethics of her behaviour. 'After all, I'm sure Sowerby would want the scandal to come out.'

'I suppose so,' Paulette admitted, 'but I still feel bad.'

'So how can I help?' Susan asked, keen to get off an area of conversation that threatened to subdue the normally bubbly Paulette.

'Well, Sowerby didn't know that much,' Paulette replied, once more enthusiastic, 'or if he did, he didn't write it down. You're a detective, so I thought you might help me. I mean, I spent the whole of this afternoon running around trying to find out more and got nowhere. You've been in CID; you'd know what to do.'

'Perhaps,' Susan admitted, 'but what did you want from the police?'

'To find out if there was anything suspicious about Sowerby's death.'

'Surely you don't think he was murdered?'

'Maybe,' Paulette replied, sounding slightly defensive. 'After all, if he exposed a big fraud, a lot of people would lose out.'

'True,' Susan admitted, 'but you said he died of food

poisoning.'

'That's the thing,' Paulette continued. 'It was liver failure from some poisonous toadstool called "Destroying Angel".'

'Poor guy, but these things happen,' Susan remarked.

'Not to Alan Sowerby,' Paulette replied. 'The one long conversation I did have with him was mainly him telling me how much he knew about food; especially fungi. He was going on about ceps and truffles and loads of other things I'd never heard of. No, he'd have known better.'

'Maybe,' Susan answered sceptically.

'Won't you do it then?' Paulette asked, sounding disappointed.

'For you, of course I will,' Susan answered. 'But don't expect too much, okay?'

'Thanks; I won't.'

'Now, what would you like your maid to do, Miss Richards?' Susan asked, keen not to let the moment slip away.

Small and not strictly necessary services and courtesies had already become part of the game: polishing shoes, addressing each other formally, and other little touches. Susan wondered if it could be taken a step further.

'Oh, let me see,' Paulette replied in an exaggeratedly haughty tone. 'Well, first of all, you can towel me down, and then serve me some more wine. Then dinner, I think.'

'Yes, Miss Richards,' Susan answered, her pulse racing at the thought of drying Paulette. She turned to take a warm towel from the radiator, holding it open as Paulette stood up in the bath. Looking surreptitiously at the black girl's body, Susan wondered if she could hold her pretence much longer. Paulette was tiny, shorter even than Susan herself, whose height had almost barred her from the police force. She was also exceptionally pretty in an impish, mischievous way, and her lack of height only served to exaggerate the size of her breasts and the fullness of the

9

hips which flared out below a trim waist and a firm round tummy. A dense tangle of black hair hid her sex, an area of her body which Susan found her eyes drawn irresistibly towards.

As Paulette turned to climb out of the bath she showed her chubby bottom for just an instant, then had backed into the towel which Susan was holding out, taking the edges and wrapping it around her. Susan began to press sections of the towel against Paulette's body, trembling with every touch of the firm flesh. She could sense a faint, musky scent, intensely feminine and mingled with a trace of some exotic perfume. Taking the towel from Paulette's hands, Susan began to rub it against her friend's back, then her waist, rising, drying the smooth flesh over her ribcage. Susan shut her eyes as she took a full breast in each hand, feeling their weight through the towel. Finally the wonderful, plump breasts that she had been fantasising over for weeks were in her hands, full, heavier than her own, the big, black nipples half-stiff under her fingers.

Susan lingered as long as she dared and then carried on to dry Paulette's upper chest and neck. If the black girl had noticed the extra attention that had been paid to her boobs, she gave no sign of it, instead putting her hands on her head so that Susan could dry under her arms. What Susan wanted to do was drop the towel and take Paulette's breasts in her hands again, kissing the nape of her neck and soothing her while she stroked her nipples to full hardness.

It was more than she dared, even though she was trembling with lust and could hardly believe that Paulette was unaware of the state she was in. She moved lower, trying to remove the temptation of Paulette's breasts, only to find herself faced with the prospect of towelling an equally alluring bottom. It was irresistible and, a moment later, she had folded Paulette's bottom in the towel. Paulette responded by sticking it out a little, which was

10

just too much for Susan. Sinking to her knees, she let the towel drop and planted a gentle, but deliberate, kiss on her friend's bottom.

That was it. She'd done it. She'd made an obviously sexual move which Paulette couldn't possibly miss nor misinterpret. Susan found herself blushing, her heart in her mouth as she waited for her friend's response; good or bad. None came, surprising Susan but tempting her to kiss the smooth skin again.

'Do maids normally kiss their mistresses there?' Paulette asked, all mock innocence.

'If they're told to,' Susan answered, her throat suddenly dry with expectation. Paulette wasn't shocked, or cross, or embarrassed, but she did seem keen to continue the game. 'Was I bad?'

Susan kissed Paulette's bottom again, this time lower and more slowly, pressing her face against the resilient flesh. She wanted Paulette to tell her she was bad and to be made to take her jeans and pants down for a spanking across the beautiful black girl's lap.

'Was I?' she repeated when Paulette didn't answer.

'Yes,' Paulette eventually said, 'but not as bad as me for teasing you.'

'Teasing me?' Susan queried, realising at once that every casual exposure of Paulette's body, every cheeky remark and every apparently accidental sexy pose for the last few weeks had been deliberate. 'Why didn't you say you wanted me?'

'I wasn't sure you'd want to,' Paulette answered, 'and I wanted you to make the first move. I'm sorry—' Paulette broke off, sighing as Susan's tongue traced a slow line up the cleft of her bottom, then spoke again, more hesitantly.

'You could make me sorry by putting the bath-brush across my behind...' she said, trailing off.

Susan stopped licking, realising there was a small problem. She had guessed that Paulette enjoyed the idea of spanking from earlier conversations, but had always hoped it would be herself who got her bottom smacked if anything ever happened. During a brief spell of duty in the Carapine Islands, Susan had been regularly spanked, not only by her boyfriend but also by his sister, which had given her a taste for it. George and Maria Lyle had been big, powerfully built Caribbeans who had found it not only exciting but highly amusing to spank Susan, an attitude which Susan had found gave her an exquisite thrill of erotic humiliation.

Getting Paulette to carry on where Maria Lyle had left off had been on Susan's mind ever since they had moved into the flat together. For all Paulette's small size, she had a vivacious, almost aggressive slant to her personality that greatly appealed to Susan. Unfortunately, now that she finally had what she wanted in her grasp, it turned out that what Paulette wanted was the same as her rather than its compliment.

'I was rather hoping you'd do that to me,' she admitted, 'please?'

'Susan!' Paulette responded, sounding more than a little frustrated.

'I am the maid,' Susan continued, aware that she sounded both defensive and rather pathetic.

'But…' Paulette began softly, and then suddenly with a sharper tone, 'oh okay, but really!'

Before Susan could respond in any way, Paulette had rounded on her and pushed her to the floor.

'Hey!' she squeaked, trying not to giggle as Paulette turned her face down and settled her bare bottom across Susan's shoulders, pressing her face to the tiles.

'Okay then, girl,' Paulette growled as she squeezed her hand under Susan's belly and fumbled for the button of her jeans. 'You wanted it; you're going to get it!'

Susan did start to giggle and kick as Paulette unfastened her jeans and tugged them down over her hips. Her panties followed immediately, Susan sighing as her bottom was bared for punishment. It had always been her favourite moment, maybe even better than the actual spanking; that exquisite instant when her pants were pulled down and her naked bottom was exposed to whoever was about to discipline her.

With Maria Lyle, it had started out on the seat of Susan's uniform skirt, then with the skirt pulled up and her panties her only protection, finally with Susan's white bottom bare. On her return from the Carapines, her experience of bare-bottomed beatings had increased, including sessions with hairbrushes, several men's belts, a cane and birch twigs. However hard her punishment, having her pants taken down had always been the most exquisite, delicious indignity. Now Paulette was doing the same, peeling Susan's most intimate garment away without a thought of leaving her any modesty.

'Right, girl,' Paulette said, her weight shifting on Susan's back as she reached for the bath-brush, 'I'm going to smack your lily-white behind until it's the colour of a tomato!'

Susan sighed and then yelped as Paulette brought the brush down hard across her bottom. It was the first spanking she'd had in a while, and she'd forgotten how much it stung, especially with a wooden implement in place of a hand. Paulette laughed at Susan's response and brought the brush down again, even harder, then once more before Susan had even time to get her breath back.

Paulette laughed aloud as she watched Susan's bottom wobble under the brush, the soft, white flesh turning rapidly pink. Even though most of her fantasies involved being on the receiving end of a punishment spanking, she was thoroughly enjoying using the brush on her flatmate's naked behind.

Each impact of the brush made a meaty smack with Susan's bottom, drawing a fresh yelp from the kicking, wriggling girl. Paulette carried on, laughing at her friend's

13

struggles and the way her bottom bounced and quivered with each smack. Susan's breath was coming in short gasps, her hips bucking to the rhythm of her beating, making her cheeks part to show Paulette brief glimpses of dark hair and the wrinkled spot of her bottom-hole.

Unlike Susan, Paulette had always felt the need of a spanking, revelling not just in the physical sensation of a warm bottom but in a wonderful feeling of release that only came with being thoroughly punished. Also unlike Susan, she didn't take her pleasure from the humiliation of the experience, indeed not even finding it humiliating. Instead, she felt that regular chastisement was something she deserved, simply for being her cheeky, teasing self.

Like Susan, however, she had wanted to play from the first, finding Susan's petite muscular figure, girlish haircut and sensitive yet determined character immensely appealing.

Only when Susan began to sob did Paulette stop spanking her, dismounting and kissing her friend tenderly before taking her gently by the hand and leading her into the bedroom. Susan followed, rubbing her bottom and looking at the floor, but with her mouth set in a happy smile.

Paulette knew how the game went. She herself had played it many times before. Susan would now be compliant to whatever she wanted; Paulette's plaything until they had both come and were lying in each other's arms.

Paulette turned and sat on the edge of the bed, motioning Susan down to a kneeling position between her knees. She saw Susan gulp, her eyes rising to look her in the face, and then travelling down over her throat, breasts and belly, coming to rest on the moist pink flesh of her pussy. Susan's tongue popped out, moistening her lips as Paulette curled a hand around the back of her head and took her gently but firmly by the hair. A whimper escaped the well-spanked girl's mouth as Paulette eased her down between her legs, watching Susan's mouth open and sighing as her friend's lips touched her vagina.

'Oh, Susan,' Paulette managed, as the tip of Susan's tongue found her clitoris and started to lap. She began to stroke Susan's hair, her thighs squeezing together as her muscles started to give the small, rhythmic contractions that came before orgasm. It was happening really fast, far faster than she had expected. She screamed as her orgasm hit her, then again, pulling Susan's face hard against her pussy. Every muscle in her body tensed, then abruptly relaxed, and she was lying panting on the bed.

A moment later, Susan climbed up on top of her and they were in each other's arms, kissing. Without a word they worked their way under the covers, Susan lying back as Paulette burrowed down the bed to return the favour she had just taken.

Detective Inspector Ted Gage kicked at a piece of charred wood and stuck his hands deeper into his pockets. The wood snapped, releasing a puff of ash into the damp morning air. Around him, firemen still worked among the burnt-out remains of what had been a furniture warehouse. 'World of Pine', a collapsed sign declared from on top of what had once been a reception desk. The rest of the warehouse was much the same: a smouldering ruin, the stock either burnt or soaked beyond restoration. Not that it had been good furniture, he considered, looking critically at a piece of wet chipboard from which staples protruded at odd angles, but it was still a pity.

What was worse was that it was the fifth similar fire in three months. The MO was always the same: a warehouse at the edge of a big trading estate, a petrol bomb through a high window and that was it. The fires had been scattered across London, but most had been in the east or north. Gage had little doubt that they were linked, and almost as little that whoever was doing it had no deep or complex motive but was simply out for kicks: a fire-raiser.

That was what made the case so difficult and so frustrating. The vast majority of crimes were committed either for gain or because people couldn't get along. In both cases there was always something to go on; leads to be traced, motives to be investigated, suspects and witnesses to interview. With the fire-raiser, it was different. He struck at night, randomly, and taking good care not to be caught on estate surveillance cameras. That was what made the bastard so hard to catch, but neither the press nor his Superintendent saw it that way.

The press were particularly irritating. On the one hand they would write serious articles on the inadequacy of the police in coping with a task that, from the way they made it look, should have been easy. Then they would produce a huge picture of one of the fires and several paragraphs of dramatic text. Gage could imagine the fire-raiser gloating over the articles, pasting cuttings on his wall in some grubby bed-sit, and when the fuss died down going out to do another one so that he'd be back in the papers. Nicknaming him the Fire Ghost hadn't helped either, a name that was sure to boost his ego and might also spawn copycats.

Detective Superintendent Keeson was nearly as bad. Gage's record was good, if not spectacular, and he had handled some pretty tough cases in his time. He got results, even if they were usually down to long experience, patience and hard grind rather than brilliant detective work. The way Keeson spoke, anybody would have thought Gage was an idiot beat-pounder, being told off for not following the book. What was especially galling was having to take orders from a woman, and a woman two years younger than him at that. Okay, so Julia Keeson did have an enviable record that had earnt her fast track promotion, but it was still annoying to be her subordinate.

Between them, the press and Julia Keeson were putting a lot of pressure on him that would not otherwise have been there. Five fires and still he had no lead. Still, it was just possible that the remains of the World of Pine would reveal clues where the previous four fires had failed to do so.

Gage turned, watching the sun rise above the skyline of Walthamstow to the east, its orange light reflecting briefly in the oily waters of the Lee Valley canal. The air had the typical feel of a summer morning, cool and fresh, promising another hot dry day. Had it not been for the smells of smoke and molten plastic, the scene would have been rather pleasant, for all the surrounding industrial squalor of Edmonton. Opposite him, across the canal, were buildings of grey concrete and crumbling red brick, a double line of pylons and a half-built flyover; hardly an idyllic scene. Nevertheless, the canal had a certain tranquillity, with its perfectly smooth surface and ragged line of early morning fishermen spaced out along the bank. For a moment, Gage wondered if one of the fishermen might be the fire-raiser, come to watch the aftermath of his crime. He dismissed the idea as fanciful, or at least impractical from an investigative point of view.

Turning back to the wreckage of the World of Pine, he sought out the owner, a Mohammed Khan, and steeled himself to the inevitable angry interview.

Paulette curled herself into a comfortable position on the bed and opened Alan Sowerby's diary. Naked under a light robe, she felt drowsy and satisfied. With one hand she began to turn the pages, the other gently stroking her bottom. She read quickly, scanning the words as her fingers, and her thoughts, lingered on the roughened lines of skin where Susan had put six strokes across her bottom with a length of bamboo.

Most of Sowerby's remarks had no obvious relevance

17

to the wine scandal he had been intent on exposing. Among his other papers were the original tasting-notes, the name of the restaurant at which he had first become suspicious, and the name of a wholesaler. The name of the wholesaler was de Vergy Fine Wines, a company that Sowerby had clearly viewed as of only moderate importance in the hierarchy of the wine trade.

As she read his diary, it soon became clear that if Sowerby was unimpressed by the company, then the opposite was true of his attitude to its proprietor. A whole page was given over to a description of Annabella de Vergy, Sowerby writing in a manner that managed to be simultaneously pompous and smutty.

Paulette read it with interest, amused at the way he pictured her as an untouchable goddess and then went on to speculate how she might look naked. The description became pretty intimate, although clearly based only on his fantasies. One piece in particular amused her, '...naturally the cunt of such a flower of English womanhood must be a neat purse of soft flesh. No swollen lips and rude red centre, no coarse black hair or dangling labia; such things are for common women, not my glorious golden Annabella. Hair like yellow duck down must hide sweet lips, firm and demurely closed, yet inside moist with the dew of Cupid, awaiting Priapus with both modesty and passion. Deeper, more secret still, her anus will be like a pink rosebud, tiny and puckered, virgin yet eager...'

Paulette laughed out loud at Sowerby's bizarre attitude. On the one hand, he viewed the woman as an immaculate ideal, impossibly perfect. On the other, he wanted to bugger her. A flush of guilt suddenly shot through Paulette at the thought that the author of the purple prose was dead and would doubtless have been horrified by the thought of his words being read. She continued anyway, reminding herself that she was now intent on exposing the scandal he had been so proud of discovering.

There was no evidence that he had done more than fantasise about Annabella de Vergy, but he had met her several times, either at her warehouse or for dinner at her home in Little Venice. Reading on, Paulette discovered that Sowerby had discovered that Annabella's company was the main victim of the scandal. He had gone to great care to inform her gently, as if she were likely to collapse in shock at the news. Given that she was the owner of a presumably successful business, this reaction struck Paulette as unlikely. After that came the most telling remark, Sowerby stating that he had told Annabella de Vergy that she was being cheated by one of her French suppliers. This had been at a dinner party given by Annabella's warehouse manager, a Philip Ruddock.

It didn't say how she was being cheated, or which supplier was involved, and after that the remarks in the diary became increasingly florid as Sowerby became more and more besotted. During July he had seen her once a week or so, still without consummating his passion. Finally the diary came to an abrupt halt in early August, obviously at the point he had left his briefcase in the Pipe of Port.

Paulette shut the diary with a snap and rolled over on the bed. Whatever Susan came up with, the next move was obviously to visit Annabella de Vergy.

Susan shut the door of her car and stood to look out across Hampstead Heath. London was spread out beneath her, towers rising against the clear blue sky, sunlight glinting from windows, the occasional movement of a vehicle, the low line of hills with their two masts to the south. The day was beginning to warm up, but the air was still fresh enough to clear the cobwebs from her head. The previous night was a blur: punishment, sex, more sex and more punishment until she and Paulette had fallen asleep sprawled naked on the bed. In the morning she had been too tired to do more than briefly inspect the state of her bottom and kiss Paulette goodbye, leaving with the clear understanding that going to bed together had been neither an accident nor a mistake.

Their sex had been good – wonderful, in fact – uninhibited and passionate, driven by having wanted each other for weeks before it had actually happened. There was a pleasant, sexy ache to her bottom: sexy because it reminded her of what Paulette had done with her hand, the bath-brush, a long-handled hairbrush, and finally a length of bamboo that they had borrowed from its normal job of propping up the cheese-plant. Not that Paulette had gotten away with it, Susan remembered, chuckling to herself at the memory of Paulette kneeling naked on the bed with her lovely bottom stuck up and six purple stripes standing out across the dark velvet of her cheeks. She shivered at the memory and turned her attention back to the cityscape.

She blew out her cheeks, still feeling a touch of tiredness, even after driving up to the Heath. Alan Sowerby had lived in Highgate and, by good fortune, one of Susan's ex-colleagues was stationed nearby. Not that Paul Berner would have been her ideal choice, she considered. As a DC, he had been brash and cock-sure, making no secret of fancying her but ruining his chances by behaving like a chauvinistic pig, both on duty and off. Since then he had gained promotion to Detective Sergeant. So much she had discovered during their brief telephone conversation, and the higher rank seemed only to have added to his laddishness and self-assurance.

Walking down to the police station, she considered her best strategy. Berner had no reason to make life easy for her, but he had always fancied her and might well be persuaded to look up the information that Paulette wanted about Sowerby on the national police computer. Better still, he might have been involved with the Sowerby case, assuming the death had warranted a police investigation.

20

That was the crux of the matter. Paulette's reasoning struck Susan as somewhat dramatic, also over-abstract: qualities that might be useful in a reporter but had little place in detection. Susan preferred a combination of hard fact and statistical analysis. Sowerby had been a gourmet, constantly sampling exotic dishes that most people would never even know about. He had died of poisoning from a lethal toadstool, the Destroying Angel, *Amanita Virosa*.

Susan had looked the species up, finding an unremarkable white fungus not unlike a field mushroom. Sowerby had been a writer, not a scientist, and it seemed perfectly reasonable to Susan that he might have made a fatal mistake. The thing was also rare and unquestionably lethal. Sowerby had been an expert on edible fungi, true, but that didn't mean he was also an expert on poisonous ones.

Susan reached the police station and jumped up the front steps. It was a tall building of red brick, the old-fashioned blue lamp still in place over the main door. The desk sergeant called for Berner at her request, and a minute later he appeared.

'Paul, hi,' she greeted him as he pushed open the door that led into the interior of the station.

'Susan, you haven't changed at all,' he replied, extending his hand. 'Still as sexy as ever.'

Nor have you, Susan thought, noting that he had waited for the exact instant that the desk sergeant was out of hearing before making his remark. Actually he had changed, she corrected herself, at least physically. A little bald patch had started on the crown of his head and his face had picked up a line or two. Even at training college, when he had been among the best-looking of the cadets, there had been something sleazy about him. Now his looks were fading but the sleaziness was more pronounced than ever.

'What can I do for you?' Berner asked affably, turning

back to Susan as he made his way along the passage.

'I was wondering if you could give me some information?' Susan asked.

'Maybe,' Berner replied. 'Look, my governor's out; let's use his office.'

'Sure,' Susan replied as she followed him up a flight of stairs.

Berner said nothing more until he was seated behind the desk in the DI's office, then flipped a cigarette into his mouth and offered one to Susan. She declined and watched him go through the motions of lighting up. She remembered his habit of smoking, something that particularly disgusted her and another reason that she had never accepted a date with him.

'So,' he asked, 'what's up?'

'I wanted to know about a man called Sowerby, Alan Sowerby,' Susan began, deciding to cut straight to the point. 'He died a few weeks ago, ostensibly of food poisoning. I need to know if his death was considered suspicious.'

'That's tricky,' Berner answered, sucking air between his teeth, an irritating mannerism Susan remembered from when they had been colleagues. 'It wasn't a case I had anything to do with, or I'd remember; and, as you well know, we're not supposed to take stuff off the computer for any old Joe Public who walks in.'

'I'm not any old Joe Public,' Susan answered. 'I'm an ex-colleague and a private investigator as well.'

'Well...' Berner answered, once more sucking air between his teeth.

'Come on, Paul,' Susan urged, 'it won't take a second.'

'Hmm...' Berner continued, wheeling the chair back from the desk and sitting back casually with his knees apart. 'Maybe, but...'

It took Susan a fraction of a second to realise what he wanted. He'd been notorious for it, boasting about how many blow-jobs he got and how many girls were eager to suck him.

'Paul—' she began to remonstrate, only to be cut off by his sly smile and a gentle shake of his head.

'Come on, Susan, it won't take a second,' he quipped, imitating her voice as his hand went to his zip.

'For goodness' sake, Paul,' Susan protested. 'You can't just—'

'Oh, yes, I can,' Berner answered, 'and it won't be the first time.'

'Don't be a dirty bastard, Paul,' Susan tried, hoping to play on whatever sense of morality he might have left. 'You just can't expect me to do that—'

'Come on,' Berner broke in, 'a quick blow-job never hurt anyone. You should be pleased to get the offer from a good-looking guy like me.'

'I—' Susan started, barely able to believe Berner's sheer arrogance.

'Jesus, you girls make a fuss,' Berner exclaimed. 'What's the big deal? You open your mouth, in goes my cock, you suck a bit, I come, you swallow, it's all over. No big deal, right?'

'No, it's not right,' Susan snapped. 'It's a really intimate thing to do! Especially if you come!'

His expression hardened at her reluctance. 'It's simple,' he said quietly. 'You want your information, you suck my cock. You don't want it, you don't have to suck me. Take your pick.'

'I...' Susan began again, only to stop, unsure how to continue. She looked out of the window to the jumble of red-brick houses and tiled roofs that stood to the rear of the station. Berner was an oily self-satisfied bastard, yet the combination of talking dirty and his very arrogance were starting to get to her. One thing was certain, he wasn't going to back down. If she wanted her information she was going to have to do what he demanded. She needed the information, but did she need it that badly?

'Come on, Susie, you know you want to,' Berner wheedled.

'That's what you think,' she answered, half-intent on not ending up on her knees with his cock in her mouth, half-wanting exactly that.

'Hey, look,' he said. 'If it's your precious pride or reputation or whatever you're worrying about, then don't. It'll just be between us, and come on, you know you'll enjoy it.'

'Isn't there something else you might want?' Susan asked desperately.

'A shag?'

'No—' Susan started hotly, then stopped. It was hopeless.

'Come on, Susie,' Berner said.

'Okay!' she snapped. 'Okay... But at least have the decency to lock the door.'

'Good point, good point,' Berner remarked as he got to his feet. 'Oh, and you can get your tits out, too. I've always wanted to see your tits.'

'Oh, for goodness' sake,' Susan answered him, starting to unbutton her blouse as the latch snapped into place on the door lock.

'Good girl,' Berner remarked, watching Susan expose the swell of her breasts with undisguised relish. 'I'm going to enjoy this. I always did think you'd look good with your face wrapped around my cock.'

'I'm sure you did,' Susan responded. 'You always were a dirty bastard. Look, you can come on my boobs or in your hand, but not in my mouth, okay?'

'Fair enough,' Berner agreed. 'But I don't see why you're so fussy.'

Because you're a slime-ball, she thought as he slouched back in the chair and once more spread his knees wide. She had reached the lowest button of her blouse and was

24

pulling the tails out of her jeans, having decided to take it off rather than risk making a mess of it. He pulled his zip down as she unclipped her bra, flopping his cock into his hand as her breasts were bared to his lecherous gaze.

'Oh, they're nice,' he leered, beginning to stroke his penis. 'Lovely and big. Did you know the boys used to call you Peaches?'

'No,' Susan admitted, somewhat flattered despite herself. She took off her bra and hung it on the back of the chair with her blouse. Berner's cock was semi-stiff, the foreskin beginning to roll back.

'Come on, show them off,' he demanded.

Susan reluctantly cupped a breast in each hand, holding them together and then leaning forward to make the best of her cleavage. Berner sat with his eyes fixed on her, his fingers moving his foreskin up and down as his cock expanded. Susan bounced her breasts in her hands and ran her thumbs over the nipples, making them erect.

'Your tits are gorgeous, Susie,' Berner said. 'Now come and get that pretty mouth around my cock.'

Susan hesitated for a moment, and then walked around the desk and knelt between his legs, his cock inches from her face. Intent on teasing him, she stroked her fingernails slowly down his shaft, making him expel his breath with a sharp hiss.

'Come on then, love, get on with it,' Berner said, his voice slightly hoarse.

She took his cock gingerly in her hand and held it, squeezing gently and feeling the thick shaft pulse. It was pale and rather fleshy, sprouting up from a nest of dark hair: an obscene sight – deliciously obscene. Reasoning that she might as well make the best of it, Susan tweaked down the front of Berner's jockey shorts and pulled out his balls, cupping them in her hand as she stroked his cock.

'You're loving this, aren't you?' Berner said thickly. 'I

always knew you were a tart underneath.'

Instead of answering, Susan gulped his cock into her mouth and started to suck. He tasted salty and male, his prick thickening quickly as she slid her lips up and down the shaft. Berner's words were coarse, insulting, but that was exactly what was starting to turn her on. That, and being made to suck his cock. To have to kneel topless on the office floor with a man's erection in her mouth was wonderfully rude, dirty, undignified, and exactly the sort of thing that excited her.

She started playing with his balls, stroking and squeezing them as his cock reached full erection in her mouth. He was quite big, much bigger than she'd have expected from its size when limp. She pulled back briefly to admire it, a fat, swollen prick rearing up over good-sized balls. Suddenly, she genuinely wanted to suck it, to feel the lovely thickness in her mouth, to work eagerly and obediently on his prick.

As she sucked and Berner began to moan, her fantasies turned to exploit the full potential of the situation. Maybe she should be stripped naked and fucked over the desk. It would be nice to be beaten first; to have his belt taken to her plump white bottom, then forced to suck him again, and finally to have him use her vagina, rough and hard until she was moaning and begging for it. Perhaps he'd even put it up her bottom, not bothering to ask, but just casually bum-shagging her while he smoked his filthy cigarette with one hand and carelessly fondled her tits with the other. Yes, that would be perfect: beaten and then buggered by a man who just took her as if it was something to do for a laugh.

Berner put one of his hands on the back of Susan's head and twisted a handful of hair into his fist. His cock was rock-solid in her mouth, a hard rod of flesh on which he was pulling her face slowly up and down, controlling her as he fucked her mouth. He pulled clear, then put the tip of his cock against her lips. She pursed them obligingly, letting him penetrate her mouth and slide it in until it was squashed to the very back of her throat and she started to gag.

'That's good,' he sighed, once more starting the same action.

Susan let her fantasy run, although determined to give him only what he had asked for and nothing more. Despite that, she sneaked one hand between her legs to surreptitiously stroke her pussy through her jeans, rubbing the swollen lips and sending little thrills through her body. As he started to grunt and thrust his hips she knew he was approaching orgasm. Despite her mounting pleasure, she still didn't want him to come in her mouth. She tried to pull back, but was held steady by the fist in her hair. His cock jerked and suddenly her mouth was full of salty sperm. He let go and Susan pulled back, only to receive a second jet of seed all over her breasts. She reluctantly swallowed his copious emission.

'Oh, Susie, you fucking gorgeous little tart,' he rasped as he hit the peak of his orgasm.

She slumped back, looking down at her splashed boobs, and aware that it was also on her chin. 'Dirty bastard!' she managed. 'I told you not to!'

'Ah, you love it!' Berner said as he relaxed back into the chair. 'Fuck me, but that was good. Do you want to come? You can do it in front of me if you like.'

'No thank you,' Susan answered pointedly, although she actually needed her own orgasm quite badly. Berner was just too arrogant, and she knew that if she let go and masturbated in front of him it would just make him all the more cock-sure. 'Could you just pass me a tissue?'

Berner obliged, and then pulled his chair towards the computer. Susan moved to let him closer to it, and then stood up, doing her best to clean up while he tapped at the keyboard. By the time she was doing her blouse back up, he had found the information she wanted.

'Sowerby, Alan,' he said. 'Died of liver failure brought on by amanitin poisoning, whatever that is. August twenty-four. No suspicious circumstances, no case.'

'Is that it?' Susan demanded.

'Yup,' Berner answered with a smug grin. 'Like you said, it didn't take a second.'

'Did you know that all along?'

'Yup.'

'You bastard!'

'Oh, come on Sue,' Berner laughed, 'don't tell me your panties aren't damp.'

'You...' Susan began and trailed off. It was pointless remonstrating with him, and he was right, anyway, her panties were very damp indeed. 'Okay, fair enough.'

'I'll see you out,' Berner offered, getting to his feet.

'Don't bother,' Susan replied, 'especially as you'd probably want another blow-job for making the effort.'

'Any time you like, love.'

Susan left the police station in a mixture of rage and frustrated excitement. Berner's behaviour had utterly humiliated her, but it was just the sort of sexual humiliation she always fantasised over. She desperately needed an orgasm but was pleased that she hadn't succumbed to her feelings and begged Paul Berner to fuck her over his DI's desk. As she came back in sight of the Heath, she began to wonder if she dared risk a sneaky frig among the bushes. It was a nice idea, but the morning had blossomed into a baking hot day and the Heath was far too crowded to take such a risk. No, her pleasure would have to wait until she got back to the flat. Once there she could strip and masturbate at leisure.

Despite Susan's resolve, things got worse as she approached the car park. The way Paul Berner had squeezed a blow-job out of her, made her show him her tits, then come in her mouth and on her breasts was just too much. She was trembling so much that she was unsure if it would be safe to drive, and her need for an orgasm was becoming desperate.

The car park was packed, her own black Rover wedged between a van and a hulking four-wheel drive. She squeezed into the narrow gap and eventually managed to get into the seat, then realised just how fully enclosed she was and that nobody could possibly see below her waist unless they were actually leaning over the bonnet of her car. Quickly, and before common sense could get the better of her, Susan undid her jeans. A moment later and they were down around her ankles, the air warm on her bare thighs. Her panties were soaking, her pussy tender and ready inside them. She pulled the gusset aside, and sank a finger between the moist lips to find her clitoris. Her mouth opened as she started to rub, using the brisk dabbing motions that always gave the best orgasm. Almost immediately she started to come, her muscles contracting in her thighs and bottom, whimpering to herself despite her best efforts to keep quiet, her whole body bucking as her orgasm hit her. Even as she came a great wave of near-panic hit her. What was she doing, masturbating in a public car park?!

Desperately pulling her jeans up, Susan smiled at a middle-aged woman on the far side of the car park who was giving her a concerned look. After waiting only a few seconds to recover her breath, she turned the ignition and eased the car out onto the road, fully aware that she was blushing furiously.

Chapter Two

Susan found herself blushing at the sound of Paulette's laughter. Ever since she had given Paulette the details of her interview with Paul Berner, the black girl had been teasing her mercilessly. The idea of Susan getting the information she wanted in return for sucking Berner's cock fascinated Paulette, who had demanded a full description. Afterwards, she had taken every opportunity to torment Susan, cheekily sucking a carrot and then licking two hard-boiled eggs held in her palm. Finally, Susan had put Paulette across her knee, bared her bottom and given her the spanking she had been angling for.

Inevitably that had led to sex, leaving both of them too tired to get up until the middle of the morning. Noon now found them at Warwick Road station, about to keep the appointment that Paulette had made with Annabella de Vergy. Paulette had been teasing Susan on the tube, laughing at her own jokes and then again at Susan's answering blushes, only relenting when Susan asked her to be serious.

'It's just possible that this de Vergy woman could be involved as a villain rather than a victim,' Susan cautioned as they walked up to the bridge over the Grand Union Canal. 'You chat away and keep her attention, leave me to observe – okay?'

'Sure,' Paulette answered. 'Which one do you think is her house?' They had turned to look at the line of buildings that flanked the canal: tall ornate structures that spoke of wealth and elegance.

'I don't know,' Susan said, 'but she certainly does well

for herself. Let's see – yes, it's the blue one next to the one with all the flower baskets.'

'She must be loaded,' Paulette remarked.

Susan could only agree. Annabella de Vergy's house was four stories tall – five, counting the attic extension. It was painted a delicate blue with white on the stonework, and was smart, even by the standards of its neighbours.

The two girls descended the steps to the tow path and walked along to the house Susan had picked out.

Their knock was quickly answered. Susan appraised their hostess as she greeted and ushered them inside. Annabella de Vergy pretty well lived up to the image Sowerby had painted of her. Tall, slim and smartly dressed in an all-too-obviously expensive silk dress, she was the very essence of elegance. Golden hair done up in a tight bun and small gold-rimmed glasses gave her a refined haughty touch; high heels and seamed stockings added a hint of old fashioned grace. Her beauty made Susan feel small and rather awkward, like a little girl in the presence of a rich and terribly respectable aunt. She glanced at Paulette, who returned her look with a cheeky smile.

'So you knew poor old Alan,' de Vergy stated as she followed them into the main room of the house. 'Dreadful news about his death, don't you think? Wine, or would you prefer something else? Mint Julep for me, I think. I find it refreshing at this time of day.'

Susan accepted the offer of Mint Julep and looked about her as de Vergy went to mix the cocktails. The room was furnished in black leather, chrome, and smoked glass: elegant, minimalist and obviously expensive. Only the heavy security bars on the windows detracted from the atmosphere, and those were clearly necessary. Annabella de Vergy's taste was modern and sophisticated, an image at odds with the comfortable dignity Susan would have expected to find in the house of a successful member of the British wine trade. Still, she reflected, that just went

31

to show how wrong it was to have preconceptions.

'So how may I help you?' de Vergy asked as she returned with the drinks on a tray.

'Well,' Paulette began, 'I'm sure you remember that Alan was after some sort of wine scandal when he died, and that he felt you were being cheated in some way. I was wondering if you could shed any more light on things?'

Annabella de Vergy laughed, and then gave a little sigh before answering. Susan pretended a casual interest but studied every nuance of movement and speech.

'Oh dear, poor old Alan,' de Vergy started. 'Yes, he was sure there was something going on, but it was all nonsense, you know. You see, Alan was a bit of a romantic, an idealist if you like, but really not very practical.'

'That's true,' Paulette agreed, 'but he was a skilled and experienced taster, surely?'

'Yes, in a way,' de Vergy agreed, 'but that was really rather the problem. You see, Alan had this wonderful, romantic image of wine. He liked to think of poor but honest French peasants tilling the soil and exerting their craft to produce exquisite elixirs, more for love than profit. Of course, it's not really like that at all, and I take a rather more practical attitude I'm afraid: buy cheap and undercut the competition.'

'So what happened?' Paulette asked, sounding both puzzled and crestfallen.

'Oh, the poor boy tasted some wines we import and thought they were fakes,' Annabella replied. 'What he couldn't see was that they were just cheap examples of famous names – Châteauneuf-du-Pape for instance. Perfectly legitimate, but not at all suited to his romantic ideals, I'm afraid. I did tell him he was being silly, but he insisted. Then the poor fellow died like that. It was really terrible. No, I'm afraid there's no scandal to uncover.'

Susan watched de Vergy carefully, weighing her as a possible liar, fraud, and ultimately murderess. It seemed very unlikely indeed. There was nothing about de Vergy's manner that suggested either nervousness or a carefully contrived act. Instead, she seemed entirely genuine.

Sipping her drink, Susan decided that the investigation was almost certainly a dead-end. Alternatively, there might be something to it, but without de Vergy's knowledge: yet it seemed much more likely that the whole scandal had been dreamt up by the over-romantic Alan Sowerby. Having been shown the man's diary by Paulette, Susan could well believe it.

'Oh, right,' Paulette was saying, sounding even more despondent than before.

'I am sorry,' de Vergy replied. 'I've disappointed you. Still, better to know now than later.'

'I was hoping for a story,' Paulette said with a touch of embarrassment. 'I'm sorry to have bothered you.'

'Not at all,' de Vergy answered easily. 'Journalism must be a tough job. Will you stay for lunch?'

They accepted; Susan became increasingly impressed with de Vergy's ease of manner as they ate a lunch of cold meats and salad in the walled garden at the rear of the house. Annabella was clearly a highly successful business woman, neither needing to resort to fraud nor the sort to be taken in by it. No, it was a shame, but the whole thing had evidently existed only in Alan Sowerby's imagination.

It was also possible to see the attraction Sowerby had felt for de Vergy, Susan considered as she watched her hostess' elegant figure emerge from the house with a bottle of chilled white wine. Not that she shared Sowerby's romantic illusions, but on a purely practical level it was nice to imagine herself kneeling naked at Annabella's feet and begging for the privilege of being allowed to kiss one of her immaculate leather shoes. There was something poised, dominant, almost regal about her that appealed to Susan's submissive sexuality, and it was a feeling she was sure Paulette would share. With a touch of amused self-awareness, Susan realised she was a little tipsy and letting her fantasies run away with her.

'Not one of mine,' de Vergy remarked as she sat back down and placed the bottle on the table. 'A sample, of Alsace. We never buy on the UK market, but they still give us endless samples. I'd be interested to know what you think.'

Susan accepted the glass, determined not to make an idiot of herself. Watching both Paulette and Annabella, she imitated their actions. The wine was heady and intense with a perfumed scent. She gave her opinion, drawing an appreciative nod from Annabella. Paulette gave a more detailed analysis, causing Annabella to raise her eyebrows.

'But then a friend of Alan's is bound to know her wines, I suppose,' Annabella remarked, 'although, if I may say so, for a friend of Alan's you seem rather – how can I put it? – relaxed, easy-going, perhaps.'

'He was as much a colleague as a friend,' Paulette admitted. 'We both do restaurant reviews, or rather, we both did. I don't really know much at all, but I've been to enough tastings to know how to go about it.'

They finished the bottle together, chatting easily. Annabella then accepted Susan's request to be shown around the house.

The upper rooms were furnished in much the same manner as the living room, only really varying in their utility. As they went around, Susan kept her eyes open for possibly useful hints, not really expecting to find anything. Glancing into Annabella's bedroom as they passed, she spent a moment admiring the heavy iron bedstead before her eyes were drawn to a photograph. It was in fine-grained black-and-white, and showed a woman lying on a *chaise longue*.

The pose was languid and intensely sensuous, the more so because the model was tightly corseted, bare-breasted and naked between her corset and the tops of her stockings.

Long black-clad legs and her nipped-in waist served to enhance her partial nakedness; high round breasts and svelte hips. Susan found her eyes drawn to the model's vulva, full outer lips showing just a hint of the smaller lips between. She was also toying with a small whip, admiring it with an expression of lazy cruelty. Susan shivered at the implications of the image, only then realising that the model was Annabella de Vergy herself.

'Do you like it?' a soft voice purred from just behind her.

Susan jumped round, already stammering an apology for intruding on Annabella's privacy.

'No, really, what do you think?' Annabella insisted. 'Paulette must see, too. Come in.'

Susan hesitated, feeling like a fly being coaxed slowly into a spider's web. Of course, it would be easy to express indifference, or approval at a merely artistic level.

'Are you shocked?' de Vergy asked, with just a trace of amusement.

'No, no,' Susan responded automatically and immediately realised that she had fallen right into the trap. She now had a choice of making some stuffy remark and withdrawing with as much grace as possible, or of admitting her true feelings. She decided on the latter. 'Actually, I think it's very beautiful.'

'Erotic?' Annabella continued mercilessly.

'Yes,' Susan admitted, knowing that if Annabella ordered her to her knees at that second, she would obey without hesitation.

'Paulette?' Annabella asked.

'Lovely,' Paulette said. 'You've got a cute pussy.'

'Paulette!' Susan exclaimed, astonished at the boldness of her friend's comment.

'Have I, indeed?' Annabella remarked, taking only a second to recover her poise. 'May I ask a rather intimate question?'

'Yes,' Susan answered.

'You two are very intimate,' de Vergy said evenly. 'Are you lovers?'

Susan hesitated for a second, and then nodded.

'In a relationship,' Annabella said, 'a truly sexual relationship, in any case, one partner always tends to dominate. Do you not think?'

'Not really, we—' Susan began, only to be cut off by Annabella.

'With the two of you it is hard to guess which is the dominant,' she continued. 'Paulette seems more aggressive, more open; but you, Susan, you have a control, a firmness about you that suggests you might like to be in charge. Overall, though, I'd surmise that you both prefer to be taken charge of. Am I right?'

'I suppose so,' Susan admitted, feeling deliciously helpless, as if she were already in Annabella's claws.

'She likes a good spanking,' Paulette put in, adding to Susan's humiliation.

'And do you?' Annabella asked Paulette, to Susan's delight.

Susan expected a sulky, contrite admission, much like her own. Instead, Paulette smiled, a mischievous grin that was mirrored in her eyes. Turning, she pulled up her skirt and tugged her panties up between the cheeks of her bottom, displaying the full coffee-coloured globes and the six darker lines that criss-crossed their surface. Susan glanced at Annabella, noticing a flush at her throat.

'Would you like me to add to that?' de Vergy asked, still cool, for all her obvious excitement.

Paulette responded positively and eagerly. Susan hung her head and gave a shy nod.

'Come upstairs,' de Vergy said, her tone anticipating their compliance.

Susan followed up the steep staircase, hypnotised by Annabella's slim silk-encased calves. Paulette took her hand, squeezing it and giving her an excited grin when she turned back. They climbed to the attic and then waited while Annabella unlocked a door that evidently led into the extension.

Susan went in after de Vergy and gazed around. As she had guessed it would be, the room was dedicated to the realisation of Annabella's fantasies. The walls were scrubbed brick, the single large window covered with a thick blind, tacked around the edges. This enhanced the impression of a cellar or dungeon, the only light coming from a yellow panel, soft and dim. Several complex structures of black iron-work and deep red leather stood against the walls, each clearly intended for the restraint of a victim. A rack of whips, canes and straps stood against one wall, with a long cupboard beneath it that Susan guessed contained further sex toys. She swallowed hard, wondering how it would feel to be rendered helpless and punished by Annabella, and sure that she would have every chance to find out.

Paulette was clearly enraptured as well, feeling the padded surface of a whipping-stool with a touch that was really a caress. Remembering Paulette's fantasies of regular punishment to keep her in her place, Susan could see what the black girl was thinking. Annabella would beat her until she was satisfied, indulging Paulette's love of penitence to the full. For Susan, the set-up was less perfect, being too contrived, too deliberate to really fit her fantasies. She would have preferred to be pulled over de Vergy's knee in the bedroom, to have her jeans and panties pulled down and to be spanked with a hand or hairbrush while Paulette laughed at her discomfort. Better still would have been the garden, squealing her way through a bare-bottom spanking like the little brat she was, Annabella not caring in the least that the neighbours witnessed her victim's pain and humiliation.

'You should both be nude,' Annabella was saying, now

haughty and commanding. 'Strip and wait here while I change. There's a bathroom on the floor below.'

Susan began to undress immediately, determined to make the best of the chance to be dominated by Annabella. As the door clicked shut, Susan turned to Paulette and smiled at the eagerness with which her friend was disrobing.

Paulette trembled with anticipation as she tugged her skirt down over her hips. The prospect of punishment had entirely dissolved her disappointment at discovering that Alan Sowerby had been on a wild-goose chase. Annabella de Vergy was absolutely wonderful, not only obviously skilled and experienced in the art of domination, but with the perfect look for it. Tall, slim and athletic in appearance, de Vergy was just the sort of woman Paulette felt ought to be chastising her.

Twice she had deliberately been cheeky, and now she was going to be punished – and punished alongside Susan, which would make the experience even better. Stepping out of her panties, she gathered up the pile of clothes on the floor and scampered downstairs to wash, leaving Susan still only half-undressed.

She passed Susan on the stairs on her return, getting a friendly slap on her bottom as she went by. Back in what she was already thinking of as the dungeon, although it was an attic room, she surveyed Annabella's equipment and wondered which piece of exotic apparatus it would be most fun to use. The whipping-stool tempted, designed to leave her bent almost double with her bum high in the air and everything showing. A pillory had even more potential, as it would leave her totally helpless and fitted beautifully with her fantasy of being punished for real.

The door clicked to behind her and she turned to see Susan, naked and lovely. Susan's reaction to Annabella seemed to be identical to hers, with no trace of jealousy. Not that there was any need to feel any; they would, after all, be together.

'You want to go first, don't you?' Susan asked.

'Please,' Paulette answered. 'I'd like to go in the pillory. Do you think she'd rather choose?'

'Go in it, anyway,' Susan suggested. 'She can always order you out. She might even beat us for trying to anticipate her.'

'That's true,' Paulette replied, hoping that Annabella would do exactly that. She opened the pillory and laid her head and wrists into the holes.

Susan closed the bar, trapping Paulette and immediately bringing the thrill of helplessness. 'You do look sweet,' Susan remarked as she clicked the bolt into place. 'I'd do you myself. In fact, I think I will.'

'Hey!' Paulette protested, but could do nothing as Susan moved behind her and fondled her bottom.

Paulette sighed as Susan's hands caressed her cheeks, squeezing and pulling them apart, her fingers moulding the flesh.

'Legs apart,' Susan ordered. 'Let's give Annabella a good show of your pussy.'

Paulette obeyed, as Susan went to the rack of implements in front of her.

'If I opened the blind, your rear view would be on show to every upper window in Little Venice,' Susan joked, as she selected a black pole with a leather cuff attached to each end.

'No, please!' Paulette squeaked.

'Don't you like to be watched?'

'Only by the person who's punishing me,' Paulette answered, as Susan attached a cuff to one of her ankles. 'Do you?'

'Yes, the more the merrier. But they mustn't know I want them to be watching. I like them to think that whoever's spanking me is doing it in public to humiliate me more. Or because they don't care whether my bum gets a public

39

airing or not, they just decide I need a spanking and do it then and there.'

'I prefer it one-to-one,' Paulette said, 'but the idea of you being Annabella's maid while she punishes me is great. Oh, that's nice; I feel really open. I can't close my legs at all.'

Susan had fixed the pole in place, forcing Paulette's legs wide and leaving her pussy open and vulnerable. All Paulette could do was wiggle her bottom, an action she knew would do little to lessen the pain of her punishment. Relaxing into her bonds, she felt her pleasure rising and her breath coming deep and slow as she waited. Susan moved around to her side and knelt submissively on the floor, her hands folded in her lap and her head hung.

'She's coming,' Susan hissed even as Paulette heard the click of high heels on the stairs. She found herself trembling as the door clicked, and she knew Annabella would be looking at her naked body, strapped and ready for punishment, legs spread to offer pussy and anus.

'What is this?' Annabella de Vergy's voice came sharp and clear. 'I ordered you to strip and wait, did I not?'

'Yes,' Paulette answered, shivering at the commanding arrogance of Annabella's tone, and wishing she could see her.

'Yes, what?!' Annabella snapped.

'Y-yes, Miss de Vergy,' Paulette stammered, then gulped as long nails traced a path over the flesh of her bottom. The nails moved down to the tuck of her cheeks and a hand closed on the plumpest part of her bottom, weighing and squeezing the flesh in a casually possessive manner. Paulette squirmed, trying to push her pussy against the exploring hand, but unable to do so.

'You do not address me by name,' Annabella said in a calm, cool voice. 'You call me "mistress", both of you. Is that understood?'

'Yes... mistress,' Paulette answered, hearing Susan say

40

the same in a tiny, meek voice.

'Good,' Annabella said, 'and now I am going to beat you. It will not be because you have presented yourself in this vulgar position, obviously in the hope of punishment, nor because you enjoy it. It will be to teach you your place. Do you understand that?'

'Y-yes… mistress,' Paulette stammered again.

'I doubt it,' Annabella sneered, 'but I suspect you will by the time I've finished with you, as will your friend – although as she is notably less insolent and has adopted a more appropriate position. I expect she already has some idea. Well, Susan, do you understand, or will you need it beaten into you, too?'

'I'll probably need to be beaten,' Susan answered quietly.

Annabella laughed, a mocking, cruel sound that made Paulette's muscles tighten instinctively. Annabella's heels clicked on the wooden floor as she walked around the pillory. Paulette saw her legs first, long and elegant, clad in the same seamed silk stockings, but now with her feet in shiny black shoes with heels some five inches tall. The board of the pillory made it hard to see more. Raising and twisting her head as much as she could, Paulette watched Annabella stroke Susan's hair as she passed, then glide effortlessly around to stand in front of the pillory.

Paulette found herself looking at Annabella's midriff, the shaved lips of her pussy directly level with her eyes. Annabella was dressed much as she had been in the picture: a neat leather corset covering her waist, breasts and hips bare. Coiled-up hair, severe make-up and lace gloves that left her red-taloned fingers bare completed the image. Paulette squinted as she looked up into her mistress's eyes. Annabella gave a light, scornful laugh and moved a step closer, her bare pussy just inches from Paulette's face. A musky, feminine scent caught Paulette, adding to her excitement.

'I think we should start with an acknowledgement of

your status,' Annabella remarked, casually. 'Let me see, now... Yes, you can kiss my anus. A bit of a privilege, really, but as you are about to be beaten anyway, I suppose it's acceptable.'

Annabella turned, presenting Paulette with a neatly rounded bottom, the cheeks high and firm. Slowly, deliberately, Annabella pulled them apart and bent forward. Paulette opened her mouth, wetting her lips at the sight of what she was about to be made to kiss. Shaved, like her pussy, Annabella's bottom-hole was set in a corona of flesh a shade darker than the delicate cream of her skin elsewhere. Tiny lines ran together between bumps of soft flesh, joining to form the dark crease of the actual hole, like lips pursed for a kiss.

Paulette gulped as Annabella pushed her bottom back another inch. She hesitated, feeling unsure of what she was about to do, then poked her tongue out. This was it, the moment she kissed another woman's anus – something she felt was appropriate for her and something she'd often fantasised over, but something she'd never actually done. Now she was going to show her subjugation to Annabella, kissing and licking her bottom while Susan watched. Still she hesitated, Annabella's scent rich in her nostrils, her anus half an inch away from Paulette's mouth.

'Do it,' Annabella ordered sternly.

Her voice overwhelmed Paulette's last reserve. Shutting her eyes and trembling, she pressed her face between Annabella's buttocks, kissing the tight little hole, then again, pressing her lips hard against it, licking, inserting her tongue, licking again, frantic for more now that she'd given in to her desire.

Annabella pulled away suddenly, laughing as she turned around. She sank to her haunches and lifted Paulette's chin with a finger.

'Beat me,' Paulette begged, hearing the passion in her own voice.

'Patience, my sweet,' Annabella said, looking full into Paulette's eyes. 'All in good time.'

She smiled coolly and tilted Paulette's chin up a little more before continuing. 'I just wanted you to know, slut, that never, no matter how excited I was, would I ever do what you have just done. How does that make you feel?'

'Dirty, mistress,' Paulette answered softly, drawing another silky laugh from Annabella.

'Good,' Annabella said as she rose, 'but we mustn't leave Susan out, must we, Susan?'

Susan shook her head meekly from her kneeling position. Paulette watched in fascinating as Annabella went through the same ritual with her friend, presenting her bottom, opening her cheeks and pushing them out. Susan kissed with a willingness that surprised Paulette. Susan's eyes were open as she nuzzled her face between Annabella's buttocks. Annabella, too, clearly took more than just a mental pleasure in the act, closing her eyes and sighing as Susan's tongue found her anus.

There was an expression of utter bliss on Susan's face as she drew away, acting to remove the slight trace of guilt that Paulette had felt at obeying Annabella's command so readily.

'Fetch a whip, Susan,' Annabella commanded, once more moving out of Paulette's range of vision. 'As she was beaten only recently, I shall be merciful. Pass me the cat with the suede thongs.'

Paulette felt her breathing quicken once more as Susan rose quickly and disappeared. There was a faint click and a swish, as if of the chosen implement being tested through the air. Paulette found the cheeks of her bottom clenching in anticipation, a feeling made stronger by her inability to see what the others were doing.

'Kneel by her head.' Annabella's voice came from behind her and, a moment later, Susan appeared, sinking to her knees and cradling Paulette's head in her arms.

43

An instant later, the whip landed on Paulette's bottom with a heavy smack, as much a push as a blow. Paulette jerked and gasped, surprised by the force of the whip. It came again before she was really ready, smacking down hard against her bottom and pushing her into Susan's arms. The feeling was very different from the sharp bite of the cane Susan had used; more erotic than painful.

Despite that, the whipping produced all the exquisite thrill of chastisement, accentuated by her helpless position and the act of abasement she had performed before the whipping had started. She began to pant and then groan as Annabella continued, using the heavy whip with unerring accuracy. Each stroke fell plum across the crest of Paulette's bottom, the spread of the thongs catching the full area of her cheeks. Susan's breasts were cradled against her face, adding to a level of pleasure that was becoming truly ecstatic as the whipping continued.

'I think I'm going to come,' Paulette gasped, amazed at her own reaction. All it needed was a touch to her clit, the lightest caress, and she would be there.

'Touch me...' she begged, immediately feeling Susan's hand slide under the pillory-board, brush against one of her dangling boobs, touch her belly, and finally settle in among the nest of curls covering her sex.

'Yes, that's it,' she managed as Susan found her clit. 'Whip me hard mistress, please... harder!'

Annabella brought the whip down with all her force, Paulette coming to orgasm as it struck and Susan's finger flicked at her clitoris. Another blow caught her at the peak of her orgasm and she screamed out, calling Susan's name, and then Annabella's as her climax exploded in her head, turning the world black for an instant and leaving her sobbing her passion into Susan's chest...

Paulette waited as they released her from the pillory, then sank to the floor, her muscles shaking in reaction to her orgasm. Susan stood to one side, flushed and smiling, clearly excited.

'Susan's turn!' Paulette enthused, hugging her friend and giving her bottom a smack in anticipation of what was to come.

'In a moment.' Annabella spoke firmly, asserting her position but rubbing her arm to clear the ache induced by using the heavy whip on Paulette. 'Susan, run downstairs and fetch another bottle from the fridge, and the glasses.'

Susan obeyed, scampering down the staircase and finding another bottle of the Alsace in the fridge. Kneeling naked on the kitchen floor, it was more than she could resist to slide the cold bottle between her thighs and rub her wet pussy against it. The glass felt hard and cold, making Susan close her eyes and purr with pleasure, only with an effort resisting the temptation of masturbating then and there on the floor.

Returning to the play-room, she served Annabella, then Paulette, and lastly herself, once more kneeling at de Vergy's feet to drink her wine.

'Very obedient,' Annabella remarked. 'Better than you, Paulette; you still have a lesson or two to learn before you make a good maid.'

'Yes, please,' Paulette giggled, looking over the top of her glass, her huge brown eyes wide and bright.

'The first of which might be to appear a little less eager,' Annabella continued. 'Now what shall we do with Susan?'

'Take her into the garden and spank her in front of the neighbours,' Paulette suggested.

'Tempting, amusing, but hardly practical,' Annabella replied. 'Unfortunately, I am a respectable businesswoman and could hardly afford the scandal. A pity, though; I'm sure old Mr Pettigrew from next door would love to see that fat white behind bouncing and wriggling through a spanking.'

Paulette giggled again. Susan looked up, her lower lip starting to quiver. Annabella had just hit upon both her deepest fantasies: threatening to exhibit her to a dirty old man, and then humiliating her by remarking on the plumpness of her bottom. She knew it wasn't really true, her bottom being pretty well solid muscle and a good deal less fleshy than Paulette's, but that just made the remark sting all the more.

'Over your knee would be nicest,' Susan suggested hopefully, looking up with what she hoped was an imploring expression.

'It would, would it?' Annabella said imperiously.

'And with you fully dressed,' Susan continued boldly. 'Not that you haven't got a lovely body, or anything—' She stopped talking, effectively silenced by the look of astonishment on Annabella's face. 'It's just my fantasy,' she started to explain, 'to be bare when I'm spanked, and for—'

'I think I understand,' Annabella cut in. 'Nonetheless, your impertinence is quite extraordinary.'

'Yes, mistress,' Susan said quietly.

'And for impertinence there is only one cure,' Annabella continued, placing her wine glass carefully on the cupboards between a leather strap and a thick paddle of polished wood. Susan barely had time to react as Annabella sat down on the leather seat of one of the bondage devices and took her by the hair. Just managing to set her glass on the floor, she found herself pulled brusquely across Annabella's knee, a smack landing on her bum an instant later.

Annabella spanked hard and fast. Susan kicked and squealed, feeling her bouncing bottom warm quickly and knowing that her cheeks would be reddening fast. Her head was down by Annabella's shoes, a hand twisted into her hair to make it impossible to get up. She heard Paulette's delighted laughter above her, the black girl clearly enjoying the spectacle of her spanking. Suddenly it stopped, leaving Susan panting across her mistress' knee.

'Pass me a paddle,' she heard Annabella order Paulette.

'No...' Susan pleaded, remembering the broad wooden implement she'd seen on the top.

'Oh yes, Susan.' Annabella's voice was gleefully sadistic.

Susan squealed loudly as the paddle smacked hard against her bottom. It hurt far more than Annabella's hand, but she was unable to do anything about it. She started to beat her fists on the floor, sobbing in her shame and frustration, kicking, wriggling frantically, but unable to get away.

'No, stop, please!' she begged. 'Annabella, mistress! Please!'

The spanking stopped as suddenly as it had begun. Susan rolled off Annabella's lap and crumpled to the floor, sobbing and rubbing her bottom. She was vaguely aware that Paulette was looking concerned, but that Annabella was sitting still, looking cool and amused as she reached for her glass.

Utterly humiliated, her bottom a hot throbbing ball, Susan pulled herself into a sitting position and spread her legs slowly apart. With her vagina open to the woman who had just beaten her, she began to masturbate, looking into de Vergy's eyes as her fingers found her clit. Annabella returned her stare, mouth slightly open but otherwise as composed as Susan was abandoned.

Already breathing fast, Susan curled her other hand under her thighs, lifting her bottom and stroking the smarting skin. She felt utterly wanton, intent on making a truly dirty show of herself as she came. Her legs inched further apart as she settled her bottom back on the floor, the boards hard against the sore flesh, her fingers burrowing down into the cleft of her bum.

As she felt the first flush of approaching orgasm, her middle finger found her anus, popping into the tight hole in full view of both Annabella and Paulette. The ring contracted, firm and damp around her intruding digit, and she was coming, screaming, squirming on the floor, rubbing frantically at herself as her back arched and her muscles spasmed.

Then it was over and she was trembling on the floor, her body damp with sweat, legs still wide apart, not caring in the least what she was showing.

'Lick me, Paulette,' she heard Annabella say. The beautiful, haughty voice was still cool and very much in charge, despite the obvious flush of pleasure on her face and the moist state of her vulva.

Susan sat back as Paulette got to her knees and sank her face between Annabella's open thighs. Exhaling slowly, she closed her eyes to the full moon of Paulette's bottom and the soft moans coming from their erstwhile mistress as her pleasure rose.

'That was something else,' Paulette said as they walked along the canal bank away from de Vergy's house.

Susan nodded agreement, rather too aware of her smarting bottom to give Paulette her full attention. It was true; Annabella de Vergy made an excellent mistress, even if she had taken the spanking a bit further than Susan would really have liked.

'It's a shame she had to go to work,' Paulette continued blithely, 'but, like she said, there'll be other times. You really throw a tantrum when you're spanked, don't you?'

'It was hard!' Susan protested.

Paulette laughed and promptly changed the subject. 'Shame about the scandal, or rather the lack of a scandal. I suppose I should have known Sowerby was on a wild goat chase; silly old fart.'

'Are you giving up then?'

'I suppose so,' Paulette sighed. 'But at least we met Annabella, so it's not a total wash-out.'

'So I sucked Paul Berner for nothing?'

'It'll teach you your place,' Paulette joked, imitating Annabella's accent.

'Unless, of course, there is a scandal but Annabella simply doesn't know anything about it,' Susan speculated. 'You saw how self-confident she is. Maybe she's being cheated and doesn't know it.'

'Maybe,' Paulette replied dubiously, 'but she seemed to know her stuff...'

'You're probably right,' Susan admitted. 'In any case, it seems pretty certain that she's not involved in any way. In all the interviews I can remember, I've never seen a guilty person so calm and offhand. One thing we do know; Sowerby never managed to have Annabella.'

'How?' Paulette queried.

'He had no idea what her pussy looks like,' Susan answered, drawing a laugh and a cheeky grin from Paulette.

Bob Tweed pressed a button as the sleek, black Jaguar approached the barrier. The driver, Annabella de Vergy, gave him the merest nod as she passed, a gesture of lofty condescension that made him want to spit. Stuck-up cow, he thought, acting as if she was better than anybody else, especially him. True, she ran a successful wine import business while he was a night-watchman on an industrial estate, but in his eyes she had no right to behave as if she were superior to him.

'Bitch,' he mumbled under his breath at the departing Jaguar. For a long moment he stood looking after the car, even when it had passed from sight, feeling resentful and self-pitying. He was still staring in the same direction when the sound of a horn drew his attention back to his job. It was a BMW, the driver hooting irritably for his attention.

'Keep your mind on your job,' the man snapped as he passed, once more drawing a sullen curse from the watchman. The man was Philip Ruddock, manager at de

Vergy Fine Wines and, if anything, even more stuck-up than his boss. de Vergy was haughty and aloof, where Ruddock was actively rude. Despite that, Tweed found Ruddock less irritating; it was easier to be looked down upon by a man than a woman.

Being Sunday, the estate was nearly empty, only a few late workers remaining. Other than the wine warehouse, only a handful of places opened on Sunday and, of those, de Vergy, Ruddock, and their staff were invariably the last to leave. They were always the last to turn up as well. Lazy bastards, he thought, turning up for work in the middle of the afternoon. Tweed slid a magazine from under his desk, and opened it at random to admire a picture of a leggy large-breasted blonde with her legs spread in a pose of crude sexual display. He sighed, thinking how good it would feel to have the stuck-up bitch de Vergy spread open like that, begging for his cock up her posh twat. Bitch, he thought once more, realising that de Vergy saw him as no more than a shadow as she drove past each morning, a servant whose name it wasn't even worth knowing. As for him ever having sex with her, it was more likely that the girl in the magazine would come to life. Besides, he consoled himself, the cold bitch had probably never had sex anyway – not proper sex, like he would have given her.

Tweed studied the magazine, quickly forgetting de Vergy and Ruddock. Half an hour later he pulled the main gates shut and activated the alarm system before taking up his torch for his first patrol of the night.

The estate proved secure, as it almost invariably did. Once or twice he had had to chase groups of kids off the roofs of the industrial units and, when he had first worked there, a burglary had happened. The thieves had been caught, the result of the network of video cameras that covered every warehouse door and every alley on the estate. None had tried since, presumably because word had gone round of how well protected the estate was. With the Grand Union Canal to one side and the railway to the other, the estate was hard enough to access as it was, while it would be impossible to get a van in and load up with anything really worthwhile.

He returned to his box, sat pensively for a while, and then once more took out his magazine, scanning the pictures of naked girls with a wistful hopelessness that came from a knowledge that the time when he might have aspired to such blatantly sexual women was long gone, if indeed any women had been so easy when he was a young man. Why, he asked himself, did women have to be so precious with their bodies? Surely a fuck or a suck wasn't a big deal?

Tweed put the magazine away, feeling depressed instead of turned-on. He turned to the bank of video screens behind him, watching the changing pictures, none of which showed more than the expected empty yards and corridors.

The night wore on, as dull and uneventful as any other; Tweed drinking the occasional coffee and doing his hourly rounds. By three a.m. he was feeling thoroughly fed up as he stared out into the night, listening to the distant rumble of a train. He had just finished his round and was considering another coffee and wishing he could risk a nap, as he had so often done in the days before surveillance cameras became commonplace.

Another sound caught his attention, so faint that he was unsure if he had actually heard it. It was the tinkle of breaking glass, somewhere off in the distance. He turned back to the screens, letting each cycle twice before deciding that it must have been a bottle breaking or something. Feeling bored and frustrated, he once more retrieved his magazine from under the desk, trying to regain something of the thrill that pictures of naked women had once inspired.

The distant clang of an alarm bell cut suddenly into his

thoughts. It was on the estate, the warning light on his panel showing for one of the big warehouses that backed onto the canal. It was de Vergy Fine Wines, he realised as he got to his feet. He swung around to glance at the screens, but the camera that covered the front of the wine warehouse showed nothing out of the ordinary.

Or did it?

Tweed peered more closely, only to have the picture change to one from another camera. He waited with a flush of annoyance, his hand poised over the button that would summon the other guard and the police. The picture returned to the wine warehouse, still showing no movement, but he immediately realised what had caught his eye. The windows at the very top of the picture showed an odd shifting light, which could only mean one thing.

Tweed stabbed his hand onto the button even as he reached for the telephone to call the fire brigade.

Ted Gage woke to the incessant ringing of the telephone. He cursed as he slowly stirred, hoping it was something trivial but knowing full well it wouldn't be. A glance at the clock showed it was nearly half-past three in the morning, and one ominous thought immediately came uppermost in his mind: fire.

Sure enough, a wine warehouse in Park Royal was burning. Gage hurried to dress, ignoring his wife's complaints as he turned on the lights to make things easier for himself. Within five minutes he was more or less ready and clambering into his car.

He drove west, gaining at least some satisfaction from his wailing siren and the pleasure of doing a ton on the Westway. As he approached Park Royal he saw the fire, orange flames lighting the horizon and a pillar of black smoke rising against the night sky.

'Shit that's a big one,' he swore, cursing the fire-raiser who in all probability was even then watching and crowing with delight over the destruction he had caused.

It was easy to find the trading estate. Flames were visible for miles, licking up through the shattered roof of the warehouse with sparks trailing high into the windless night. Fire engines thronged the yard outside the warehouse, the team's hoses turned onto the face of the burning building.

With the warehouse backing directly onto the canal it was difficult to get at the heart of the fire, but after a long struggle it was brought under control and finally checked, leaving the warehouse a burnt-out shell.

As soon as the worst of the crisis was past, Gage identified the white helmet of the senior fireman and walked over to him.

'DI Gage,' he introduced himself. 'I'm in charge of an investigation into a series of these warehouse fires. Any idea how it started?'

'Don't quote me on it yet, but it looks like a petrol bombing job,' the officer replied. 'And I think I can tell you why the roof went up like that.'

'Oh?'

'Brandy. Apparently there was a pallet of it stacked by the office. The whole lot would have gone up like a bomb.'

'How do you know it was there?' Gage asked.

'There are bits of brandy bottles all over the place – blown clear by the blast.'

Gage sighed, preparing for the sixth round of futile investigation followed by criticism from his superiors and the media.

Chapter Three

'Susan! Wake up!' Paulette called, the words barely registering to Susan as she drifted slowly out of her sleep. 'Annabella's warehouse has burnt down!'

'What? You're joking?' Susan managed, her sleepiness draining away as the adrenaline began to run.

'No, I'm not,' Paulette insisted from the kitchen. 'It's on the radio. De Vergy Fine Wines, in Park Royal – that must be it. They're saying it's another attack by the Fire Ghost.'

'I'm coming.' Susan rolled out of bed and dashed into the kitchen in time to catch the end of the report.

'I can't believe that's a coincidence,' she said as the newsreader moved on to another item.

'Surely you don't think Annabella did it?'

'It needn't be that simple. What I'm saying is that there's a high probability of a causative link between our visit to Annabella and the fire. It would be wrong to speculate on the nature of that link, but right to investigate it.' Susan hurried from the kitchen.

'Well, er – yes,' Paulette agreed, although slightly lost.

'I'm going over there…' Susan called from the bathroom over the sound of water cascading into the basin. 'Would you find me the address?'

'Inspector Gage, can you confirm that this is another attack by the Fire Ghost?'

Ted Gage paused, trying not to show his annoyance to the cluster of cameramen and reporters facing him. 'At present,' he said, speaking clearly and slowly, 'I can only say that we are investigating a warehouse fire as part of normal police procedure.'

'But it looks like the work of the Fire Ghost, doesn't it?' another demanded.

'I have no further comment at this juncture.'

'Are you saying it's not the Fire Ghost?'

'As I said,' his annoyance grew a little more, 'I have no further comment at this juncture. A full statement will be released in due course. Now, if you will excuse me, I have several important matters to attend to.'

Gage turned and walked away, ignoring the continuing barrage of questions and crossing back into the haven of police tape. Despite his comments to the press, he was depressingly sure that the fire was the Ghost's sixth strike. The MO was pretty well identical to the others. A rear window had been broken and a petrol bomb hurled through it. Forensic had already identified the shards of the bomb, despite the sea of broken glass inside what remained of the warehouse.

The difference with this attack was that, instead of landing on material that was merely flammable, the bomb had landed within feet of a pallet of brandy. According to forensic, the cardboard boxes must have caught, burning until the brandy started to boil inside the bottles and then exploded with enough force to blow out the roof and scatter burning debris over everything else. The result was a revolting mess of half-burnt cardboard, shattered wine bottles and charred pallets, all of it swimming in an inch-deep sea of ruined wine and water from the fire hoses. Gas cylinders in the Portakabin that served as an office had also gone up, adding to the mess and completely gutting the office. The smell was abominable, making the normal mixture of smoke and melted plastic seem quite inoffensive.

The last people to leave had been the owner, Annabella de Vergy, and the manager, Philip Ruddock, who had shut the warehouse several hours before the fire started. Both had been at home when the fire happened. Both lived alone and so could not provide alibis, but Gage hardly felt he needed them to. The arson attack was, after all, too similar to the other Fire Ghost attacks to be anything else.

As he walked towards his team he saw a pretty female talking to Sergeant Yates. Expecting a pushy reporter, Gage sighed and steeled himself to get rid of her. 'Excuse me,' he began as he approached, only to have the sergeant turn and address him.

'This is Susan MacQuillan, guv,' the sergeant said. 'Used to be a DC with central, a few years back.'

Gage turned to her, unable to avoid having his eyes drawn to the lovely swell of her breasts beneath a tight T-shirt. 'Pleased to meet you, Miss MacQuillan. I'm DI Gage.'

'Hi,' she smiled. 'Can we have a quick word?'

'Sure.' Gage found himself immediately drawn to her friendly manner. 'What is it?'

'It's to do with the fire,' Susan began. 'A friend of mine – a reporter – has been investigating a wine scandal. Now, she took over the investigation from another writer who recently died of food poisoning, leaving Paulette, my friend, with very few leads. One lead was that the original writer had thought that Annabella de Vergy was one of the victims of the fraud. Only yesterday Paulette and I interviewed de Vergy. Given that the warehouse fire occurred only some twelve hours after Paulette and I saw her, it seems highly probable that our transmission of information is in some way linked to the fire. Annabella de Vergy herself appears to have no knowledge of the scandal, although she cannot be ruled out. More probable is a case in which she mentioned that the scandal was still being followed up to a third party, who then panicked and set the fire in an attempt to destroy any evidence. So—'

'Hang on, hang on,' Gage interrupted, Susan having

reeled off the explanation at a speed that had left him far behind. 'So you're saying the fire was deliberate and caused by someone involved with de Vergy Fine Wines?'

'More or less, yes.'

'And this is based entirely on speculation?'

'No,' Susan replied indignantly, 'it's based on an analysis of probability. I have no hard evidence, but the probability of the three events – Alan Sowerby's death, Paulette and my interview with de Vergy, and the fire – not being causally linked are tiny. I would estimate—'

'Stop, hold on. Who's Alan Sowerby?'

'The writer who died of food poisoning.'

'And you don't have any hard evidence?'

'No…' Susan admitted, 'but—'

'Miss MacQuillan,' Gage broke in once more, 'I cannot base an investigation on such vague speculation. You must know that.'

'Sure,' Susan conceded, 'I don't expect you to. But bear it in mind when you're interviewing.'

'Fortunately,' Gage was becoming slightly irritated by the pace and intensity of Susan's approach, 'there isn't any need for further interviews. The fire has an MO that fits perfectly with the previous five warehouse fires started by the arsonist they're calling the Fire Ghost.'

'I'm sure it does,' Susan persisted, 'but that in no way alters my reasoning.'

'What reasoning? Your theory is pure speculation. Any three events might be linked, the way you put it. It's obviously just chance—'

'No, no, you don't understand—'

'Stop!' Gage had heard enough. 'Look, I know you were in the force and I do have some respect for your opinion, but if I go off on some hare-brained side-track the Super will have my guts for garters. If you can bring me some more concrete information, then I'll listen. Until then, be a love and leave it out, okay?'

Susan made to say something more and then stopped, leaving Gage with the satisfied feeling of having won the argument, and a slight sense of unease because he hadn't entirely understood her explanation.

Susan walked across the slowly drying puddles of the yard, feeling intensely irritated. The disinclination of the police to follow lines of reasoning based on probabilities had always infuriated her. It was not as if she thought such intangible ideas should be acceptable in court, merely that, in the absence of hard evidence, using probability as a tool often produced results.

Shrugging off her annoyance, she turned her mind to the main question raised by the fire. Was Annabella de Vergy involved in some way? After interviewing her and then playing with her, Susan had been convinced of her innocence. Following the fire, it was no longer possible to be so sure. Assuming that a link existed, then anybody who had spoken to Annabella also became suspect. There had been only twelve hours between them leaving Annabella's house and the fire. If her reasoning was correct, then there could only be a small number of possibilities.

One of those possibles had to be the man Annabella was now standing with at the far side of the yard. He was shorter than de Vergy, red-haired and very red-faced. Dressed smartly, carrying a briefcase and with the subtle air of natural arrogance that Susan had learnt to associate with English public-school types, she found herself filled with an instant dislike. Telling herself not to be irrational, not to say prejudiced, she approached the couple.

'Susan, what are you doing?' Annabella asked in surprise as Susan greeted her.

'I wondered if I might help,' Susan offered, deciding on a pose of friendly usefulness. Of course, if Annabella was linked to the fire, let alone Sowerby's death, then she would hardly hire a private investigator to look into it. Bearing this in mind, an acceptance from her would put her innocence beyond any reasonable doubt. In Susan's experience, no criminal, however confident, would actually hire someone to investigate them.

'Help?' Annabella asked, sounding puzzled.

'I didn't mention it yesterday,' Susan replied. 'I used to be in the police. I'm a private investigator now.'

'Really?' Annabella's tone of slightly amused disbelief annoyed Susan, even though it was by no means the first time she had faced such a reaction.

'Are you really cut out for that sort of work?' the man asked.

'I have a moderate track record,' Susan replied, trying not to sound defensive.

The man merely gave her a look of scepticism; Annabella responded instead. 'It's very sweet of you, dear, but I'm afraid there's not much to do. The police think it's the work of that serial arsonist, the Fire Ghost. They've been after him for months, so I don't suppose you could do anything, anyway. Oh, by the way, this is Philip Ruddock, my warehouse manager. Philip, Susan MacQuillan. She's terribly sweet; she and a reporter friend of hers thought we might be being cheated in some sort of wine scandal and came over to tell me yesterday.'

'I hardly think they'd be qualified to judge such a thing,' Ruddock answered with an arrogance that further infuriated Susan.

'Oh, no,' Annabella continued, 'it was Alan Sowerby who thought he'd found a scandal, something to do with an exporter selling table wines as quality wine. Of course, I said it was nonsense; just poor old Alan being an idealist.'

'Sowerby did at least have a moderate palate,' Ruddock put in, 'but he was no businessman. Now if you'll excuse us, we are very busy.'

Susan left, seething at their attitude, particularly

Ruddock's. Annabella had been condescending, and probably more so than she would have been had Susan not submitted to her sexually. That was a common reaction though, if annoying; many of Susan's partners had expected her to be meek and submissive in ordinary life, just because she enjoyed sex that way. Such relationships never lasted. Annabella was arrogant, but Ruddock was both rude and arrogant. He was an unpleasant little shit, but she still knew that next time she fantasised over being sexually humiliated by a man, Ruddock's image would creep into her brain, whether she liked it or not.

What had been a casual interest in an investigation, done purely to help Paulette and fill in time until another case came her way, had now turned into a burning need to get to the bottom of things. Of course, there was also the chance that the fire genuinely was another Fire Ghost attack and that, by further investigation, she would only make an idiot of herself. There was also the fact that nobody was paying her to make the investigation, yet her natural stubbornness wouldn't let her back down.

No, she would see it through, and preferably with police help. Paul Berner, for all his cock-sure arrogance, had a brain, and it was possible he could be persuaded to take an interest in the case. Given that the investigation into the Fire Ghost was obviously getting nowhere, it should be easy for anyone involved with the metropolitan detection squad to get onto the team. That was what she intended to get Berner to do, even if it meant sucking his cock for him every day for the next year.

Bob Tweed watched as the small, curvaceous woman walked towards him. On a normal day he would have knocked off some hours earlier. But with the fire at de Vergy Fine Wines, an apparently endless succession of policemen and reporters had wanted to talk to him. All in all, he felt thoroughly pleased with himself. He would now be on television and in the papers: famous, if only briefly and only by chance. Still, it was a good feeling.

He half-expected the woman to come and speak to him, as so many of the other people who had visited the fire site had done. Looking at the way her big breasts strained against the fabric of her T-shirt he was hoping she would, too, if only so he could admire her at close quarters. But instead she turned towards the rank of cars drawn up against the trading estate fence and made for the small black one she had arrived in.

As she bent a little to open the door he was treated to a view of a bottom every bit as round and shapely as her breasts, the contours shown off beautifully by tight blue jeans. He sighed, imagining how it would feel to get his hands on such a ripe young body. Any woman who dressed the way she did was asking for trouble, he considered, and then decided he was wrong. She wasn't actually dressed all that provocatively; it was just that with a body like hers it was hard not to look sexy.

She smiled and nodded as he raised the barrier for her, a friendly easy-going gesture, very different from the way most people treated him. Watching the car go, he shook his head, wishing once more that he was young enough to be able to set his sights on such gorgeous women.

Susan parked the Rover in the shade of a dirt-encrusted sycamore and got out. The Grand Union Canal ran to one side, as smooth as glass, the surface reflecting the brilliant blue of the sky and the shapes of the buildings that flanked it on the far side. She had driven nearly three miles to reach the side of the canal opposite to the trading estate on which de Vergy Fine Wines was based, but had at least managed to get fairly close to the back of the ruined warehouse.

She walked down the tow-path. To one side was wasteland overgrown with straggling brambles, sycamore and buddleia – to the other the canal. Across the canal, the tall brick walls of the warehouses fell straight to within inches of the water's edge. Sergeant Yates had told her how the fire had been started. One of the rear windows had been smashed with a chunk of brick and a petrol bomb thrown in after it.

Reaching the section of the canal opposite de Vergy Fine Wines, she considered it carefully. Forensic would have already gone over the ground; the solid concrete of the canal path making it unlikely that they would have found anything. What interested her was the actual physics of the thing. To have thrown the piece of brick and then the bomb from the six-inch wide strip of ground that ran under the windows would have been nearly impossible, not to say highly dangerous, for the fire-raiser. It had therefore presumably happened from where she was standing.

With all the windows now blown out and showing only as soot-blackened frames, it was impossible to tell which window had been smashed first. Still, they were all some two feet high and about six feet long. Given the width of the canal, it would have taken a fairly impressive piece of throwing to have smashed a window and then put the bomb through the hole – unless…

Susan stood pondering, forming and discarding theories but always sticking on the fact that she really needed to know more about the other five fires. Given that Gage was disinclined to be helpful, that meant Berner. Rather looking forward to the prospect of sucking his cock again, she turned to go, catching a movement across the wasteland as she did so.

Peering between tall fence stakes, she saw a man spraying a graffiti tag onto a half-demolished concrete wall. The first word looked like 'Fire' and he was now working on an 'h' that followed what was surely a 'G'. Finding a gap in the railings, Susan stole onto the wasteland, using bushes for cover until she was near the man. As she rounded a great pile of rubble, he came into her view. He was at the mouth of a sort of cul-de-sac where a bulldozer had pushed an alley into the rubble. The wall he was spraying was the last remaining piece of whatever structure had once stood there. She sank into a crouch and moved a flower-laden buddleia branch to one side, watching as he finished his tag. As she had thought, he'd written 'Fire Ghost'.

The letters were three feet high and a brilliant scarlet, to which he now added an equally vibrant orange. Susan watched, wondering if this could really be the elusive arsonist who had eluded the police five times. She had heard no reports of distinctive tags found near the scenes of the other fires, nor did it seem credible that he would be so stupid as to place his tag mere yards from the scene when it was still crawling with police officers. Still, stranger things had happened.

Skinny and dressed in loose casual clothes, he looked about eighteen. Susan was sure she would be unable to catch him if he ran, yet she had no way of summoning help without risking losing him. A bold front might work, especially if he was drunk, as the nearby can of super-strength lager suggested.

No, it was hopeless; he was undoubtedly faster and probably stronger than her, for all his scrawny body. She would probably be able to overpower him by putting him in a hold, but getting him to a police station would be a different matter. Brawn was out; brains would have to do, as usual.

'You're not really, are you?' she asked, stepping boldly out from cover.

The lad turned sharply and stopped, his initial expression of alarm fading as he looked at her.

'Seriously, are you the Fire Ghost?'

'That's me, babe,' he answered, straightening up and putting on a pair of sunglasses.

63

'That's neat,' she said, sounding awed, even as she thought how insecure he looked in his trendy casuals and dark glasses. 'I'm Susan.'

'Hi. Like my tag?'

Susan nodded and went to sit on a block of brickwork that had once formed part of a chimney. He returned to work with the orange spray paint. Just as Susan was about to start a careful line of questioning intended to first win his trust and then find out if he really was the Fire Ghost, another voice sounded from nearby.

She looked round to see a second young man coming towards them with a four-pack of the super-strength lager in his hand. A third was behind him, also carrying cans. In age they were similar to the first, one tall and even thinner but with a finely formed face and bright eyes, the other solidly built and distinctly fat. They were both clearly drunk.

The first lad, who insisted on being called Fire Ghost, introduced Susan to the others, calling them Taz and Beadle. Neither showed any concern at her presence, which increased her conviction that they were merely impressionable youths struck by the glamorous image of fire-raising. They were also beginning to make her feel uneasy, the lanky Taz in particular joking at her rather than with her. After a while he sat next to her, pointing at her breasts, making as if to weigh them in his hands, and winking at the others – all with no attempt to hide what he was doing.

Susan made what she hoped was a suitably cutting remark and turned back to where Fire Ghost was finishing his tag. Leaving was beginning to seem like a good idea, especially as she was certain he was not the genuine article. On the other hand, she felt an odd compulsion to stay. She recalled the endless fantasies she had had about just such situations as this. In some she'd imagined herself in a prison cell with three or four sex-starved inmates.

Another favourite was being gang-banged by bikers in a remote roadside café. The present situation was a lot milder than either, yet it was real, and the little voice in her head telling her to go for it was being shouted down by another telling her to get away as fast as possible. Promising herself she'd let it happen on another occasion but knowing full well she wouldn't, she got to her feet.

'I've got to go,' she said.

'Hey, I thought we were going to have a party!' Taz complained.

'Yeah, come on,' urged Beadle, 'have a beer.'

Susan turned to him, spreading her hands in a gesture of resignation. There was a sound behind her, a light touch at her waist, and suddenly her top was up around her face.

'Hey!' she protested as Taz twisted the T-shirt and trapped her arms above her head, 'that's not funny!'

'Get her tits out, Beadle!' Taz cried.

Beadle hesitated only an instant and then stepped forward, barely visible to Susan through the thin material of her top.

'No!' she shouted as rough hands closed on her breasts, fondling them for a moment and then flipping the cups of her bra up to reveal their glory. She felt them spill free and knew they were bared for the leering lads. They felt incredibly prominent; the whole focus of her body, naked and vulnerable.

'Nice tits, Susan,' she heard, then kicked and twisted and managed to break free.

They stood watching and she sensed indecision. Her brief show of true defiance had got the message across; she didn't really want them messing with her.

'Hey, I was only fooling,' Taz said as Susan hastily covered herself. They were in front of her, and steep piles of rubble made retreat difficult. Taz was standing with his arms held wide in mock apology. Beadle stood to the side and a little behind Taz, nursing his assaulted shin. Fire

Ghost was still kneeling by his tag, quietly surveying the scene.

Susan hesitated; an angry word or a determined look and it would be over, and if she wanted to she could fetch Gage and Yates to lock the three youths up. If they didn't have the sense to disappear, that was, which she somehow suspected they wouldn't; Taz obviously thought he'd merely played a joke, Beadle looked hurt rather than resentful, and Fire Ghost just looked stupefied.

Another voice, deep inside her head, was calling her a fool for not playing along. All she'd had to do was giggle a bit and let them get on with it and she'd have been stripped and molested in a way that would have given her a lifetime's supply of memories to masturbate over. But she hadn't had the guts. Resisting was too deeply ingrained. Now her chance was spoilt and the moment had passed... almost.

It was such an opportunity. The temptation was just too, too much...

'Don't hurt me and I'll toss you off,' she suddenly blurted at Taz before she could stop herself.

A crafty grin spread slowly across the youth's face.

Susan realised she'd taken the right line: not too willing, not too aggressive.

A hand went to his zip, drew it slowly down, and slipped inside his grubby jeans. With a little jerk he pulled his limp cock and hairy balls out into the open. Beadle and Fire Ghost gawked. Susan moved forward, her eyes riveted to Taz's genitalia. She reached out and gingerly cupped his balls, her thumb stroking the upper surface of his cock. He sighed. His shaft moved under her thumb, swelling as she slowly squeezed it in her palm. Beadle stepped closer and tentatively touched her breasts.

Susan began to gently pull the stiffening flesh back and forth, feeling it thicken and swell. Beadle moved behind her, growing bolder as she made no protest at having her

66

breasts fondled through her top. Fire Ghost watched with fascination.

'You'll do as I say, won't you?' Taz croaked, his voice a cocktail of arousal, uncertainty, and malicious glee. Susan trembled. She nodded, unable to tear her eyes from his increasingly impressive cock.

'Get her top up, Beadle,' Taz ordered. 'I want to see those lovely big tits again.'

Susan felt Beadle's hands go to the hem of her T-shirt and tug it up. Her bra followed, and for the second time in a few minutes her breasts burst into the warm sunlight. She continued to milk Taz as four clumsy hands mauled her breasts and sought her nipples. Beadle stopped, leaving Taz free to enjoy the feel of her, and suddenly eager fingers were tugging at her jeans. Taz pulled her arms up, and her top and bra followed and were tossed to the rubble. Her jeans were yanked open, and Taz lowered her hand and curled her fingers back around his erection.

Beadle wrestled her snug jeans down over her hips, and Fire Ghost at last plucked up the courage to molest her vulnerable breasts. The jeans were quickly down to her thighs. Taz pushed her down until she was kneeling. She let him position her without complaint. His hips jerked forward and his shiny helmet touched her lips. She kissed it. Her bottom was exposed, her white panties stretched taut across her cheeks. Taz pushed and his cock slipped into her mouth, thick and salty, stretching her jaw.

Beadle's hands invaded her panties. Susan shut her eyes in utter bliss as the fat boy eased them down. Her bum was naked, stuck out towards him, the cheeks apart, her rear entrance and her pussy on show.

'Looks like her old man's given her arse a good whacking!' Beadle sniggered, sending a pang of humiliation through Susan as she realised that the results of Annabella's rough handling were still visible.

Beadle felt her bottom, one hand stroking her cheeks

and then creeping round to cup her pussy. She knew the other hand would be on his cock, getting it ready for his turn with her. A thumb slid into her vagina, making her gasp with the lovely shock of penetration.

Taz started to wank into her mouth. Fire Ghost was tormenting her breasts, squeezing each soft globe in turn and teasing the nipples. Her eyes were shut, her senses drinking in the taste of Taz's cock, the feel of Fire Ghost's hands on her breasts, and the agitating thumb in her pussy.

'I'm going to fuck her.' Beadle's voice strained with the excitement. He gripped and lifted her hips for easier penetration.

'Hey,' Taz snarled. 'I want her cunt first!'

'But you're getting a gobble,' Beadle whined.

'Look, if anyone's going to fuck her first, it's me!' Taz insisted as he pulled his glistening cock out of Susan's mouth.

Susan knelt meekly in the dirt and brick-dust, with Fire Ghost still fondling her dangling breasts. She opened her eyes and peeped at his cock, now in his hand and fully erect. She sighed and dipped her back, improving the access for whoever won the argument to fuck her first.

'You always get your way,' Beadle whined again. 'You had Jilly first after her party.'

'Well she is my fucking girlfriend!' Taz snapped.

'Says who?'

'Please…' Susan whispered, abandoning any pretence of unwillingness. She was desperately aroused, but it seemed the stupid youths were close to forgetting her and coming to blows instead.

The arguing ceased and there was a long pause. Then hands – presumably Taz's – gripped her thighs and her ankles were nudged apart. He shuffled between them. She again braced herself. Fire Ghost moved around to her face and his long cock prodded against her lips. She peeled them apart and swallowed him hungrily. She felt a push against her bottom and then a long column of rigid flesh prised her pussy open and filled her. Taz started to pump, gripping her hips and banging against her bottom. She was in ecstasy as she sucked on Fire Ghost's erection. A hand took her wrist and guided her fingers around Beadle's cock.

She knew the youths couldn't last long, but even as she strove to achieve her own orgasm before they were all spent, Fire Ghost jerked and erupted in her mouth. Susan swallowed his seed as he slumped back on his haunches, wheezing unhealthily.

Beadle pushed him aside like a spoilt child claiming a treat, and stuffed his own bursting erection between her glistening lips. He squealed and ejaculated immediately, giving Susan little choice but to drink his offering too, and then fingers clamped into her hips and she felt Taz erupt deep inside her.

The two smug youths withdrew. Susan sank to the ground, barely noticing how uncomfortable she was on the brick rubble, and started to masturbate, desperate for her own release. Her audience gawped at the luscious sight before them as her approaching orgasm made her writhe and gasp in earnest. She started to come. She whimpered in ecstasy, hitting one beautiful peak and then another. As her pleasure gradually ebbed she relaxed, feeling soiled, dirty... and utterly happy.

The youths said nothing, but their movements were a little awkward as they rearranged their clothing and looked at one another, a little sheepishly.

'Could I have a beer?' Susan eventually asked. Feeling sore and a little ashamed of herself she accepted a can from Taz, propped herself onto one elbow, and opened it. A deep draught did something to take the edge from her sudden thirst and the salty male taste from her mouth.

'You are one dirty bitch!' Taz enthused.

Susan took another swig of beer and sat up. Her panties

and jeans were still tangled around her ankles, clean and fairly dry, although her knees and one thigh were covered with brick dust. There was also the matter of the mess in her pussy and between her inner thighs. She sighed; it seemed pointless asking if any of them had a tissue, so she resigned herself to going home with soggy knickers.

'We've got to tag her,' Fire Ghost said as Susan reached for her panties.

'Yeah, right,' Beadle agreed.

'Come on boys,' she remonstrated. 'That was nice, but I've had enough.'

'Sorry, girls we have get tagged,' Taz said, and suddenly grabbed Susan's ankles.

'Hey, No!' she squealed as Beadle gripped her arms and pulled her backwards. 'Get off me!'

Susan struggled as Taz and Beadle forced her down. For all her determination not to get covered in spray paint, she couldn't help laughing, a reaction that encouraged them. Soon she was helpless and spread-eagled on the ground.

'Oh, come on…' she begged as Fire Ghost approached with his spray cans. 'No, please, not paint! Get off me, you little bastards!'

Despite herself, Susan was still laughing. There was no real cruelty in their actions, just high spirits and a total disregard for her dignity. Tagging her was simply a playful ritual – humiliating, true, but no more humiliating than what she had just done for them.

'Stay still or you'll spoil the design,' Fire Ghost said as he shook the can of scarlet paint.

'Okay, I give in, you little sods,' Susan conceded, her struggles subsiding.

Fire Ghost started at her breasts, judging the size of the tag carefully to end at her pussy. Taz and Beadle continued to hold her down, evidently not trusting her promise of submission. Taz also kept her legs as far apart as her jeans

70

would allow, adding the further humiliation of having her pussy held vulnerable while she was done.

Susan stared up at the sky while Fire Ghost worked the paint over her body, pondering what induced her to get into such situations. It was because she had an insatiable sexual appetite, she knew.

Fire Ghost started with the orange, tickling Susan where the spray caught her tummy. She giggled, looking up into Beadle's plump grinning face. She sighed, raising a final muted protest as the spray caught her pubic hair, and then yielded completely. They could do as they liked, suggest any humiliation their dirty little minds could come up with, and she'd just go along with it.

Fire Ghost added brilliant yellow and crimson low-lights before declaring himself finished.

'Stand up and I'll do mine on your bum,' Taz said.

'Okay,' Susan acquiesced, 'but pull off my jeans and panties; I don't want them ruined.'

Taz cheerfully stripped off her remaining clothes, including her shoes, leaving Susan completely naked. She got carefully to her feet, trying not to spoil Fire Ghost's artwork, then stood obediently with her hands on her head as Taz applied a rich green paint to her bare bottom. Looking down her front, Susan could see the start of the 'Fire Ghost' tag, the letters somewhat distorted by the swell of her breasts. Taz followed with silver, a much simpler tag than Fire Ghost's and clearly suited to the roundness of her bottom. Beadle went last, using her back as a canvas for a crimson and silver tag.

'Are you all done, now?' Susan asked patiently.

'Yeah, that's the lot,' Taz confirmed. 'Just let the paint dry for a bit.'

Susan stayed still, wondering how she must look, naked and painted. In a way, she supposed, it made her their property; a deliciously submissive thought. The three sat drinking lager and admiring their handiwork, looking

71

extremely pleased with their efforts.

'So when's the next fire?' Susan asked casually.

Fire Ghost started to speak, only to be interrupted by Taz.

'He hasn't been feeding you that shit, has he? He's not the real Fire Ghost; he wouldn't have the guts.'

'Turn round, let's have another shot of the one on your bum,' Paulette laughed, winding her camera on.

Susan turned and posed to show off the 'TAZ' tag on her bottom, placing her hands on her hips to give a proud, cheeky pose. The camera clicked.

'Now bend over a bit and stick it out,' Paulette instructed.

Susan obeyed, giggling as she adopted the rude pose requested by her girlfriend. The camera clicked again.

'One more, and that's the end of the film,' Paulette announced. 'Let's have a good one of the front.'

Susan turned and pushed her boobs out, making the best of the 'Fire Ghost' tag. Paulette made her move a little and then took the final picture, the thirty-sixth, of Susan's painted body. She was stark naked in most of them; towards the end adding coloured pop-socks and then high-heels to make the pictures subtly ruder.

'He's a good artist,' Paulette commented, 'even if he's not the real fire-raiser.'

'I'm sure he's not,' Susan replied. 'Even at first, I was pretty sure. If any of them was capable of it, I'd say it was Taz.'

'You're dead lucky, Susan. I'd never have had the guts to go for it when they started.'

'I nearly didn't,' Susan admitted, 'but I'm glad I did. I do feel a bit ashamed, as it goes – but not much.'

'Nothing a good spanking won't put right.'

'Maybe, when I'm clean and pink again instead of multi-coloured,' Susan said. 'Besides, I've got to go and see Paul Berner and try and get him to involve himself this afternoon. If we start playing spanking games we'll be here all day.'

'I'll remember that,' Paulette called after Susan as she went into the bathroom. 'I offer you a nice spanking and you'd rather go and give some lout of a policeman a blow-job – thanks!'

'It's work, and you can spank me later—' the sudden hiss of the shower cut off her words.

Susan sighed as she mounted the steps to Heath Police Station. It had already been a long day. It had taken ages to get all the paint off, and she even had to shave her pussy to be completely rid of the artwork.

Afterwards, all she'd wanted to do was curl up in bed until it was time for Paulette to serve her dinner. As it was, she was facing the prospect of trying to persuade Paul Berner to join a team any career-minded policeman would have been doing his best to get out of. He did have a genuinely enquiring mind but, at the end of the day, she knew it would be her willingness to grant sexual favours that would swing the balance. Even on the telephone, he had hinted at what he would expect for any further assistance, and she hadn't even told him the extent of the favour she wanted.

As she went through the process of announcing herself to the desk sergeant, explaining why she wanted to see Berner and then waiting for him to come down, Susan pondered the events of the day. The more she thought about it, the more likely it seemed that if there was a scam at de Vergy Fine Wines, then Ruddock was the man behind it. If Annabella was involved, then she was a stunningly good actress.

Remembering how Annabella had maintained her role as the cool aloof mistress almost to the point of orgasm, Susan began to have doubts. Maybe Annabella wasn't so innocent. One thing she was certain of: a link existed.

The probability of the three events being coincidence was negligibly small.

Berner finally appeared but, to Susan's relief, was unable to secure the use of anywhere sufficiently private to allow him to make use of her sexually. Instead, they used the reception interview room, far too close to the desk sergeant to risk more than a feel of Susan's boobs and bottom. After satisfying himself with a grope, which Susan accepted without protest, he fetched coffees and asked her to state her case.

Susan accepted the coffee and began to explain her ideas. He listened attentively, making the occasional comment and then sitting back. She watched as he sipped his coffee, clearly deep in thought.

'Well?' she finally asked, exasperated by his lack of response.

'This is the deal,' he said, suddenly leaning forward. 'I'll ask for a transfer to the Fire Ghost team, and then I'll do what I can. In return, I want you as my plaything until it's over. That means what I like, when I like. Okay?'

Susan sighed. It was more or less what she'd expected, the only difference being that she'd thought that by this stage she'd already have been on her knees with his prick in her mouth.

'Detective Sergeant Paul Berner,' she said, getting to her feet. 'You're a filthy bastard, but it's a deal.'

Berner accepted her hand and shook it, grinning from ear to ear.

Chapter Four

Susan nodded and smiled as the security man raised the gate for her. He returned a lewd grin, a reaction that Susan had come to accept as normal. She drove to the far end of the estate and parked next to the cordon of police tape that still shut off de Vergy Fine Wines from the public. What was left of de Vergy Fine Wines, she corrected herself, looking at the gutted roofless ruin and the mess of blackened debris around it. The sun had dried most of the yard, leaving ashes and an unpleasant black paste. There was still a scent of boiled wine in the air, mingled with smells of smoke and wet cardboard. A single man guarded the wreckage, a young PC who gave Susan an officious look as she climbed out of her car. He stood immobile as she kicked off her sandals and pulled on wellington boots.

'Is DS Berner here yet?' she asked.

'Yes ma'am,' the constable answered, 'but he's gone for coffee. Are you Miss MacQuillan?'

'That's right,' Susan replied. 'Can I go in?'

'Er... I suppose so,' he answered uncertainly.

'Thanks.'

One glance inside the warehouse told her that there would be very little to find. For a start, forensic would have taken anything obviously useful in tracing the cause of the fire. Secondly, there was very little to take in any case. A burnt-out forklift stood near the entrance. The portable office was barely recognisable; an iron base with a few pieces of wet charred wood and paper scattered across its surface. A large roll of police tape lay on one corner, the blue and white stripes incongruously bright among the drab surroundings.

The main warehouse floor was a carpet of the revolting black paste she had seen outside, presumably compounded of soot, cardboard, broken glass, wine and water. Here and there pieces of roof, bits of pallet, and miraculously unbroken bottles had survived, protruding from the black muck like pieces of flotsam in an oil slick. Susan grimaced at the smell, hitched her skirt up a little, and began to pick her way across, using bits of roof and charred pallet as stepping-stones.

At the far end, a burnt-out piece of machinery stood on its own in an area separated from the rest of the warehouse by a breeze-block wall, now half-collapsed. The machine was large, a massive and complex construction of steel that had withstood the heat. It appeared to be for doing something with bottles, but Susan found it impossible to guess what.

The sole surviving structural part of the interior was the lavatory. Stepping over the remains of the door, Susan poked her head inside. Everything was covered in soot and the floor was awash, but everything looked in working order. She found herself amused by the thought that, of the entire structure, only the lavatory should survive.

She backed away and turned to the main body of the warehouse. The end she was at was the least damaged, a fair number of bottles remaining intact. Susan pulled one from its matrix of soggy cardboard, guessing that its position at the very bottom of the pallet furthest from the door had saved it. The label was wet but legible, declaring it to be from a wine co-operative at a place called Choray in the Loire valley. She peeled off the damp label and put it carefully into a plastic bag.

A theory began to form in her mind.

'Hi, Susan.'

She looked up to see Paul Berner standing in the

warehouse entrance. He was holding two plastic beakers.

'Come out,' he called, 'I've got you a coffee.'

'Thanks, Paul,' Susan acknowledged him, and picked her way gingerly across the floor.

Berner watched with amusement, grinning at her fastidiousness.

'Yuck,' she said as she reached him, 'that stuff's revolting.'

'What's the fuss? You've got wellies on.'

Susan shrugged.

'You're not going to find anything,' Berner continued. 'Forensic have been over it already, and the Fire Ghost MO is pretty standard. Stone and petrol bomb through a high window at the back; bang, up it goes. No fingerprints, nothing on the security cameras. He obviously stakes the places out first, so old man Gage has got most of the team going through endless security tapes in the hope that he's stupid enough to have actually gone into an estate. The idea is to look for faces appearing on several of the tapes from different estates, but they won't find anything. I'd be doing that if I hadn't asked to look round here.'

'No trouble getting on the team then?' Susan asked.

'Just the opposite.' Berner grinned as he sipped his coffee. 'You'll remember our little bargain, though. Once we've looked round, I'll decide what to do with you.'

'Here?' Susan was horrified.

'Why not?' he said with a shrug. 'It's private enough, with young PC wet-behind-the-ears on guard. I might have you suck him off, actually,' he chuckled, 'I reckon he'd blow his fuse in ten seconds flat.'

'You're filthy, do you know that?' Susan retorted, but only succeeded in making Berner laugh all the more.

'What are you after, then?' he asked once he'd calmed down, looking around at the mess.

'A couple of things,' Susan replied, glad to be back to the real purpose of their meeting. 'For starters, how come they had a pallet of brandy delivered just before the fire? Wine doesn't burn, brandy goes like a bomb. Don't you think that's a bit suspect?'

'You're too suspicious, Susan,' he answered. 'They're a wholesale wine warehouse, supplying mainly restaurants. It's hardly surprising that they stock brandy. Name me a restaurant that doesn't sell brandy?'

'Vegan ones?' Susan suggested half-heartedly. 'Point taken, but it still seems odd. Do you know when it was delivered and why it was so close to the office?'

'No to your first question,' Berner answered, 'but presumably at the end of last week. It wouldn't have been Sunday, but it was near the office because that's where the deliveries come in and they hadn't had time to stack it elsewhere.'

'Maybe it came in on Saturday and was waiting for a warehouseman to stack it during the week.'

'That sounds likely.'

'I still don't like it,' Susan said, turning to look down the length of the warehouse. Something jarred about the whole situation, but she couldn't think what it was. Also, if the brandy had been there before Sunday, then the idea that the information she and Paulette had transmitted to Annabella had led to the fire was flawed. Unless the brandy had been there anyway and Annabella and Ruddock had moved it.

'Who left last on Sunday?' she asked.

'I'm not sure. We could ask security,' Berner suggested.

'Could you do that?'

Berner nodded and walked away, leaving Susan deep in thought. The situation was becoming increasingly complex; a maze of possibilities in the middle of which her theory was slowly taking shape.

It was impossible to tell if the brandy pallet had been moved to the side office; all that was left of it was a rough square on the floor of a slightly different consistency than its surroundings. There was no shortage of bits of brandy-bottle though, many having been blown clear when the pallet exploded. Some even had intact labels, showing a brand name and an address in Athens. Susan waited until the constable wasn't looking, chose one from just outside the door, and slipped it into her bag.

When she returned to the warehouse she began to search for readable labels, using a piece of lead piping to poke in the muck. A surprising number had survived, although very few of the bottles were unbroken. There had been several different wines, but all showed the same address in Choray.

Susan was still searching when Berner returned with the information that Ruddock had left some minutes after de Vergy on the Sunday evening. She smiled, her theory almost complete.

'Are you done?' he asked.

'I'm thinking.'

'Think away.'

'What are you up to?' she asked, watching him pick his way over the remains of the office.

'Oh, just thinking what to do with you. If you're sure you're finished here, that is. I wouldn't want to break your concentration.'

'Oh, come on Paul,' Susan pleaded, 'not here, it's filthy! If you're that desperate for it, I'll come back to your flat for a bit and we can go to bed. Wouldn't that be nice?'

'Delightful,' Berner replied, 'but not nearly as much fun as what I have in mind.'

'Paul,' Susan wheedled, 'it's horrid in here. Let's go to your flat—'

'Another time,' he interrupted, thoughtfully picking up the roll of police tape.

'No, Paul,' Susan begged, seeing the way his mind was working. 'Not with the tape – not in here!'

'Do you remember training?' he asked.

'Yes.' Susan sighed, knowing exactly what he meant.

'Do you remember Collet and that other kid… Spenson, I think he was called.'

'Yes.'

'Do you remember them tying you up with tape for a laugh?'

'Vividly,' Susan said, not adding that her sole regret at the time had been that they'd stopped at tying her up.

'It really turned me on,' Berner mused, looking at the roll in his hand.

'I'm sure it did. And where do you intend to indulge this perversion?'

'Here,' he replied casually.

'Seriously, Paul, I don't mind being tied up, if that's what turns you on, but this place is revolting. Besides, if the constable looks in he can hardly miss us, and bang goes your career. Come on, take me home and you can tie me to the bed.'

'I sleep on a futon,' Berner answered. 'Come on now, and stop whining.'

Susan sighed. 'Don't blame me if you get dismissed for whatever the breach of regulations is for putting women in bondage during an investigation.'

Berner sniggered and started across the debris-strewn floor, gesturing for Susan to follow. She obeyed, knowing further complaint was futile, and picked her way from solid piece to solid piece. With her gaze fixed on the hazards under foot, it wasn't until she had almost reached the remains of the partition wall that she realised Berner had gone into the toilet.

'Paul, not in there, please!' she begged, realising his intention. Being tied up amid the filth and stink of the burnt-out warehouse was bad enough, but to have it done in a lavatory was truly disgusting.

'Come along, Susie,' Berner chided.

She entered, resigning herself to her fate. After all, it was certainly going to be a humiliating experience, and once things got going she would probably enjoy it, if only she could overcome her distaste at the smell and filth of her surroundings.

Berner pushed her back into one of the cubicles and followed. 'Take your skirt and blouse off,' he instructed. 'It wouldn't do to get them dirty, now would it? Your bra had better come off too, but not your panties.'

'Oh, so you're a panty freak too, are you?' Susan goaded.

'I wouldn't be so cheeky if I were about to be tied up,' Berner snapped. 'Come on, get your kit off.'

Susan stripped to her knickers, removing each item carefully so as not to touch the walls or floor and handing them to Berner. He hung them on the hook on the back of the cubicle door. Finally she stood in nothing but white panties and wellington boots. Berner looked at her and nodded thoughtfully.

'Nice… very nice,' he remarked. 'Shapely, but not flabby; plenty of tit. I always did say you had the best body in our year. A shaved pussy, too… I do like that. Give me a spin.'

Susan turned slowly, displaying her panty-clad bottom to him.

'Have you been spanked?' he asked. 'I can see faint marks.'

'Y-yes,' Susan stammered, feeling a faint blush colour her cheeks.

'I always did wonder what pressed your button,' he said, with a hint of victory in his tone. 'Now I know. Didn't it hurt?'

'Yes… but in a nice sort of way,' Susan answered meekly, wondering why she felt she had to justify her pleasure in being spanked to him.

'Hmm, interesting,' Berner remarked. 'Hold your hands out, wrists together.'

Susan turned back and did as she was told, acutely aware of her naked breasts as he strapped her wrists together with the blue and white tape.

'Now kneel on the bog seat,' he instructed, 'and rest your hands on the wall.'

Susan flushed with humiliation as she climbed awkwardly onto the lowered lavatory seat and leant against the wall. The pose forced her bottom out, making her panties tighten across her cheeks. It also meant kneeling in the layer of soot which coated the top of the seat. She hung her head as he strapped her wrists on either side of the thick iron pipe that led down from the cistern. She was genuinely helpless, unable to protect herself from him in any way, her position leaving her naked body completely vulnerable.

Her breath started to quicken as he lashed her ankles together and wound the tape around the base of the bowl, making it impossible for her to do more than wriggle her bottom from side to side.

'You're enjoying this, aren't you?' Berner asked, squeezing her bottom with a possessive familiarity that sent a new tingle of submissive pleasure through her.

'Y-yes,' she admitted. He sniggered again.

'You've no idea how cute you look,' he went on, squeezing her bottom with more and more familiarity, 'naked except for your wellies and panties.'

He put the tape down, and then started to fondle her breasts, weighing them and rubbing his palms against her nipples.

Susan began to whimper with pleasure as he explored her breasts. Each touch on her nipples sent a little shock through her, her inability to resist adding to the thrill.

'You do look very sweet,' he said, letting go of her breasts and standing back a little. 'Well, I think we'd better have these pretty knickers down now, don't you?'

Susan moaned as he reached for the waistband of her panties and drew them slowly down over her bum. Her bottom felt fat and prominent, as it always did when her panties where taken down; be it for a good spanking, or in preparation for a long fuck. She instinctively dipped her back.

'That's right, stick it out, show me everything,' he breathed. 'You're gorgeous, Susie. I'm not surprised people want to spank you. I'm not really into it, but with a backside like yours, I can see the temptation.'

'Do it, then,' Susan moaned as he settled her panties around the tops of her thighs and began to caress her buttocks.'

'Maybe,' he said quietly. 'After all, you're tied up, so I can spank you when I like, can't I?'

'Yes,' Susan agreed, her voice little more than a whimper.

Berner's hand moved from the cheeks of her bottom to her thighs, stroking the smooth flesh, squeezing gently as if to test its quality. Susan put her head back and began to moan in earnest as his hand moved between her legs, cupping the mound of her pussy, the heel of his hand grinding directly onto her clitoris. He chuckled softly at her excitement. Her breath was coming fast and hard, the muscles of her midriff, thighs and bottom contracting rhythmically.

He stopped suddenly, leaving her in an agony of desire.

'Touch me!' she begged.

'Uh-uh, we can't have you coming, not just yet,' Berner teased.

'Bastard!'

'Now, now – such language,' he chided. 'Maybe I should beat you, or maybe I should just fuck you quickly and leave you for an hour or two.'

'No, Paul, have mercy!' Susan begged. 'Spank me, please!'

'That I like to hear,' he said. 'Say it again, beg for mercy.'

'Mercy, please,' Susan responded. 'Spank me, fuck me, but don't leave me. Please, please…!'

'Nice. You really are getting me quite excited, Susan. I

think I will fuck you now.'

'Go on, then,' she breathed.

'Say please.'

'Please, Paul, fuck me… please.'

'That's what I like to hear. You have such a pretty pussy, too, especially from this angle. Your sex-lips pout really sweetly and you're all wet and ready. I like the shaved look, too.'

Susan strained to peer back over her shoulder. Berner was nursing an erection, his cock spearing up from his open trousers like a flagpole.

'Please, Paul,' she begged, sorry that his threat to spank her seemed to have been no more than a tease, but desperate for the feeling of his cock inside her.

He moved closer and she felt hands on her hips. His cock touched her pussy, rubbing in the wet flesh, and then suddenly stabbed inside. Susan grunted and gasped with the shock of his rough penetration, gripping the pipe as he started to fuck her with hard short strokes. His groin thrust rhythmically against the cheeks of her bottom and shoved her forward. Squirming in her bonds, she pleaded for more without a thought for who might hear.

Suddenly he was still. 'Stop squealing,' he hissed. 'You'll alert young wet-behind-the-ears!'

'Sorry…' Susan said limply.

'I'd better gag you.'

Susan waited while there was a rustle of clothing, and then her skirt was wrapped over her head and secured in place with more of the tape.

'Can you breathe okay?' she heard him ask. She nodded; the skirt hadn't really gagged her, but she was happy to play along.

A finger touched between her buttocks, tracing a slow line until it found her anus. It probed the tight entrance. She gulped as the muscle relaxed, and she rocked back slightly in the hope that he'd push it right in.

'Ready,' she heard, as the finger disappeared. For a moment she thought he was going to bugger her, but it was her pussy to which he prodded his helmet. Again it eased into her, slowly this time, stretching her vagina and sliding deeper until it was fully embedded and she could feel the bulge of his balls against her pussy. His hands locked on her hips and he started to fuck her, slowly at first, then faster, making her grunt into the gag as his hips slapped against her bottom and his cock worked in and out of her vagina. She heard him curse. He went rigid and strained against her bottom, forcing her face uncomfortably against the wall, and then she felt his cock pulse rhythmically and his semen erupted deep inside her.

He pulled out, breathing heavily.

Unable to move, and with her thighs aching from the awkward position, she hoped he would untie her now he'd had his fun. She hadn't come, as she knew she wouldn't without at least some attention to her clit, but once free she intended to sit down on the toilet and relieve herself, regardless of what he thought or how dirty her bottom got. She needed it badly, but could do nothing until he chose to untie her.

Something touched her anus and she squirmed with pleasure. She relaxed the delicate muscle to assist the intruding object. It pushed in a little way and then stopped. She shivered, knowing that whatever it was it would be sticking out of her bottom, protruding obscenely from between her taut buttocks. It was a deliciously dirty thought. She eagerly anticipated the expected touch on her pussy; maybe even a tongue, if he was in a generous mood.

But nothing happened. She began to wonder what he was doing.

'Paul?' she mumbled uneasily, after what seemed an unreasonable period without a remark from him, or indeed any sound at all.

There was no answer.

'Paul?' This was getting less funny by the second. Her desire evaporated. 'I'm getting very uncomfortable here... Paul?'

Still no response; no sound.

She turned her head, unable to see more than vague patterns of light through the layer of cotton wrapped around her head. Nothing moved within her field of vision. The bright sunlight from the collapsed roof showed enough for her to realise there was nobody there.

Berner had left her alone.

Not only had he tied her up and taken advantage of her, but he'd left her kneeling on a lavatory seat with her panties pulled down and nothing else on but wellington boots. She knew how she must look, kneeling in an obscenely blatant position, tied and gagged, her bottom stuck out and plugged by a mystery object.

She started to sob with frustration, wriggling on the seat but unable to loosen the tough tape that bound her in place. The smell of burnt wine was starting to get to her as well, strong in the warm stillness of the warehouse. She considered calling for help, but abandoned the idea. If the constable came in and found her it would be unendurably embarrassing. On the other hand he would free her... or would he? A young lad like that, presented with a helpless girl.

Remembering the thoughtless passion of Taz, Beadle and Fire Ghost, Susan decided that the temptation for the young officer would probably be overwhelming. He could do what he wanted to her and then deny it. After all, it would be obvious that Berner had left her like that, and Berner's job would be on the line if the story got out. Yes, she decided, he might well risk it.

The realisation unsettled her, and her desperation grew. 'Paul!' she mumbled again, although she knew it was pointless.

She waited for what seemed like an age, moving her legs as much as the bonds allowed to ease her aching muscles. She heard a noise, and then footsteps squelching across the warehouse floor. Praying it was Berner, Susan strained to try and see over her shoulder. She started to struggle, despite knowing the futility of trying to escape.

Someone was about to find her!

There was a noise close behind and she knew someone was there – watching. She stopped squirming and stayed very still, expecting to hear a voice at any moment.

Nothing; not even an exclamation of surprise.

She started to wonder at his intentions, or whether it was Berner tormenting her.

The sound of a zip answered at least half her question.

Susan started to tremble, waiting, completely at the mercy of whoever was there. The object in her rear passage was pulled slowly out, and she sensed that the mystery man was intending to replace it immediately with his own object. She was going to be buggered while tied and kneeling on a toilet seat, an act that would be incredibly humiliating for her. She waited, expecting the swollen tip of a penis to push between her buttocks and touch her anus at any moment.

The man seemed to be taking a long time but, just as Susan had decided he might have thought better of it, something did touch her. Relief mingled with disappointment as the firm roundness of a man's cock touched not her anus but her pussy. The cock was rubbed in her wetness, just as Berner had done, making Susan wonder if it was him. Then it penetrated her with one long thrust and she didn't care any more.

Hands curled around her body and weighed her breasts as the silent stranger started to fuck her with steady powerful strokes. Her back dipped and her head flopped in ecstasy as the hands worked on her breasts and fingers pinched her erect nipples. Her pleasure was mounting inexorably, and then she moaned her despair as the man suddenly and silently came and immediately pulled out.

Once more she was left alone, sobbing in frustration. She was pretty certain it had been Berner again, and she silently cursed his chauvinistic selfishness.

This time the wait was shorter. Footsteps sounded behind her only a minute or so later.

'Sorry I was so long,' Berner said in a tone of cheerful unconcern. 'I wanted to get something to paddle your backside with, but this place is remarkably clean for a trading estate. Still, I found a nice piece of wood in a skip. It's not too dirty. Oh, and I've got my camera.'

Susan could only whimper as she was photographed in her utterly humiliating pose. The camera clicked several times before he was satisfied. There was a pause, and then something hard smacked gently across her bottom.

'Nice?' Berner asked.

Susan hung her head in meek acceptance of her beating, past caring and knowing that when she did come it was going to be an orgasm to end all orgasms. Her thighs and arms ached and her pussy was sore, but the whole experience was just too good to end before she had come. The piece of wood smacked across her bottom again, rather harder. Susan wiggled her bottom for more, the third and still harder smack catching her full across her cheeks.

Berner's body touched her flank, a hand curling under her belly to find her pussy. Susan sighed in bliss. He was going to frig her while he beat her; the perfect way to come. His fingers started to rub her clit as he brought the wood down on her bottom again. She could feel her bottom bounce as the wood struck, her buttocks wobbling under the punishment. Her muscles strained against the bonds, adding to the bliss of being beaten and masturbated at the same time.

'Would you like me to talk to you?' Berner asked. 'To tell you how fat your bottom is and how rude you look with your cheeks spread? I can see your little arsehole and your shaved cunt-lips, Susie. That reminds me, where's that lipstick I put in your arse to keep you amused while I was gone? Ah, here, a bit dirty, but that won't matter.'

Susan felt the lipstick being pushed into her anus. She groaned as it popped in, not just from the pleasure of having it put in her bottom, but also at the thought of how rude it must look. Berner put his hand back under her belly and found her clit as the wood smacked against her bottom again. She knew it wouldn't be long as he started to rub. The smacks were hard but no longer hurt as much, a sure sign that she was going to come soon.

She started to buck, pushing her bottom back and squirming frantically to get better friction against his fingers. He sniggered arrogantly and the beating became harder, faster, taking Susan to the brink. A rhythm started, his rubs and smacks working in unison. Her muscles spasmed. She tensed, trying to scream but unable to. She needed to kick and squirm but the bonds wouldn't let her. Then it came, a rush of pleasure that exploded in her clitoris and ran through every nerve in her body. For an instant she was incredibly sensitive, aware of the heat between her legs, her anus tight around the intruding lipstick, her bottom throbbing and hot, her spine arched into a tight curve, her wrists and ankles lashed and straining. Bright lights exploded in her head, and then everything went dark.

It was over, and she hung limp in her bonds. Every muscle in her body ached as Berner started to loosen the tape.

'Thank you,' she gasped as her skirt was pulled clear of her head. 'That was really special.'

'Don't mention it,' Berner said as he pulled the lipstick out of her bottom.

Paul Berner walked across the gutted warehouse with a grin that ran from ear to ear. Behind him Susan picked her way carefully through the debris. He turned to catch a shy, abashed look and a little smile, which made his grin broader than ever. Underneath her skirt he knew she was bare.

The thought sent a pulse to his cock, despite his recent orgasm. Susan was so lovely – and dirty beyond his wildest hopes. Not only that, but she was his until the Fire Ghost investigation was over, maybe longer. Her ideas about a link between the fire, the death of Alan Sowerby, and some sort of wine scandal interested him, although they were hard to take seriously. On the other hand, during the time they had served together, he had learnt to respect her knack of spotting when something dodgy was going on.

The young PC gave them a curious look as they came out of the warehouse. Berner returned a formal nod, and caught a questioning glance from Susan. He shook his head and smiled, knowing exactly what the question was. He got into his car, drove to front gate, and waited for Bob Tweed to raise the security barrier.

He looked back, smiling to himself as Susan's black Rover pulled up behind him. He watched her look at Tweed, and Tweed smile back; not his normal leer but a knowing, satisfied smirk. Paul Berner's grin broadened as he saw Susan's mouth drop open, her cheeks blush a furious red, and realisation dawn in her lovely wide eyes.

Susan slid down in the bath until the water was up to her chin. Closing her eyes, she took a moment to concentrate on the delicious feeling of Paulette massaging her thigh muscles. Her tension faded slowly under her friend's fingers.

Five minutes later, feeling warm and relaxed, she told Paulette to listen and concentrated on the ideas she had formed while at de Vergy Fine Wines.

'This is my reasoning,' she began. 'Firstly, the whole idea rests on Sowerby's refusal to believe that certain wines were what they claimed to be. That presumably means they were watered or adulterated in some way. Therefore the original fraud must have occurred at the point of production. Annabella's outfit is distributing the wines, not producing them, but our reasoning demands that Sowerby's death, our following his investigation up and the fire are somehow linked. I also discovered that the brandy pallet that exploded had been delivered before we spoke to Annabella, and that Ruddock left some minutes after Annabella on the Sunday evening. Okay?'

'So far,' Paulette answered.

'So, this is the theory. A producer in France is making bad wine, presumably very cheaply. They then make an agreement with de Vergy Fine Wines to import and distribute it. Sowerby gets onto it and is poisoned, to prevent him exposing the scam. Annabella and Ruddock decided to quit and destroy the evidence, so they imitate a Fire Ghost attack and destroy the warehouse and all the adulterated wine. Believe me, what's left isn't going to yield much to analysis.'

'Are you sure Annabella's in on it?' Paulette queried.

'Not necessarily. What I don't know yet is whether Annabella takes an active part in the buying and handling of the wines, or if Ruddock does all of that and she just heads the company. If he does, then she might not be involved at all, but simply have told him about our visit. The presence of the brandy might be coincidence, but more probably it indicates that he, or they, intended to fire the warehouse and brought the date forward when they discovered our interest. True, destroying the warehouse immediately after we'd shown an interest looks suspicious, but with Sowerby dead and all the evidence destroyed, they would be safe from prosecution regardless.'

'So the trail's pretty dead at this end,' Paulette put in.

'Yes, but not in France. I only found two addresses in the remains of the warehouse: the brandy supplier, who is a big British wholesaler of Greek brandy, and a co-op in the Loire valley which produces several wines.'

'So you're going to France?'

'No, you are. There's an eleven o'clock ferry from Portsmouth to Caen. You're on it.'

'But—'

'Work can wait a few days. You're a freelance, aren't you? I'm better employed here seeing how things develop, and besides, it's not often I get the chance to be the plaything of a man with a mind as twisted as Paul Berner's. I always thought of him as the sort of pig who'll make you suck him, bend you over for a thirty second stuffing from the rear, and then refuse to help you come. He's actually quite imaginative, and definitely perverse.'

'Slut,' Paulette said playfully.

Robin Riddell stood looking out from his parent's tower block flat high over the lights of west London. Ever since Monday afternoon he'd been unable to get what had happened out of his mind. Lust and guilt warred in his mind, creating feelings so strong that sleep was impossible. The girl Susan had actually sucked his cock while Taz was fucking her, an act dirtier than anything he had done before. Okay, he was no virgin; he'd fucked Clare and had Jilly after her birthday party. Jilly had also helped toss his cock for him when Taz wasn't around – not once but several times. Susan had been different, rude, uninhibited: sucking and fucking with a frantic eagerness. And she'd fingered herself and come in front of them, not caring at all what they saw.

The thought of Susan's tits sent his hand to his cock. They'd been big and firm, with good-sized nipples. As fine as any he'd seen in magazines, and he'd not only had a good feel but put his tag across them. That thought started his guilt again. They'd held her down while they tagged her, and she hadn't stopped struggling until it was too late. It had been a joke though, and she hadn't minded in the end, laughing and showing it off, obviously proud of herself.

Again, it wasn't the first time. Jilly had had a 'Taz' tag put on her bum more than once, and the first time they'd held her with her skirt up and her knickers pulled well down. She'd giggled all the time, though. Feeling puzzled and confused, he started to stroke his penis. Whatever they'd done, the memory was too much to ignore.

An orange glint somewhere out among the lights beneath him caught his attention. It came again, moving, flickering, clearly not a streetlight. It was somewhere down by the canal, among the industrial estates of Park Royal:

Fire.

Forgetting all about his fantasising, he hastily grabbed his clothes. As he dressed, he watched in absolute fascination as the fire sprang up. It caught fast, the orange flicker becoming a line of flame, then a great gout as something exploded. Fire-engine sirens cut across the night, flashing blue lights moving along the Westway into his range of vision.

Fully dressed, he grabbed his bag of spray cans from the top of the wardrobe. The flat was dark, his mother sleeping; undisturbed by the distant wails of the fire-engines.

He shut the flat door carefully and made for the lift. This time he was determined; he would leave the 'Fire Ghost' tag while the flames still burned.

Then they'd notice it: they had to.

Half an hour later, he was pushing his way through a gap in a fence that led onto wasteland across the canal from the burning warehouse. The place had been easy to find; orange flames reflected in the sky and occasionally visible along roads or between gaps in buildings. A great pillar of smoke also showed against the stars, a black column to guide him to his destination. Near his destination, anyway; Robin had no intention of risking getting caught and reasoned that it would not be until morning that the far side of the canal was investigated, if at all.

His torch illuminated a path across the wasteland, the gradually dying fire throwing weird shadows of orange and black across the scene. Unlike the last fire scene, there were no great heaps of rubble to provide convenient surfaces for tagging, and it was some while before he found a brick wall that suited his purposes. A distant cluster of bright violet-white streetlights illuminated the surface, giving him enough light to go about his work.

With the thrill of illicit activity that tagging always gave him, he selected the red can and began the careful work of spray-painting. He was a good artist, he knew: maybe the best in the area. Certainly far better than Taz or Beadle. Finishing the red, he started to add the orange, getting halfway through the second word before a noise made him spin, his heart leaping into his mouth.

He froze. Behind him, as tall and lank as Taz, hands thrust deep into the pockets of tatty jeans, spiked red hair like a halo around his head, was a man. Robin could make out very little of his features, but something told him that he had just met the real Fire Ghost.

Chapter Five

Ted Gage stood looking at the wreckage of Crazy Joe's Carpet Madhouse. The scene was depressingly familiar, the only difference being that it was less than a mile from the last fire. There was soot and charred wreckage in a sea of filthy water, police of various sorts going over the mess, reporters and onlookers standing outside the cordon of police tape. This time Detective Superintendent Julia Keeson herself had come down. She was trying to dispose of the media, a job that Gage was glad not to have, for once. Otherwise her presence was a nuisance, although at least it meant she got to appreciate the difficulties he was labouring under from first-hand experience. Paul Berner was also there, talking to Susan MacQuillan. Gage found both Berner and MacQuillan somewhat irritating, to say the least.

'Sir,' someone called.

He turned to see Sergeant Yates coming towards him.

'Something you should see, sir,' Yates announced. 'There's some graffiti on the far side of the canal.'

Gage went with the sergeant, interested in anything that might provide the slightest clue. Having found their way to the opposite bank of the Grand Union canal, they were directed onto a strip of wasteland that separated the canal from a main road. There, plastered on a brick wall, was the legend, 'Fire Ghost'.

Robin Riddell leant eagerly forward across the stained Formica of the café table. Opposite him, his leg cocked up onto the bench and a cigarette dangling carelessly from between his fingers, sat the man on whom Robin had styled himself. Thin, lanky, his red hair formed into spikes, the Fire Ghost was pretty much as Robin had imagined him. He also had restless eyes and a wide loose mouth that gave the impression that he was amused by everything around him: a cynical, knowing amusement. He had also told Robin to call him Paul, a confidence which filled him with pride.

'Quit?' he laughed, in response to Robin's question as to whether he felt it would be wise to stop fire-raising while he was ahead of the game. 'No way. Why should I? They'll never catch me, and it's my life. It's fun. I enjoy it.'

'There's a lot of cops after you,' Robin insisted, awed by his new friend's coolness.

'Who cares?' Paul replied easily. 'They ain't going to catch me, like I said. See, there's two types of guy in this world: the winners and the losers. I'm one of the winners. Seven times now, and they ain't had a sniff. It's easy. Pick a target they ain't expecting, find a side with no cameras, wait until the soft sods are all asleep, and bang!'

'Neat. When are you going to do another?'

'Maybe soon, maybe not. I'll tell you, because I can see you're a bit like me. You don't give a fuck for the pigs or any of these lah-di-dah shits who think they know what's right. I've done places down the East End and up Lee Valley and around here. Next one's going down on this big estate in Merton. I've looked it over. It's a snip. You can come and tag it if you want.'

'Really?'

Paulette drew her car to a stop in the central square of Choray. The village was tiny, no more than a couple of dozen houses, several of which had signs declaring their owners to be vignerons; wine makers. None had claimed to be a co-op. Trying her halting French at the single small hotel, which appeared to lack even a name, she discovered that the place she wanted was a mile outside the village on the road leading south.

She yawned, deciding to have lunch and an hour's sleep before tackling the co-op. The ferry trip and the long drive across France had been tiring, leaving her feeling hot, sticky, and in need of sleep.

The hotel had space, despite its small size, and even managed to provide an adequate lunch. Finding the room comfortable and provided with a shower, she locked the door, washed, dried herself and fell naked onto the bed. A minute later she was asleep. She dreamt of Annabella de Vergy, picturing herself tied over a trestle at the dominant beauty's mercy. The image was so vivid that, when she woke up, she was unable to resist masturbating.

In her fantasy she was Annabella's pet slave on a plantation, being beaten while spread naked on silk sheets. Even when she came she was no more than half-awake, returning to a more peaceful sleep afterwards. By late afternoon she once more felt ready to tackle the world and left the hotel, taking the road south.

The co-op was obvious. Set on the brow of a hill where the land began to fall away towards the Cher valley, the great structure of concrete and wood made a sharp contrast with the squat buildings of yellow limestone in the village. As she stopped on the verge, she saw that the co-op had an air of bustle and industry quite different from the sleepy atmosphere of Choray and the other villages she had passed through since she had left the autoroute at Blois.

She stepped from the car and adjusted her clothes and hair. She and Susan had worked carefully on her image. If the co-op was involved in a major fraud, they were hardly likely to welcome journalists and might well not even welcome casual passing trade. The best bet had seemed to be to hope that the manager was male, in which case he was highly unlikely to refuse Paulette's polite request to be shown around.

To maximise her chances, Paulette had dressed carefully. Her striped T-shirt clung to her braless breasts, giving the occasional hint of her nipples and exaggerating the breadth of her chest. It was also tucked tightly into her cut-down jeans to show off the trim lines of her waist. The jeans were also tight, hugging her bottom and the swell of her pussy; the frayed shortened legs allowed just a hint of her bottom-cheeks. The idea was to give an impression of unintentional sexual display; a naïve girl dressed for a summer's day, and unaware of the effect of her choice of dress.

A welcoming sign at the gate removed her first possible obstacle, advertising local wines and wines from the south of France. Visitors buying and tasting the co-op's produce were clearly welcome. The appearance of the suited man among the people working in the yard removed her second. The instant he saw her he flashed his white teeth and his eyes glinted in a way that was more than familiar to Paulette. At no more than five and a half feet, slim, and so dapper as to seem more in place at a wedding reception than in the yard of a wine co-operative, he presented an image she regarded as typically French.

'Ah, mam'selle,' he welcomed smoothly, making Paulette wonder what it was about her that was so transparently British, and then realising that the number plate of Susan's car was visible to him, 'may I help you?'

'I was wondering if I could taste some of your wines?' Paulette asked, thankful that she was not going to have to try and communicate in French.

'But of course,' he replied, his smile even broader. 'Allow me to introduce myself. Christian Charrier; I am the manager here.'

'Paulette Richards.'

He took her hand and kissed instead of shook it. 'Enchanted,' he leered. 'Or is that wrong in English?'

'No, not really.'

'Ah, I am so clumsy,' he went on. 'To know the words of a language is one thing; to speak like a native, quite another.'

'No, really, you speak very good English.'

'Thank you, but you flatter me,' Charrier continued, casually taking her arm. 'Perhaps you would permit me to personally show you around?'

'Fine,' Paulette answered, feeling somewhat taken aback and wondering if she hadn't overdone the look of sexual availability.

He led her into the low whitewashed building that bore a sign indicating it as the tasting room, and poured two glasses of a fresh sharp white wine. She made a polite comment, although she would have preferred something with more flavour. Charrier responded cheerfully, explaining the background of the wine and then leading her through a connecting door into the main body of the co-op.

Paulette looked round, wishing she had a greater knowledge of wine, and wondering how she was supposed to find out whether or not the co-op was involved with fraud. Great tanks of concrete, fibreglass, and stainless steel stood around the spacious room. To one side, a machine that was evidently a bottling plant clicked and whirred. The two men operating it cast lustful glances at her.

As Charrier continued the tour, Paulette started to feel very self-conscious. It was obvious that Charrier was chatting her up, and obvious that the workers knew it. Maybe they even regarded it as a familiar routine, judging from the knowing looks that were passed without much concern for whether she saw or not. In other circumstances she would have made a polite excuse and left, but she needed to be able to study the co-op. As they returned to the tasting room, Charrier became bolder, allowing his hand to stray onto the curve of Paulette's bottom and passing a remark that was clearly intended as a compliment on the size and firmness of her breasts.

Paulette found herself at once flattered and repelled. Charrier certainly had charm and an open, appreciative attitude to her which she found refreshing. On the other hand, there was something oily, almost serpentine about his character, and physically he was not really her taste at all. She liked men to be big, muscular, and strong enough to dominate her physically without really thinking about it. Charrier was only a few inches taller than her and bony, although his bronzed skin and sinewy hands suggested at least some strength.

She accepted another glass of wine, this time red and rather thin. The idea of letting herself be seduced in order to investigate the co-op had changed from an amusing joke to a very immediate reality. Charrier had obviously decided that he had made a conquest.

They continued to talk, Paulette sampling each of the four main wines produced by the co-op and the two brought in from the south. The glasses were large, and even with her limited knowledge of wine, Paulette knew that tasting samples were never filled to the brim. Still, allowing him to pour cheap wine into her was making the idea of being seduced by him more acceptable, so that when the other workers began to leave and Charrier offered to show her the cellar, she followed without hesitation.

'Temptation,' Charrier declared as he closed the heavy wooden doors behind him at the bottom of the cellar steps, 'could be defined as a woman's body. Do you not think?'

Thinking of Susan, Paulette readily agreed with Charrier's rather over-dramatic philosophy.

'And yours,' Charrier continued, 'is provocation beyond endurance.'

Without warning he pushed her against the wall and was upon her. Paulette responded to his kisses, at first half-heartedly and then more warmly, letting her mouth open under his. He moaned as he mauled her breasts, then sharply tugged the T-shirt up, letting them spill softly into his hands. Paulette shivered as his thumbs found her nipples, then sighed as his mouth disengaged from hers to suck on one hard bud of flesh. She held his head, her passion rising as he moulded and licked her breasts.

She did not resist while he undressed her. He kissed her body and peeled her clothes off to leave her standing naked in the dim yellow light of the cellar. He murmured endearments in French, few of which Paulette understood, except that he clearly had a thing about her being black, and that she had in some way teased him into making his advance. She took very little notice, not worried about his fantasies as long as she got what she now needed; a good fuck. Suddenly he pulled away, leaving her naked and panting against the wall.

'Would you perhaps allow me to indulge a little penchant?' he asked, as breathless as she and slightly hesitant.

'I'll try,' Paulette whispered, hoping his fantasy would be to her taste.

'Come.' Charrier's eyes glinted hungrily, and he took Paulette by the hand.

She allowed him to lead her into a smaller room; a chamber of the local yellow stone lined with racks of bottles. In the centre stood a large barrel on a trestle.

'Get on the barrel for me, my little one,' Charrier said with a catch of urgent lust in his tone.

Paulette hesitated for a moment, and then straddled the barrel. Her mouthwatering breasts squashed against the smooth wood as she lay forward. Bracing her feet against one end of the trestle and gripping the other with her hands, she managed to get fairly comfortable. The position forced her thighs wide open, as she knew it would, and held her pussy vulnerable and exposed. She felt gloriously available and extremely rude, knowing that when he moved behind her he would be able to see every detail of her pussy – and her anus.

Charrier appeared in front of her, holding a coil of rope.

'May I tie you?' he asked hoarsely. 'Say if you'd prefer otherwise.'

Paulette wavered between lust and caution. To be tied over the barrel fitted so well with her fantasies that it was almost irresistible, yet Charrier was undoubtedly a suspect for fraud, possibly even murder. Then again, he had no reason to suspect her of being in any way involved with an investigation, or even to know that there was an investigation. Also, if he was the sort of man who could murder, backing out now might very well be the wrong thing to do.

Yes, she decided, the wisest course was to let the Frenchman fulfil his fantasy. Not that she had a great deal of choice any more. Even as she pondered her predicament he had busily tied one of her ankles to the trestle and looped the rope underneath. Paulette shivered, the thrill of bondage getting to her despite the danger – or possibly because of it.

'You are such temptation, my dear,' Charrier said as he finished securing her to the barrel. She was now utterly available to his every whim.

'In the seventeenth century, and before,' Charrier continued, walking around Paulette and looking at her naked perfection, 'when a whore was taken, she would be tied behind a cart and brought to the village square. There she would be stripped, tied to a stake, and left for the ridicule of the people. Perhaps she would be pelted with refuse, perhaps spat on by the village women, but most often she would be whipped...'

He was now standing in front of Paulette and slowly undid his belt, with clear intent. She watched, hypnotised by his words and the movement of his hands. The belt was a good two inches wide, much broader than would normally be used on a man's suit trousers, and made of a heavy, supple leather.

'A fitting punishment for a whore, do you not think?' Charrier goaded as he moved behind her again, his fingertips lightly following the contours of her back. 'Yes, it is a terrible sin to tempt men with your flesh, and for sin we must have expiation, must we not?'

Paulette couldn't answer. She was trembling, and beginning to understand what Susan meant by sexual humiliation. She had been tied up often enough, spanked even more often, but always by indulgent men who only called it punishment because she asked them to. In practice, they'd always been so taken by her body and unashamed sexuality that they'd have done anything she asked. Charrier clearly desired her as much as any of them, but he had called her a whore, and was going to beat her as a punishment for it; beat her without knowing it was what she really wanted.

'Don't you see? You are to be whipped like the whore you are,' Charrier said as he idly stroked Paulette's raised bottom. 'Only then will I give you what you crave; my penis.'

Realising that an acquiescent silence was not the reaction he would expect of a girl who was about to be whipped, Paulette began to whimper and stopped trying to control her trembling.

Charrier snickered.

Paulette could not see him, and could do nothing but wait passively for her beating to begin.

But the Frenchman was clearly in no hurry. He explored her buttocks, saying nothing as his fingers slid between them and loitered on her rear entrance with a casual intimacy that had his victim sobbing with frustration.

Charrier snickered again and his hand left her. There was a long pause. Paulette closed her eyes and braced herself, waiting for the whistle of the belt and the explosion of pain across her backside.

Nothing happened.

Her breathing quickened with the agonising frustration of her helplessness, and the sure knowledge that she was about to have his belt taken to her behind. Her buttocks clenched in anticipation. The tension was almost unbearable.

'Do it…' she begged, finally unable to endure the waiting any longer. 'Please… beat me.'

Again she heard his cruel laugh, only this time it was immediately followed by the first stroke. Paulette gasped, feeling her buttocks bounce under the harsh impact. The belt was heavy and stung, a sharp pain delivered with a force that pushed the air from her lungs. The second smack caught the fattest part of Paulette's bottom, the third the junction between buttocks and thighs. She made no effort to hide her response, squealing and wriggling as best she could in the restraints.

Charrier laughed as he beat her, calling her a whore and then lapsing into French as he became more excited. At first she answered him back, calling him every name she could think of, then subsiding to whispered curses and finally whimpers as her buttocks began to throb and the familiar urgent ache began to build in her pussy. Her whole bottom was a mass of pain, incredibly sensitive; the centre of her awareness as the leather smacked against it again and again.

'Fuck me, Christian,' she whispered, breathless and urgent for the Frenchman's cock inside her.

He stopped the beating immediately. She heard a dull thud as the belt dropped to the stone floor, and then the sound of a zip. She sighed in anticipated as his cock nudged between her thighs and then pushed a little way inside her pussy. He paused for a moment, and then the air was wrenched from her lungs as he lunged forward and filled her aggressively. Fingers locked onto her hips and he began to fuck her with strong, slow motions, each of which pressed his belly against the well-beaten flesh of her buttocks.

Paulette began to grunt as his strokes quickened, each one sandwiching her against the barrel, the fiery pain in her bottom contrasting with the pleasure in her vagina. Tied and helpless, there was nothing she could do but let Charrier take his pleasure from her body.

'Harder,' she begged, drawing a new flurry of energy from the Frenchman. He began to moan and mumble her name. She knew he was coming. He pulled away. An instant later something splattered across her bottom, and she knew he had ejaculated on her tenderised flesh. It felt gloriously undignified, and she wondered how she must look for him. Incredibly lewd and wanton, that was for sure.

'Help me come,' she begged, hoping that Charrier would have the decency to consider her.

He didn't. He merely made a noise that sounded to Paulette like disgust.

'Please...' she implored again, feeling incredibly frustrated and annoyed at his casual assumption that it was all over just because he'd come.

He snorted contemptuously, but from the corner of her eye she saw him walk to one of the racks and take a bottle, after considering two before making his choice. He moved back out of her view, and a moment later the cold glass was pressed against her wet labia.

'Thank you,' she sighed, rubbing with little side-to-side motions of her hips. 'Oh... that's so nice. Oh, thank you, Christian... thank you for beating me, thank you, thank you...'

Charrier laughed his same cruel laugh, and in that instant she erupted, screaming her passion in the empty cellar, her mind fixed on the sheer dirtiness of the condition she was in as her orgasm welled up and burst in a shock that speared right through her body.

Charrier untied her even before her orgasm had fully subsided. She was vaguely aware that he was apologising for beating her in a tone that indicated genuine regret and sought mitigation.

'You tempted me too much,' he said, almost angry in his attempt to justify his actions.

'It's all right,' Paulette tried to reassure him. 'Calm down. You might have asked first, but I didn't mind.'

'No?'

'Actually,' she admitted, 'it made it rather special, knowing that you didn't know, if you see what I mean.'

'*Extraordinaire*!' Charrier enthused. 'Normally girls protest when you try, love it when it's being done, and then complain afterwards.'

'Not me,' Paulette said as she climbed off the barrel and stretched her stiff limbs. 'Do you think I could have a wash?'

'Of course, how thoughtless of me. There's a basin in the office, upstairs and to the left. Don't worry, everyone has gone home.'

Despite Charrier's assurance, Paulette checked carefully before slipping out of the cellar, then poked her head above the parapet before emerging from the stairwell. Appearing naked from the cellar in front of half a dozen French workmen was beyond her idea of showing off. The place was empty, so she hurried across to the office. She washed quickly, listening for Charrier's footsteps. Whatever he was doing, it clearly didn't involve coming back upstairs and so, with her heart in her mouth, Paulette quickly wiped herself dry and moved to the filling cabinets at the far end of the room.

It took no time at all to find what she wanted. The files were clearly labelled and in seconds she was holding the de Vergy Fine Wines file in trembling fingers. The top sheet was an invoice copy, showing that Annabella and Ruddock imported all six of the co-op's wines. Even as Paulette turned to the next page she heard the firm sound of the cellar door being shut.

'I've brought your clothes, Paulette,' Charrier's voice sounded as she hastily replaced the file and scampered back to the basin, making a pretence of finishing her ablutions as he appeared and placed her clothes on the desk.

He grinned at her nudity and made a joke on the state of her bottom. Paulette did her best to return a bubbly smile, even though her heart was pounding in her chest.

'And will you be a passing delight for me, my dear,' he asked, watching Paulette slip into her panties and wince a little as they touched her tender bottom, with obvious relish, 'or perhaps you are staying locally and would care to see more of me and the Loire?'

'I shouldn't really be doing this,' Paul Berner said as he dropped a sheaf of papers in front of Susan.

'You shouldn't really tie girls to lavatories, either,' she said, 'at least, not at incident sites. Have you got some blank paper and a pen?'

'Sure,' Berner confirmed. 'D'you fancy Chinese or Indian?'

'Aren't you going to cook?' she queried, looking up from where she was spreading the reports of the seven Fire Ghost attacks across his coffee-table.

'Cooking's not really my thing.'

'Chinese, then.'

Berner fetched the pen and paper, leaving Susan absorbed in the details of the arsons. After telephoning for the take-away he went to the fridge for beer. Susan took hers with a murmur of thanks, not even glancing up from her work.

Feeling somewhat ignored, he crossed to his favourite armchair and slumped into it, sipping his beer and thinking about Susan and sex. When it came down to it, she was perfect; willing, wanton, and submissive. And the sex was good – very good. He felt a familiar tingle in his groin as he savoured the way her breasts strained against her T-shirt as she leant over the coffee-table.

Waiting for the Chinese to arrive, he started thinking about what he could do with her, once she had finished with the work. It was not going to be easy to top what he had done the day before, but one or two interesting ideas came to mind. Watching her perform with others came top of his list; making her do things to them, not because she particularly wanted to, but because it gave *him* pleasure.

The chime of the doorbell interrupted his fantasy. Susan was still engrossed, so he got up and fetched the meal. Even when he placed the delicious smelling food in front of her, she merely mumbled a thank you and reached for a prawn cracker.

'Give it a rest, Susan,' he chided. 'You've got all evening to do that.'

She looked up. 'Sorry, you're right. Let's eat, and then I'll run it past you.'

'Haven't you had enough work for one day?' he asked petulantly. 'I thought we might have some fun.'

Susan smiled and stuck her tongue out, reaching for her plate as he took a draught of his beer.

When they had eaten she worked for another ten minutes or so, and then gathered the papers into a neat stack.

'Right,' she began purposefully. 'Seven arsons, seven warehouses on seven different industrial estates. A pattern of sorts, but short of putting a team on every estate in London, not a very useful one. On the other hand, a number of factors separate the first four attacks from the later three. I take it you lot have noticed that?'

'Er – well, no,' Berner began. 'Sure, the last three have all been by canals, but so was the first. Anyway, that's surely just a question of sides of estates that face onto canals being unguarded. After all, in the second attack he used a railway in the same way.'

'That's not really accurate,' Susan continued. 'The first attack was in Enfield and the warehouse backed onto the New River. That's small and not open to water traffic. The next three all have no road access, but easy enough foot access to the sides on which the attacks were made. True, the railway shields the one in East Ham nicely, but numbers three and four have a park with a narrow belt of scrubby woods and a broad belt of wasteland respectively. Five, six and seven, though, all have broad navigable canals by them. To throw a petrol bomb through a broken window, say twelve feet up and twenty feet away, is fairly easy, but to throw one across a canal as much as sixty feet wide and hit three times out of three, takes a bit of doing.'

'So the guy's a good throw,' Berner suggested. 'What do we do, arrest all known cricketers?'

'Very funny. No, we assume the bombs were not in fact thrown from the far bank, but from a boat actually on the canal. All three are on navigable canals, but also on lonely stretches with no overlooking roads. It would be simple, but involves a major discrepancy from the psychological profile DI Gage had done. Where is it?'

Berner watched as Susan rummaged for the sheet and scanned it quickly before continuing. '...inadequate... attention-seeking... ah, here we are. "Suffering from a deprivation of regular mental stimuli" – that's bored, to you and me. Leaving the jargon aside, the Fire Ghost seems to be some bored kid who wants to feel he's something special, or maybe look big in the eyes of his mates. Apparently, he might well be expected to have some pseudo-political justification for his acts, probably involving class warfare. What he isn't very likely to have is a riverboat.'

'That's a bit speculative,' Berner objected.

'Nonsense,' Susan said. 'We haven't many hard facts, so I'm building a theory. I'll test it, and if it fails, I'll build another. Eventually one will work. You've got to admit it's a better technique than waiting for the next blaze and hoping Fire Ghost will make a mistake. He uses a simple formula. As long as he sticks to it he's unlikely to be caught, unless enormous resources are devoted to the problem. Anyway, according to my theory we have Fire Ghost and an imitator. The imitator is well-off, presumably has a motive, and I think I know who it is.'

'Annabella de Vergy, presumably,' Berner said, 'but your reasoning is circular. You're after de Vergy and so you've constructed your theory to fit her. It won't wash, let alone stand up in court.'

'I don't expect it to,' Susan replied, 'and, if you want the truth, I'd rather Annabella de Vergy was innocent. It's Philip Ruddock I'm hoping is the bad apple, but unless he has sole charge of the buying at de Vergy Fine Wines, I'm afraid Annabella is at least an accessory.'

'You're away with the fairies,' Berner observed as he reached for his beer, the fifth in a line of bottles that was slowly building across the table.

'Thanks for your confidence,' Susan said indignantly. 'All I can say is that, so far, none of the facts run in contradiction to my theory, although I admit I do need a lot more before reaching any definite conclusions. Oh, and another thing: Dr Potheroe, Gage's pet psychologist, points out that the spacing of the first four fires suggests that each fire creates a satiation of Fire Ghost's need to burn things followed by a period of increasing need before setting another fire. He says the gaps fall with a five percent margin of error when compared with averages determined by some other psychologist. The last three have been much more closely spaced.'

'It's all too theoretical for me,' Berner insisted. 'But I'll tell old man Gage, if you don't mind me pinching your ideas. At least he'll think I'm keen. He's a bit of a plodder, so don't expect him to take much notice.'

'I don't. And you can pinch as many of my ideas as you like. That's me done, anyway. Can I have another beer?'

'Sure.' He got up and went out to the kitchen. 'You're lucky, you know,' he called back, 'I was going to take you out to a car park that's got a bit of a reputation, but I reckon I've had a beer too many.'

Susan was a little puzzled. 'A car park with a reputation?'

'Voyeurs.'

Susan's stomach lurched with excitement at the thought. 'I – um… I've only had one beer,' she called. 'I could drive.'

Berner's hand hovered in the fridge over a bottle as he looked back at her from the kitchen. Was there nothing she wouldn't get off on?

Susan lay back in the seat of Paul Berner's BMW, shivering with pleasure and the exquisite shame of public exposure. Her top was up over her breasts, her skirt rucked up around her waist while Berner kissed the sensitive skin of her tummy and worked his fingers against her pussy through her knickers. Twice faces had peered in through the windscreen, one owlish and bespectacled, the other lean with staring eyes. Their attention certainly had the intended effect on her, but she was glad of Berner's protective presence. The sheer lust written on both men's faces had been frightening.

He kissed her for a while, then transferred his attentions to her nipples as his hand moved down the front of her panties to find the wet flesh of her pussy. A finger slid inside her, his palm rubbing her mound. As her excitement rose, the idea of being made a public exhibit became more appealing. When she'd accepted Berner's suggestion, she'd known that she would enjoy it in the end, but that hadn't made the shame and embarrassment of being seen

111

any less – nor any less exciting.

Berner's hand had left her pussy and was tugging at her panties. Susan sighed as she lifted her bottom off the seat to let him pull them down. She looked down. The interior light illuminated her pussy, a little pink flesh showing as her panties were taken down to her ankles and her knees fell apart. Berner edged himself back a little, pushing Susan hard against the door. His head was between her open thighs, kissing and licking at the soft skin. Slowly, his kisses moved towards her pussy. Susan closed her eyes in ecstasy and cupped her breasts and stroked her aching nipples. He was kissing her pubic mound, the stubble of her hair tickling her into a state of distraction. Finally, he started to kiss her pussy, awkward in the confined space. His tongue found her clit and began to flick against it, making her moan.

'Oh Paul… that's nice,' she sighed.

She opened her eyes, wondering if they were being watched. Sure enough, the owl-faced man was standing a little way away, his face a mask of intense lust, one hand down his trousers, masturbating himself shamelessly. He was about fifty and fat, his clothes suggesting not just wealth but extravagance.

'We – we're being watched, Paul,' she whispered between gasps. 'S-some sad fat man with his hand down – uh – his trousers.'

To her horror, he reached across her and began to wind the window down.

'P-Paul!' she squeaked.

'Offer to toss him off,' Berner mumbled from between her juicy thighs.

'I – I'm not sure, I...' Susan faltered, as her last shreds of reserve began to melt away.

Berner chuckled and put his lips back to her pussy. Susan moaned as his tongue once more found her clit. The window was down, the owlish man looking right at her, hopeful yet distrusting. Susan looked back, eyes wide, mouth a little open, trying to pluck up the courage to speak to him. Berner began to explore her bottom. He stroked the cheeks, burrowing between them, a finger finding her anus and popping just inside. Susan whimpered with delight, feeling her orgasm simmering in the pit of her stomach.

'S-slow down, Paul...' she gasped. 'Perhaps we shu-should st-stop—'

The owlish man shuffled closer. His hand jerked inside his trousers. Suddenly Susan really wanted to plunge her own hand down there; to grip the evidence of his desire for her.

'Oh, God... I'm going to do it,' she gasped, and reached out into the cool night air. The man ducked back a little like a cautious animal. The tongue between her legs flicked expertly over her clit and she groaned and clutched at the air, desperate now to curl her fingers around the stranger's erect cock.

He hesitated and watched her warily, evidently not convinced of her good intentions.

'Come here,' she urged huskily, feeling deliciously dirty. 'You'll – uh – you'll love what I can do for you.'

The man licked his lips, and then started to unbutton his trousers as he sidled closer again. They gaped, and his white underpants bulged out into the night. Susan stroked the bulge, and shivered at the realisation of what she was doing. It felt large and warm beneath her exploring fingertips. She felt her pussy open to admit Berner's thumb, and his finger moving in her bottom, rubbing the membrane between rectum and vagina. His tongue worried her clit again, and suddenly it was just too much. Nothing mattered but extracting all the pleasure she could.

Tugging aside the slavering stranger's underpants, she pulled him sharply until he was flat up against the car and she could stuff his monstrous cock into her ravenous mouth. She was shocked by his size, but there was no going back now. He wheezed as she sucked his helmet and masturbated his shaft. Berner's fingers worked incessantly inside her, his tongue lapping at her clit. She was already coming as the stranger jerked and her mouth filled. She swallowed and revelled in the lasciviousness of her behaviour. He pulled out, and his cock twitched just inches from her spellbound face. It glistened in the dim light, coated in his own seed and her saliva. The sight made her hungry for more. She licked at it eagerly, and then gobbled him back into her mouth, sucking desperately with stretched lips as she reached her climax with pussy, anus, and mouth all full at once.

The man's cock was already shrinking as he finally pulled away from her. Susan still felt dirty and submissive, despite her recent orgasm. She knew Berner would still want to fuck her, and hoped he would do it as publicly as he could. He sat up as the stranger slithered back into the shadows, forgotten.

'Fuck me, Paul,' Susan whispered. 'Over the bonnet if you want to. I don't mind.'

Berner grinned as he turned the key in the ignition. 'I don't think that would be too wise for a man in my position. Let's get back to the flat, pronto.'

Chapter Six

Paulette waited in the Cave Co-Operative de Choray. She had deliberately turned up early, in the hope of finding some evidence to support the idea that activities at the co-op were fraudulent.

This was proving no easy task. Even from a quick glance, it was clear that specialist knowledge would be needed to know what was and what was not legitimate practice in a winery. It was also highly unlikely that anything incriminating would simply be left lying around, especially when casual visitors might see into the main building – or inspectors visit, for that matter.

There was also the slightly galling notion that the workers evidently felt entirely secure about her being in the winery. They treated her with a familiarity that bordered on insolence, and she suspected that if it hadn't been for her association with Christian Charrier, then the incomprehensible but clearly rude remarks and the occasional pat of her bottom would have been even less restrained.

However, she felt she had made one or two observations that suggested everything was not entirely above board. Firstly, there was the fact that they produced only four wines and yet had sixteen tanks, each annotated with a distinct legend written with chalk on tablets of slate. Even allowing for their wines from the south and capacity for over-production, sixteen tanks seemed rather a lot.

Secondly, there were the annotations themselves. Each gave a range of data, most of which was incomprehensible to her. But one part wasn't. Each slate included a figure followed by a dash and the legend 'g/l H_2SO_4'. Paulette recognised the formula as that for sulphuric acid, which, she was certain, was not a naturally occurring constituent of wine. Could they be adding it for some reason? If they were, then she had no idea why, but the idea did fit with the theory that the co-op's wines were adulterated in some manner.

'Ah, Paulette, my little one.' Charrier's oily tones made her start guiltily. 'You are eager, I see. I trust my colleagues have kept you entertained?'

Paulette nodded, certain that if she were to complain to Charrier about having her bottom pinched, he would only laugh.

'Today,' he continued, 'I will show you a French vineyard, to me the most beautiful sight on Earth. We will inspect my own properties and then take a picnic in a charming forest... no, wood?'

'Copse, maybe?' Paulette suggested.

'Perhaps,' Charrier continued. 'You English have six words for everything. What matters is that it is mine and we will be quite alone. We will stop in the village for bread and perhaps a local cheese. But first, the most important thing.'

He turned and signalled to one of the workers, a pot-bellied man who had been far too familiar towards Paulette. 'François, a bottle from the cellar – the '89.' He turned back to Paulette and said, 'This is not something we export, but a reserve intended for ourselves. Generally the local wines take little time to mature, but myself and two others own parcels of Côt, a magnificent red grape that was once the pride of Bordeaux as well as the Loire.'

'How many special wines do you make?' Paulette asked.

'Just this, and a little Pinot Noir,' he answered. 'Also a sweet Chenin, like the wines of Vouvray, but only in the hottest of years. This year, I think, maybe we will, but it is impossible to be sure until the vintage.'

Paulette glanced around again, now aware of what at least some of the extra tanks were for. It was certainly impossible to draw any conclusions without greater knowledge.

François returned with a bottle, which Charrier took with exaggerated delicacy. Pausing only to take a cold bottle of white wine from the refrigerator in the tasting room, he showed her out of the co-op; Paulette caught several remarks from behind her and a knowing leer from François as they left.

After a brief stop in Choray, they drove east. Christian soon pulled off the road onto a dirt track, and stopped the car in the shade of a grove of poplars. On her way down to the Loire, Paulette had expected a more or less unbroken monoculture of vineyard, an image she had formed from pictures of Southern France and the Central Valley in California. The Touraine was very different. Patches of vine were frequent, but interspersed with numerous woods and copses. There were also other crops, notably sunflowers. Pasture, numerous ponds, and untended land all combined to produce a pastoral scene of far greater beauty than she had expected.

Charrier had stopped by one of the larger expanses of vines, beyond which an oak wood shimmered in the heat haze. He got out of the car. Drawing a deep lungful of air, he waved his hand expansively at the landscape.

'This,' he said with evident pride, 'is les Ormeaux; seven hectares of Sauvignon and Chenin. The vineyard was named for a group of elms that stood at the far end, now sadly gone. The grapes, as you see, are ripe. In some days, the vintage will begin.' Paulette followed his finger to where he was indicating bunches of greenish-yellow grapes among the foliage of the vines.

Charrier took the basket in which he had packed the wine and food from the car, and Paulette followed him along the edge of the vineyard. He occasionally pointed

117

out some feature or recounted a tale. He made no mention at all of what they had done the day before.

She accepted this at face value, keen to sample more of Charrier's 'penitence', but more than a little uncertain about the wisdom of doing so. Bearing in mind his curious predilection for punishment as repentance for showing herself off, she had deliberately chosen a long white dress that morning. Belted at the waist, it showed so little flesh as to be positively demure, yet she knew full well that even a weak light would show her silhouette through the material. While less obvious than her cut-down shorts and stripy top, it seemed unlikely that Charrier would fail to be tempted.

At the end of the field the vines gave way to smaller bushes with grey-brown wood and more rounded leaves. Peering closely, Paulette saw that they were blackcurrant bushes, the fruit already ripe.

'Cassis,' Charrier explained, noting her interest. 'Blackcurrants, in English. I make a cordial for drinking at home. A few drops of cassis in white wine or, better, sparkling wine, makes an excellent aperitif.'

'Kir,' Paulette responded, counting the bushes; they seemed very numerous for a drink used only a few drops at a time for home consumption.

'Yes, kir,' Charrier agreed. 'I see you know it. Anyway, here we have our picnic spot. Perfect, is it not?'

He had stepped between the bushes, and Paulette found that the ground sloped suddenly away and then levelled out into a clearing. Thick oaks surrounded the space on all sides, and a carpet of lush grass covered the wood floor. Dappled sunlight made patterns on the grass, and large yellow butterflies flitted in the beams.

'Beautiful,' Paulette admitted. 'You're lucky to own all this land.' Charrier shrugged.

As she walked down into the shallow bowl, she found herself entirely cut off from sight. Here, she thought, would be a wonderful place for sex. She could strip, lie naked in the grass, and indulge herself however she pleased with little risk of being caught. She smiled at her companion, wondering if he had had the same thought when deciding to come to the glade. Charrier smiled back, a touch of wickedness in his look confirming Paulette's suspicions.

They spread out the picnic, making themselves comfortable on the soft grass and sipping glasses of white wine as they talked. Paulette drank without restraint, indifferent to how tiddly she became. Physically, Christian Charrier was unappealing, but mentally he had what was effectively a direct line to her clitoris: the desire to punish her. Had he been a foot taller and reasonably heavily built, he would have been perfect. As it was, she knew that a bottle of wine would quickly dispel any misgivings she might have.

He opened the red wine, and poured the top inch out to let it breathe while he explained how futile merely pulling the cork was. He seemed to view this error as an English habit, an idea that amused Paulette when she thought of the obsessive care Alan Sowerby and people like him took with bottles of fine wine. Thinking of Sowerby brought her somewhat down to earth. It was not impossible that Charrier, the man who was currently seducing her with wine and flattery, had murdered Sowerby in a particularly horrible way. She shivered, glancing at his face. It was quite relaxed, the over-large nose projecting up at an angle, the sallow cheeks creased with a grin as he recounted a story about some Belgian visitors to the co-op.

'Have some bread and pâté,' Charrier suggested, the very normalcy of his remark breaking the rather grim sensation that had been creeping upon her.

She accepted the piece he was holding out. Watching him pour the red wine, she took a bite of the bread, checking for mushrooms in the pâté with her tongue, despite herself. It was definitely okay, but the process of checking drew a strange look from Charrier.

'Don't you like it?' he asked, sounding hurt.

'No, no, it's very good,' Paulette stammered. 'What's in it?'

'Oh, goose livers, duck livers, pheasant livers, herbs, a little pepper. It's locally made. So is the cheese.'

'Mmm, delicious,' Paulette assured him. 'Could you pass my wine?'

It was delicious, and completely different from the wines she had tasted the day before: rich, smooth, and spicy, with flavours of smoke and aromatic wood.

'Excellent,' she announced. 'Why don't you sell this? I've never tasted anything like it.'

Charrier laughed before answering. 'In a good year, on the best land, with a skilled vigneron, it is possible to make wine like this. Even then it costs two, maybe more, times as much to make as the ordinary wine. This is not Champagne, where fools will pay five times the worth of a wine because of its name. No, it is not worth our while to sell it. It is better to keep it to drink ourselves and use it to inflame the passions of dusky maidens from across the seas, no?'

'I thought you found me a temptation,' Paulette laughed, 'a temptation who needed punishment for flaunting herself?'

'Very true,' he replied, 'as is true of all women. To tempt with your bodies is your nature, to be beaten is a natural consequence of your womanhood.'

'Do I get another belting, then?' Paulette giggled, keen not to be drawn into a discussion of Charrier's bizarre philosophy.

'You are truly extraordinary,' Charrier replied. 'So few are the women who know their darker desires, but you... you know, and you have no shame.'

Paulette shrugged. She had never understood why sex should be thought of as shameful. A smacked bottom gave her physical pleasure, and if her bottom was smacked as punishment, a new dimension was added to that pleasure. That was the way she felt; a harmless sexual urge. Guilt was for when you hurt someone.

'So you truly want another taste of my belt?' Charrier continued.

Paulette nodded, remembering the way he had beaten her, and anticipating more. Her lips felt suddenly dry, so she took a large mouthful of wine. She watched as he stood and looked down at her with a strange mixture of lust and contempt. Her lower lip trembled, and her hands moved automatically to the cord that held her dress tight at the waist.

'I'm naked underneath,' she told him softly.

'I know,' he replied. 'Do you think I have not noticed? Your breasts and legs show against the light and it is obvious that you have no panties on. Well, you want to tempt, now you must show it all. Take your dress off.'

Paulette obeyed, rising to her knees to pulled the dress up around her waist, slipping the cord loose and pulling it up over her head. Naked except for her shoes, she knelt in front of him, angled her head back, and parted her knees to present her breasts and sex openly. He scrutinised her body; the tell-tale swell at his crotch indicating his excitement.

'Whore,' he said at last. 'Get up.'

She rose, expecting to be told to position herself for punishment.

'Finish your wine,' he ordered, instead.

She gulped it down, spilling it in her eagerness, a deep red rivulet meandering down her chin and throat.

'I am going to whip you,' Charrier continued, 'but not with my belt, and not here. Follow that path...' he pointed. 'Do you know what a birch tree looks like?'

Paulette nodded, at once realising what he had in store for her. Susan had told her what it felt like to be made to

121

pick birch twigs for use on her own bottom. Now Paulette was to have to do the same.

'Good. You will pick the twigs I tell you to and then, when there are sufficient, I will whip you with them. Come.'

She took the path indicated. Charrier occasionally pointed to a choice birch twig, which she would snap off. The process was every bit as forceful as Susan had described it, her anticipation of her coming beating rising with each twig added to the bundle and the knowledge of how much it would hurt. The fact that she was not only naked but moving further and further away from her clothes only added to the sensation. Charrier maintained a stern aloofness, but failed to conceal his rising excitement.

'I am not without mercy,' he remarked as he pointed to a section of twig. 'As your derrière still bears the marks of my belt from yesterday, that is why I will use the birch. As you will discover, it produces a very different sensation.'

He laughed, a cruel, mocking sound that did nothing to make Paulette believe that lessening the pain of her punishment was at all important to him. She picked the twig he had indicated and added it to her bundle, now a spray of leafy birch at least as broad as her bottom.

'Enough, I think,' he decided. 'I think perhaps it would also be amusing to have you select a place for your own whipping.'

Paulette nodded and looked around for somewhere reasonably comfortable. They came into another clearing, similar in size to the first, yet more silent and lonely. A fallen oak lay across it, blocking their path. The trunk formed a perfect whipping place; just right to position her bottom at the perfect angle for punishment. A secret part of Paulette wanted to suffer as much as possible.

'Here,' she said softly. 'Over that tree-trunk… please.'

'My pleasure,' Charrier nodded. 'Then make yourself comfortable.'

Paulette passed him the birch. Her pulse was thumping; a concoction of fear and excitement. She knew the beating would hurt, and that Charrier would undoubtedly take his own pleasure when her bottom was a burning ball of pain. The thought made her feel weak and totally compliant.

She walked to the oak and bent forward, pressing her stomach to the rough bark. Her hands hung down and touched the cool grass. She was unable to see what Charrier was doing, and that increased the delicious uncertainty of the situation.

'I will tie you,' she heard him say.

Paulette did not resist, submitting meekly to having her ankles tied to a branch. Charrier fixed her legs well apart, running a hand casually over the exposed mound of her pussy as he straightened up. Paulette found herself as open and helpless as she had been over the barrel.

Charrier appeared in front of her, holding a length of twine that she recognised as the sort used to tie vine shoots to their supporting wires. She tried to relax as he leant over her, pulled her arms into the small of her back, and lashed her wrists tightly together.

'We shall, I think, see just how much you truly enjoy being beaten,' Charrier said casually. He squatted and lifted Paulette's chin, so he could look deep into her wide eyes. 'But your body is making me unsettled, so first...'

He knelt and opened his trousers. His hands were inches from Paulette's face as they worked to free a half-stiff cock. Her lips peeled apart hypnotically as he offered it to her. His hand closed gently in her hair, drawing her closer, and she let him feed it in. She swallowed the thick shaft; tasting him. It stiffened instantly as she sucked and he pumped it slowly between the tight softness of her lips.

He expressed his pleasure in French, but just as Paulette was wondering if he intended to come, he suddenly pulled away.

'Ah, my little whore,' he chided, rising to his feet, 'so eager, so dirty. That was a great pleasure, but we must not hurry, must we?'

He moved out of sight again. Something tickled her thighs: the leaves of the birch she had picked. She shivered, fighting down a panic rising more from not being able to see than from the thought of what was about to happen. The tickling continued, making her squirm. The leaves flitted against her pussy.

'Now, I will beat you,' Charrier announced theatrically, and without further warning her bottom exploded with pain. She squealed and bucked, her buttocks feeling as though a thousand needles had spitefully pricked them.

'Curse as much as you like,' Charrier said over her expletives, 'nobody can hear you.'

Again the birch sliced down, lashing into her fleshy cheeks and upper thighs. Again Paulette squealed and bucked against her bonds. Her bottom was alive with the overwhelming sensations of the birching. A third blow fell, and then Charrier set about beating her in earnest. Poor Paulette begged him to stop with every stinging bite of the twigs.

Charrier merely laughed, calling her a whore as he thrashed her squirming buttocks. She kicked and shouted. She cursed him, even while the pleasure of her beating began to build. The strokes rained down mercilessly.

Through the burning haze Paulette realised she was going to come.

'Harder Christian!' she implored, as she started to tense in the first flush of orgasm.

He immediately changed the angle of the birching, bringing the bundle down between her buttocks instead of across them, then changing to strokes that came up between her spread thighs, impacting directly onto her pussy. Paulette screamed more loudly than before as the birch slapped against her vagina, then suddenly the pain was gone and she was riding a wave of pure pleasure. Every muscle in her body tensed as her orgasm hit her, starting in the flaming centre of her vulva and spreading to explode in her head.

The last thing she was conscious of was the tension of the twine binding her wrists – then everything went black.

Paulette found herself momentarily disorientated, then remembered where she was. She knew her bottom had been thoroughly beaten. She shook her head, still dizzy from her shattering orgasm. In addition to the pain in her bottom and thighs, her wrists and ankles hurt, while the rough bark of the trunk was definitely uncomfortable.

'Untie me, Christian,' she breathed. 'That was lovely, but I've had it.'

'One moment,' Charrier replied from over her shoulder. 'I hardly think this is fair. You have had your fun, and now I will have mine.'

'Sure, you can do anything you like – but untie me first,' she said, not wanting to deny him, but badly needing to rub her bottom and stretch her limbs.

'No, no. You are as I want you, just so.'

'Christian,' she complained. 'Please.'

He said no more, and Paulette resigned herself to being bound to the tree for a while longer yet. She adjusted her position as best she could to minimise her discomfort. Then something greasy nudged between her tender buttocks.

'Christian?'

A lubricated finger pressed against her rear entrance, and then pushed inside.

'Oooh... Christian.'

'Do not worry, my little one,' he encouraged, wriggling his digit back and forth.

'I... no...' Paulette stammered. The finger withdrew, and something bulbous and firm replaced it. 'No, Christian,

125

not in my bottom...'

'Ah, but it is so beautiful,' he panted in her ear, as his cock pushed its way into her well-lubricated anus. 'So, so beautiful.'

Paulette moaned as his cock slid into her bottom. She could feel her anus stretched around his shaft. It hurt a little, then less as he began to slide in and out and eased his passage. His groin pressed against her sore bottom-cheeks with each cautious push. His laden balls started to slap against her pussy, and he was grunting and breathing hard as he moved. Despite herself, she began to moan softly, slowly coming to terms with the sensation, and finding that she rather liked it.

Her pleasure was mounting again when Charrier stiffened and pushed his cock in to the hilt. Paulette realised he had given her the final delicious indignity, and come in her rectum. She also understood exactly what Susan meant by erotic humiliation.

As before, he was both apologetic and defensive once he had ejaculated. Paulette kissed and thanked him for an exquisite orgasm. Her bottom hurt, as she knew it would for a while, yet the pleasure had certainly been worth it and, despite her aches and pains, she mentally listed birching as something worth trying again.

Charrier returned to his normal effusive self as they walked back towards the picnic site, apparently oblivious to Paulette's nudity as he pointed out various types of edible fungi among the leaf litter to either side of the path.

'There are truffles, too, but they are not so easily found... And here we have something you should avoid with great care.' He prodded an ordinary-looking white toadstool with his shoe. Paulette bent to look, finding it not dissimilar to an ordinary field mushroom, except that the gills were white.

'What is it?' she asked.

'*Amanita Virosa*,' he replied. 'It is deadly poisonous,

and there is no cure. You call it, in English, Destroying Angel.'

Ted Gage looked thoughtfully across the table. Opposite him sat three individuals, and his irritation with each of them was increasing steadily. First there was Detective Sergeant Paul Berner. Not only was Berner full of himself, but Gage suspected that he was involved in a relationship with the pretty girl by his side.

Susan MacQuillan irritated him partly because she was young and smart. She also irritated him because he was against private investigators, full stop. Finally, there was the fact that she was attempting to intrude a theory into the Fire Ghost case that would make it considerably more complex and harder to solve.

The third person was Dr Potheroe, a police psychologist and a man Gage could usually rely on to provide some theoretical backing for cases. Gage considered the entire subject to be mumbo-jumbo, but still valued Potheroe for his ability to blind juries with science. This time, however, the doctor insisted on backing MacQuillan's over-complicated theory about there being a second arsonist involved in the case.

'So,' he began cautiously, 'let me get this straight. You feel that the pattern of arsons shows two fire-raisers with distinct modes of operation. The original Fire Ghost, who is an insecure male with a background of mental illness and commits arson for the thrill of it. Also an imitator, who is at least reasonably affluent and motivated by some practical consideration?'

'Exactly,' Susan MacQuillan replied.

'A fair lay summation,' Dr Potheroe added.

'I agree,' Berner put in.

Gage looked at Berner, suspecting that the sergeant had no more idea of what the others were talking about than he did, but knew a good bandwagon when he saw one.

'And also,' Gage continued, 'that the second arsonist is either Philip Ruddock, Annabella de Vergy, or both, their motive being to cover a wine fraud which may also be linked with the death of a writer called Alan Sowerby?'

'Exactly,' Susan repeated.

'Conceivably,' Potheroe said. 'Miss MacQuillan's theory is based entirely on estimated probabilities of specific events being connected or not connected. The mathematics behind her calculations is sound, but her initial estimate's inevitably somewhat conjectural. Statistically, her results fail to meet the ninety-five percent confidence limits generally considered a valid scientific proof, as I am sure she will be the first to admit.'

'True,' Susan responded, 'but still—'

'So you think there are two arsonists, but don't suspect the de Vergy Fine Wines staff?' Gage asked, eager to avoid another spat of statistical analysis.

'Essentially—'

'Yes or no, Dr Potheroe,' Gage interrupted.

'Yes, but—'

'Good,' Gage cut in again. 'Paul?'

'I agree with Dr Potheroe,' Berner answered, 'but I do think Miss MacQuillan has a point and that it would be wise to investigate de Vergy Fine Wines. I'd like that opinion to be on the record too, sir.'

Slimy bastard, Gage thought. Berner's answer covered all eventualities. If Susan was right, then Berner would get the credit. If she was wrong, then he would merely appear to have been exercising reasonable caution in investigating every lead that came up. At the end of the day, though, it was he, Ted Gage, who had to take one or both theories and kick them upstairs to Julia Keeson. The first idea had the backing of Potheroe and was therefore safe. The second was simply too wild to impress the strictly practical Detective Superintendent. Nevertheless, he could hardly ignore it if it had Berner's backing. Gage thought for a moment and then made his decision.

'Right,' he addressed them. 'Thank you for your advice, Dr Potheroe, and also for your input, Miss MacQuillan. If the most recent three fires are connected and your idea is correct, then it seems reasonable that the arsonist is connected with one of the three companies involved. I intend to investigate all three for possible motives and if Miss MacQuillan's idea is correct, then the details will undoubtedly come out in the wash. In the event of there being a link to the death of Alan Sowerby, which I frankly doubt, that too will certainly come out. Any questions?'

Susan MacQuillan started to speak but thought better of it, instead thanking Gage and leaving with the others. Gage sat back, feeling thoroughly pleased with himself. His decision not only advanced the investigation but covered his back, and might just possibly produce a lead in what was fast becoming the most frustrating case of his career.

Robin Riddell turned the corner and glanced nervously along the street. Visiting Jilly was a perfectly reasonable thing to do, he told himself. They had been friends for years. What was making him nervous was not that he shouldn't be where he was, nor even that she was now Taz's girlfriend. It was that he knew exactly what he wanted to do with her. There had been something sexual between them for a while. By her own admission, she liked to watch him masturbate and had several times lent a helping hand, squeezing his balls or holding the base of his cock right up until the moment he came. They had fucked at her birthday party, but that had been in a haze of drink and dope, not to mention having to take turns with Taz and Beadle. Now he wanted her full attention, and was sure that the kudos of his knowing the real Fire Ghost would be enough to make the difference.

There was no sign of Taz. Not that Robin had expected

there to be. Taz was helping his uncle at a car auction and was guaranteed to be gone for the day. Robin made for the shop from which Jilly's parents sold bric-a-brac. As he pushed the door open, his heart sank. He had expected Jilly's mother. Instead, Jilly herself was minding the shop, seated behind the counter with a steaming mug of tea in her hand. If she was in charge of the shop, then sex was hardly practical.

'Hi,' she greeted him enthusiastically. 'Have you come to keep me company?'

'Yeah,' Robin answered, picking his way among the clutter.

'Tea?' Jilly asked. 'The kettle's just boiled.'

Robin accepted the tea and made himself comfortable in the low armchair behind the counter. Jilly, poised on a high stool which let her see the shop properly, was well above him. A customer came in and Robin took the opportunity to admire his friend's body while she served. Jilly was of average height and slim, pretty with her face framed by long blonde hair currently decorated with pink streaks. Her ears were pierced, as was her nose, a touch that greatly appealed to Robin. She wore a dress of bright blue that suited her hair and ended well up her thighs. He found his eyes drawn to her legs, working up from bare feet to her thighs, slim but full and soft enough to be thoroughly female. As he watched she bent forward to indicate something to the customer. He stared entranced as her skirt came up to reveal the tuck of her bottom and a slice of white cotton patterned with blue flowers.

Robin felt his cock stiffen as he admired the soft curve of Jilly's bottom. She turned unexpectedly, catching him looking. For a moment their eyes met, and then she smiled. He smiled back, blushing faintly.

'Over there, sir. No, right by the end,' Jilly addressed the customer again, only this time bending further over the counter so that Robin's view up her skirt was even better. Her flowery panties were tight across her sweet, firm buttocks, and slightly caught between them. Checking to make sure he was genuinely invisible from the shop floor, he put a hand down his trousers and squeezed his already stiffening cock. Perhaps Jilly being alone in the shop wasn't such a bad thing after all.

He stopped playing with himself while Jilly served the customer, returning her wink when she looked at him. The bell signalled the departure of the customer.

'Do you like my bum?' she asked, with the mixture of coy uncertainty and openness that had always attracted him.

'It's nice,' he answered. 'In fact, you're really pretty all round.'

'Thanks,' she tittered. 'Do you want to do it in front of me again?'

'Here?'

'Yeah, come on. Nobody can see you down there, and the bell will warn you if anyone comes in.'

'You like to watch me, don't you?'

'Yes I do. You've got a lovely cock, Robin, and I think it's really nice the way you do it in front of me. I really like to see the pleasure on your face. Come on, just for me.'

'Would you go further?' he asked tentatively.

Jilly paused, settling herself back on the high stool. Robin waited for her answer. 'I don't know,' she said. 'It's really the way you don't mind showing me how excited you are that I like. Anyway, we can't really in here, can we?'

'S'pose not,' he admitted glumly.

'Do it for me, please?' Jilly pouted.

Robin looked up into her eyes and slid forward on the chair, letting his legs loll apart. Her eyes travelled slowly lower as he put his hand to his zip and drew it down. The idea of masturbating in front of her excited him; her uninhibited delight in watching boosted his ego. This time he was sure he could get more, if only he had the patience to let her get really turned on instead of coming before she was ready.

Her eyes were fixed on his crotch as he pulled his cock out. Watching her expression, he began to stroke it. He did it slowly, alert for the sound of the bell, but becoming more excited as his cock stiffened in front of her. Patience was everything, patience and getting her to pay attention to her own body.

'At least let me see your knickers,' he prompted.

Jilly giggled and swung her legs around, parting them just a little so that her panties showed. The material was tight over the bulge of her pussy. Robin felt his cock harden in his fist. Jilly giggled again as it swelled to full erection. He pulled his T-shirt up, opened his jeans, and started to masturbate properly.

'Show me your pussy,' he begged, indicating the front of her panties with his eyes.

'Robin!'

'Please, Jilly. I'm doing it for you.'

'Well… okay,' she conceded, a little flustered.

He watched as Jilly licked her lips, glanced guiltily at the door, and then parted her legs a little further. He began to pull harder at his erection as she slipped her fingers into her panty gusset and pulled it aside, revealing the moist pink flesh of her pussy in a nest of tawny hair. Her vagina looked wet and ready.

'I'm going to come, soon,' he breathed. 'Put a finger in.'

She looked at the door again, and then slipped a finger into the moist crevice. He watched it slip in, his breathing becoming quicker and deeper. His cock felt as if it would burst at any moment, yet he held himself back, determined not to come and spoil his chances. She was obviously getting horny, sliding the finger in and out and dabbing at her clit. Her panties were stretched to one side, showing everything as she masturbated for him.

'You're beautiful, Jilly,' he gasped, his eyes riveted to her pussy. 'I wish you were naked. Would you strip for me?'

'Of course,' she blurted, her voice husky with passion. 'Oh, Robin, of course I'd strip for you. You're really sweet, and your cock's so lovely. Spurt in front of me, Robin. Spurt for me.'

'Lock the door,' he groaned. 'Let's fuck,'

For a moment she hesitated, and he thought he'd blown it. Then she jumped down from the stool and hurried to the door, quickly shooting the bolts and flipping the sign to 'Closed'. She rushed back behind the counter, sank to her knees, and grabbed his cock. Robin nearly came as her fingers curled around it and started to pull with a frantic urgency.

'I – I want to fuck you, Jilly,' he protested, putting his hands over hers to slow the pace with which she was wanking him.

'Oh, God, okay,' she sighed. 'I'll sit in your lap.'

She rose and turned, and pulled up her dress again to show him her panties. Robin sighed and reached forward, feeling the softness of her bottom. He gripped her panties and pulled them aside. She lowered herself, a little clumsily, onto his lap. He aimed his erection, and watched the tip ease into her pussy and the shaft slip inside her. She sighed as though sliding down into a hot bath. He grasped her hips and began to bounce her on his lap. She gripped the arms of the chair for balance. Determined not to spoil the moment by coming too quickly, he slowed his pace. Jilly put a hand to her pussy and started to masturbate once more.

She flopped back against his chest, and gasped, 'I want to come.'

Robin reached round and squashed her breasts in each

hand, finding her nipples already stiff under his fingers. Her hands were between their legs, stroking his balls and the juncture of his cock and her pussy. All he could do was give little shoves with his hips and feel her tits. Her back arched and she twisted, trying to kiss him. Their lips met awkwardly. He felt her pussy contract around his cock, heard the sigh of pleasure deep in her throat, and smiled to himself triumphantly as he realised she was coming.

He was on the verge of an orgasm himself.

'Not in me,' she panted, sensing his imminent crisis and fearing the spectre of an unwanted pregnancy.

Equally as fearful, Robin pushed her forward and his cock bobbed out just as his semen splattered against her bottom and thighs.

She slumped back down against his heaving chest and their lips mashed together in another artless kiss. Robin hugged her close as a fierce elation welled up inside. They remained like that, gently rocking, until the doorbell rang insistently. Jilly ducked down to adjust her dress and retrieve her panties. Robin peered over the counter and saw an elderly lady shoving at the door and glancing at her watch.

'Customer, Jilly,' he said unnecessarily.

'Coming,' she called loudly as she smoothed her dress down, before lowering her voice to whine at Robin, 'Yuck, I'm all sticky.'

Robin got to his feet, unable to stop himself from grinning as Jilly fumbled with the bolts to let the woman in. He was sure the old bag would know what they'd been up to, and his chest swelled with pride. He smiled at her like an imbecile, and received a suspicious look in return.

He went into the back room, leaving an embarrassed Jilly to serve the woman. He was singing as he made tea, utterly happy and well pleased with himself. Possibly Jilly would now want to go out with him, or at least have regular sex. It was a shame she was going out with Taz.

The thought of Taz brought him down to earth. For one thing they were friends, even if he did resent playing second fiddle all the time. Everyone looked up to Taz, Jilly included. So did he, but he had always wanted Jilly, and now wanted her even more. Maybe if he told her about the Fire Ghost she would think him cooler than Taz.

The bell chimed and Jilly came into the back room, giggling and holding her hand over her mouth.

'Did she notice?' Robin asked.

'I'm not sure,' she twittered, 'maybe.'

They chatted as they drank tea, Jilly bright-eyed and smiling, Robin eager to impress. She reacted to his revelation that he had met the real Fire Ghost with what he interpreted as awe. Basking in the warm glow of her worship, he told her everything that Fire Ghost had told him, including the details of the planned fire in Merton and that he had been invited to go along and tag the site.

Chapter Seven

Ted Gage stopped outside the door and double-checked the number. Set in a neatly cultivated garden, the block of apartments spoke of an affluence well beyond the reach of his pay. He smiled, a faintly malicious grin born from the pleasure of the prospective arrest of someone who had obviously done well for himself. Following the lead suggested by MacQuillan, Potheroe and Berner, he had dug into the affairs of the three companies that had been the latest victims of the Fire Ghost attacks.

Both Mohammed Khan's World of Pine and Annabella de Vergy's wine warehouse had been showing healthy profits. Crazy's Joe's Carpet Madhouse had been heavily in debt, having become badly over-extended when they expanded from a smaller premise. The insurance, however, had been fully paid up, leaving the proprietor, Joe Cooper, with enough ready cash to escape bankruptcy and reorganise his business on a smaller scale.

It was a clear, understandable motive, far more appealing to him than Susan MacQuillan's complex speculations. Julia Keeson agreed with him as well. Cooper also had a record. He had been clean in recent years, but had a long list of minor chicanery going back to when he was a teenager. Gage had decided on a blunt aggressive approach, accusing Cooper of the arsons, hinting at the existence of damning evidence, and hoping for a clean confession. It might not work, but it was worth a try, and the technique suited Gage's style.

His radio buzzed to life: it was Paul Berner, telling him he had the fire-escape covered. Gage rang Cooper's bell, and waited only a moment before the intercom chimed.

'Who is it?' a crackling voice enquired.

'This is Detective Inspector Gage, Mr Cooper. There are one or two points I need to clear up.'

'All right, come up,' Cooper replied, the door lock clicking even as Ted Gage put his hand to it.

He strode into the lobby. A brass plaque displayed the flat numbers and inset cards showed their current occupants. Gage found which floor Cooper's flat was on and punched the call button for the lift. Berner arrived shortly after the lift, having satisfied himself that Cooper had no intention of immediately making a run for it.

Cooper let them in and offered coffee. Gage accepted as he studied Cooper for signs of nervousness. Nothing was immediately obvious, Cooper showing no more than a normal level of reluctance to welcome policemen into his home. Paul Berner declined the coffee and chose to study the details of the flat rather than the suspect.

'What can I do for you?' Cooper asked as he handed Gage a mug of instant.

'It concerns the fire at your warehouse,' Gage began.

'Don't tell me you've caught the Fire Ghost?'

'Unfortunately not, Mr Cooper. In fact, we have good evidence that the attack on your warehouse was not a genuine Fire Ghost attack, but an imitation designed to appear like one.'

'Oh, yes?' Cooper sipped his coffee.

Gage paused. Was there a hint of sarcasm in Cooper's voice? His attitude seemed cocky, amused even. Possibly it showed innocence, and then again it might be the reaction of a confident villain. Gage smiled inwardly. He had known a lot of cock-sure villains, and not a few of them were still locked up.

'Yes,' he said, deciding to cut straight to the point and hope to bluff Cooper, 'and a great deal of that evidence points directly to you, Mr Cooper.'

'You're joking!' Cooper gasped, his mouth gaping in a disbelief that Gage felt was somewhat overdone. 'What, you reckon I did it myself? But I was down the Bell that night. Anyone'll tell you.'

'Not you personally, Mr Cooper,' Gage continued, 'but the evidence points to your being involved. Now are you going to tell us the truth or are we going to have to do it the hard way?'

'Hang on a minute,' Cooper protested. 'Why would I want to burn my own warehouse down? I only opened it a couple of months ago!'

'Because you were about to go bankrupt, Mr Cooper,' Gage answered flatly.

'No, no,' Cooper blustered. 'We had it all worked out. I was taking my rescue plan to the bank tomorrow. You can check with them.'

'I know that,' Gage countered, 'and I also know they would have rejected your plans, as do you.'

'No, seriously, it was sweet. We had good customers, I'd just overdone it on the stock a bit, that's all.'

'Overdone it by just under a million pounds?' Gage turned the screw, enjoying himself immensely.

'Okay, so I fucked up,' Cooper conceded, 'but that doesn't mean I torched the warehouse!'

Gage had seen Cooper's manner before. It was typical of the sort of tough background Joe Cooper evidently came from. He wouldn't break until the evidence was shoved right under his nose: maybe not even then. Gage had known villains of Cooper's type who'd continued to protest their innocence – even when they'd been convicted with evidence that damned them without question. It was pointless to continue or to arrest him without more evidence.

'Very well, Mr Cooper,' he sighed. 'We'll leave it at that for now, but don't think we haven't got our eyes on you.'

They left Joe Cooper vehemently protesting his innocence.

'What do you reckon?' Gage asked Berner as they walked back to the car.

'He's a thug,' Berner replied. 'He's done well for himself, but at heart he's a thug.'

'I can see that. But do you reckon he did it?'

'I don't know,' Berner said thoughtfully. 'He certainly wouldn't have done it himself; I'd put money on his alibi checking out. But if Susan's right about the attacks being done from a canal boat, we can try and link him in with the hire or ownership of one.'

'Good. And check on his known associates, as well. He must know half the villains in London.'

'Searching them out... interviews... checking alibis...' Berner said. 'It's a long grind.'

'That's what gets results – unless you can come up with a better idea.'

'Actually,' Berner said thoughtfully, 'I think I can.'

'Oh yeah? Well, spit it out.'

'I reckon Cooper and the boys who work for him are a pretty close-knit mob. Close enough for any one of them to be in the know if any other was responsible for the arson.'

'Yes,' Gage agreed, cautiously.

'So, we get someone to infiltrate and found out what they can.'

'Wouldn't work.' Gage shook his head dismissively. 'It'd take too much planning to get it right. We don't have that kind of time on our side.'

'Come on, guv, the investigation's been dragging on for months now. It's about time we got an arrest.'

'And don't you think I know that?!' Gage snapped. The whole damned episode was really stressing him out.

'So guv,' Berner egged him on conspiratorially, 'let's do something to get a few results.'

Gage considered Berner's proposal for a few minutes, and eventually said, 'And who would you suggest we use to do this? There's no way I'm asking for volunteers at such short notice.'

'We don't have to,' Berner smiled. 'We've got Susan MacQuillan.'

Paulette sat in the garden of the hotel, feeling uneasy and not at all confident. Since the previous day with Christian Charrier, she had become convinced that he was Alan Sowerby's murderer. From their first sexual encounter, she had considered him not just sadistic but not entirely in control of himself. Taking pleasure in punishing her was one thing, but there was something almost demented about the way he went about it, something very different from Susan's playful behaviour or Annabella's poised dominance. She shivered at the thought of what they'd done together, even as she tried to convince herself that before he'd shown her the Destroying Angel it had been okay. After that she'd felt distinctly unsafe, despite the logical fact that he had no reason to really harm her.

Getting away was a distinctly attractive prospect, yet she had no samples from the co-op, and was sure a longer search of their files would provide some interesting reading. But the idea of facing Charrier again unsettled her immensely, especially as he was bound to want a last sex-session before she left. She got up and walked towards the hotel reception, only to falter as she pondered Susan's reaction if she returned to England with no samples.

Susan, Paulette was certain, would brave Charrier. And Susan would probably break into the co-op and copy the papers she needed. Paulette knew she had to do the same, especially after the lengths Susan had been to to help her. She sat back down and finished her coffee, wondering how best to go about the task.

Twenty minutes later she was parked outside the co-op,

praying that Charrier had already gone to lunch. He hadn't, but was in the tasting room with a party of tourists. He smiled as she entered, indicating that she should wait in the office. She went in, smiling at the secretary who was typing at the desk by the filing cabinets. The secretary smiled back and returned to her work.

Paulette pretended to study a map of the region as she waited, picking out Choray village, the co-op, and the wood to which Charrier had taken her. Her bottom still hurt. It had been good, and the orgasm had been wonderful, but the next time she allowed someone to birch her it would be a more sympathetic partner.

The sound of a chair being pushed back drew Paulette's attention. The secretary was getting up, reaching for her bag and giving Paulette another polite and silent smile. Barely able to believe her luck, Paulette waited for the secretary to leave and then turned to the filing cabinets. She could just hear Charrier still talking, and the occasional murmur of amusement or amazement from the tourists in the tasting room. With her heart in her mouth, Paulette moved stealthily to the cabinets and pulled the relevant draw open. The file on de Vergy Fine Wines was where it had been before. She pulled it out and began to scan the letters and order forms. As she had expected, without exception they were signed by Philip Ruddock.

Susan had asked for enough data to allow her to estimate how much wine the co-op supplied to de Vergy Fine Wines. With trembling fingers Paulette photocopied several order forms and an annual summation for the previous year. The damned machine seemed to be the loudest she'd ever used. Surely someone would hear. Hastily stuffing each copy to the bottom of her bag, she listened for the soft drone of Charrier's cultured voice. She moved to the ajar door and listened. Damn! He was thanking the tourists... accepting an order... he needed a new invoice pad...!

Paulette stuffed the file back in the draw, pushed it shut,

and sank into the secretary's chair just as the door opened. Her heart was thumping, and she was sure Charrier would be able to hear it. She gave him what she hoped was a friendly smile and tried to look as natural as possible. What might have happened if she'd been caught didn't bear thinking about.

'A minute more, my dear,' Charrier said smoothly. 'Could you give me that?'

Paulette passed the invoice pad he pointed to and watched him leave the office. She breathed deeply and her tension start to subside. She had done what was needed and now only had to collect her samples and get clear. Susan's job had always struck her as exciting, but having tried it she would stick to what she knew best in future.

The tourists had left, and Paulette went through to the tasting room as Charrier was shutting the door behind them.

'A glass of Sauvignon?' he asked, indicating an open bottle of white wine on the table, its green glass beaded with condensation. 'So, you are going back today. A pity.'

Paulette accepted the wine and shrugged, smiling at him with as much candour as she could manage.

'I will miss you, my Paulette,' he said softly, raising a hand to stroke her hair.

'And I'll miss you,' Paulette lied, although his sudden and unexpected gentleness had rather taken her aback.

'Maybe we could meet in England?' he suggested. 'I am there often. In fact, I was there for an exposition only a few weeks ago.'

'That would be nice,' Paulette said, feigning real interest. 'Perhaps I could ring you.'

'Of course.' He took a business card from an inside pocket. Paulette studied him as he wrote his home details on the back. She remembered the violent, almost demented quality of his lust. He was remarkably composed on the surface, but the sadistic beast was never far below.

Paulette shuddered just as he looked up. His eyes searched hers.

'Are you all right, my dear?' he asked silkily as he handed her the card.

'Y-yes, I'm fine,' she stuttered. 'May – may I buy some wine?'

'Buy some wine?' Charrier chuckled. 'Of course you cannot buy some wine. You must take some, with my complements. I will fetch some bottles from my own stock.'

'I'd like a mixed case of the ordinary ones as well, if I may,' Paulette insisted. 'I really don't mind paying.'

'Come, come,' Charrier said. 'They are good enough wines in their way, but all from our lesser vineyards, and last year was not a great success. No, for you only the best. I will bring some Côt and bottles of a Chenin Doux my father made in seventy-one. It is true nectar.'

'That's really generous,' Paulette persisted, 'but I promised to take some back for my friends, and it won't be fair to expect too many of your special bottles.'

'Very well,' Charrier shrugged, 'but you must not pay. I insist.'

'Thank you.' Paulette wondered about Charrier's apparent reluctance to part with the ordinary co-op wines. It might be because he didn't want too many adulterated bottles around, and yet he had been willing enough to have her taste them. Evidently, whatever they were doing was harmless, if not legal. Harmless unless you happened to be Alan Sowerby, she corrected herself.

François was sent to fetch the wines. Paulette returned Charrier's goodbyes with as much warmth as she could muster. Finally everything was packed into Susan's car. Paulette gave Christian Charrier a final kiss and turned the ignition key with a strong sense of relief. Ahead of her was the long drive to Caen, then the night ferry and the shorter drive up to London. It was a long journey yet, armed with the possible evidence of the Choray co-op's involvement with the wine scandal, she knew it would seem to take even longer.

'Fair enough,' Susan at last decided. 'As long as there's a heavy to keep an eye on me; it could get a little dangerous.'

'Nice one,' Paul Berner grinned. 'I knew you'd be up for it.'

'You've got guts,' Ted Gage added. 'I'll give you that.'

Susan smiled. Her adrenaline was already pumping at the prospect of infiltrating Joe Cooper's boys. The fact that she was certain they had nothing to do with the fire only added to the thrill. The operation appealed to her sense of devilment; it promised the excitement she thrived on, and Berner and Gage would end up with egg on their faces when she proved their theory wrong.

She was also confident of handling any one of Cooper's men, especially with a police heavy in the background. She would pick the best looking of them, seduce him, enjoy their sex together, and use her carnal expertise to extract any information available.

'I've done worse,' she told Gage. 'I'm not a private investigator for nothing.'

'Maybe, but you just look so...'

'Sweet and innocent?' Susan suggested how he might finish his chauvinistic sentence. 'Yes, I do, and it gets them every time.'

Berner chuckled to himself. 'Innocent, she most definitely is not.'

Susan sipped her glass of gin and orange and looked around. The interior of the Bell was much as she had expected it to be. Loud music blared from speakers set high on walls painted a deep reddish brown. Smoke filled the ceiling space, spiralling up from numerous cigarettes. The customers, mainly male, had a consistency about them that was reflected in the fact that the majority seemed to know each other. As a lone female, she was somewhat conspicuous, yet not outrageously so. Twice she had declined drinks from hopeful suitors who did not belong to the group she had her eye on.

Cooper's friends had been pointed out to her by DC Reynolds, a tall, heavily muscled policeman now involved in a game of darts with a group of the regulars. Two of the men who actually worked for Cooper were there, along with three others. All were in their late twenties, two apparently brothers. Two had girlfriends with them, which ruled them out of Susan's scheme. Of the remaining three, she had to go for the one who actually worked for Cooper.

He was a tall blond with a lean and craggy face. He was the loudest and brashest of the group, laughing and joking with the two women in a manner that made their partners defensive. She could see him having the arrogance not to take no for an answer, especially when drunk and turned on. The prospect set her pulse racing; a reaction to the thrill of action combined with a touch of fear. True, the operation was simple enough, and the prospect of sex with the man was not unappealing, but to play the evening exactly right was going to take some skill.

When his turn to buy the round came up she made her move. Waiting until he had signalled the barman, she moved behind him, deliberately pressing her breasts against his arm. He turned at the feel of soft female flesh, as she knew he would.

'Could I get in next to you?' she asked.

'Sure love,' he leered, his eyes glued to the offending bosom, and then he moved just a fraction to allow her to squeeze beside him.

'Four pints of lager, a lager top, and two rum and blacks, mate,' he shouted, holding two empty pint glasses across the bar without tearing his eyes from the generous curves stretching her T-shirt.

One of the barmaids served Susan. She ordered another gin and orange, and then looked up and smiled at the man.

'You on your own, love?' he asked.

'I was supposed to meet a girlfriend, but she hasn't turned up,' she answered flightily.

'Really?' he grinned. 'You're not from round here, are you?'

'No, my friend is. It's a real pain; I've come miles to see her.'

'Well you've met me now,' he winked, 'so it's not all bad.'

Susan giggled, and then passed some money to the barmaid.

'No, no, let me.' The man grabbed her wrist in a large hand, and then said to the barmaid, 'Put it on my round, love.'

'Thanks,' said Susan, feeling the power in his grip, and noting with a little amusement that every female was his 'love'.

'You look really lonely standing all on your own,' he was saying over the general din of the crowded bar. 'Come and join us. We're having a right laugh.'

'Sure,' Susan agreed, and followed him back to their table.

Phase one had been simple enough, she thought as he introduced her to his friends, clearly delighted with himself for having picked her up. The two remaining unattached men shot her companion looks of jealousy as she sat down.

Her 'date' was Billy Ryan, elder brother to Tod Ryan, who was with his girlfriend, Stacy. The other girl was Terri, and the men were Michael, Luke and another Billy.

Once she'd relaxed a little things went easily. She giggled and tittered inanely, and flirted incessantly with Billy Ryan. Her attention was accepted with enthusiasm, and by the time the next round of drinks arrived his arm was around her shoulders. She snuggled closer into him, although he was incredibly arrogant and her dislike for him was increasing steadily. But if anything, that made the prospect of setting him up even more appealing.

After a few more pints he squeezed her close, almost crushing the air from her lungs, and mashed his lips on hers, drawing lurid whoops and remarks from the other men and giggles from the stupid girls. Susan did her best to respond sexily to the aggressive kiss, only pulling away and slapping his hand playfully when he mauled her breasts. The reaction seemed well judged as Stacy immediately made a remark in Susan's defence. Billy Ryan laughed and took a huge mouthful of his pint.

'Later,' Susan whispered in his ear as he put the glass down, a remark that increased his brashness even more.

She could see Phil Reynolds through the door into the games room, still playing and occasionally glancing her way. Given the amount of drink Billy Ryan had put back, it seemed likely that she would only need her back-up for a lift home, yet the presence of the powerful young policemen gave a very welcome reassurance.

Last orders were eventually called and Susan felt a knot of tension in her stomach.

As the other Billy returned to the table with the final round of drinks, Luke hailed someone across the smoky bar.

'Oi, Dave, over here!' he shouted.

Susan froze as she saw the man being hailed. He was a thickset, pugnacious man with close-cropped hair and a broken nose… and Susan knew him.

He was Dave Symmes, a petty criminal she had once struck a deal with, exchanging evidence against his associates for enough time to get out of the country. She didn't stop to wonder what he was doing back in London; what mattered was that he knew she was a private investigator, and that she didn't play by the rules.

'All right, Luke,' he grunted.

Susan quickly rubbed an eye to hide her face as he started across towards them. She had mere seconds to decide what to do. It was impossible that he wouldn't recognise her. When he did, her only option would be to scream for Phil Reynolds and make a hasty exit. But that would ruin the operation, and she wasn't used to failure. For a second she toyed with the idea of bluffing it out; admitting who she was but saying it had nothing to do with her presence in the Bell. She abandoned the idea instantly; there was no way they would believe her. Even as Tod Ryan dragged his chair aside to let Dave Symmes pull a stool up, a desperate plan had formed.

Ducking her head down she slapped her hands to her mouth, and mumbled to Billy that she suddenly felt sick and was about to throw up. As she dashed for the door, sending a chair flying, she heard him roar with laughter at her inability to hold her drinks like him and his mates.

Once out in the dark car park she calmed a little and considered her options. She could take what was probably the sensible option and abandon the operation, or she could hang in there and hope, which was pretty likely, that Dave Symmes was with his own mates and would rejoin them before they all left the pub. Not one to give up easily, she decided upon the latter.

Ryan didn't come out to see if she was okay, which just about summed him up. More worrying, however, was that Reynolds hadn't come out either, which suggested he'd not been overly vigilant and hadn't noticed her hasty exit.

About ten minutes later Ryan and the gang staggered out of the pub in raucous spirits. Ryan threw an arm around Susan's shoulder, belched loudly, asked indifferently how she was, and was already laughing at some wisecrack from his brother before she had time to answer.

Susan steeled herself to continue. It was clearly too late to back out now. She cursed herself for not making sure Gage and Berner chose a more intelligent minder than

Reynolds.

They piled into a van, with Billy Ryan in the driving seat despite the quantity of lager he had consumed. Susan climbed into the front beside him, squashing up as Luke climbed in too. She started to relax just a little, but then heard the one thing she had been dreading; Dave Symmes' voice outside the van.

'You lot going back for a party?' he asked.

'Yeah, pile in,' Luke invited, as Susan pressed herself into the shadows.

The doors slammed shut and the van rattled and lurched out onto the road. There was no way out. They were going to someone's flat and, when they got there, Symmes was going to recognise her. The only thing she could think of was running the moment she got out of the van. They'd wonder what the hell she was up to and it would be the end of the operation, but at least she should get away to safety – and that was all important now.

Billy Ryan was stroking her thighs between gearshifts, steering with one hand and smoking at the same time. Susan let him get on with it, hoping beyond hope he'd get picked up for drunken driving before they got to their destination. She knew she was shaking, but prayed he would put it down to excitement, when a face suddenly appeared next to hers.

'Where we going then?' Symmes asked close to her ear.

'My place,' Billy Ryan answered as Susan tried to hide her face in shadow, trying not to look too suspicious.

'Right,' said Symmes. 'Ain't you going to introduce me to your new babe?'

'Susan, this is Dave, the ugliest git this side of the East End,' Billy chuckled.

'Look who's talking,' Symmes objected, and then turned his attention to the girl who was clinging to Billy. 'Hi, Sue... Fuck me!'

Susan knew the game was up. 'Hi,' she responded,

managing a wan smile.

'Fuck me!' he repeated, incredulously. 'You're Susan MacQuillan!'

Susan struggled to release her wrists. The sump oil with which they covered her before dumping her among the trees next to a railway yard meant that she might eventually be able to free herself. If she couldn't, then a railway worker would doubtless find her in the morning, but given the state they had left her in, that was an option she wanted to avoid if possible. With her wrists and ankles strapped together and her knees drawn up to her chest and taped in place, she was completely incapable of movement. She was also wearing nothing but her panties, once white, now filthy with oil.

After Dave Symmes had revealed who she was, she tried to talk her way out of it. But, predictably, her protestations of innocence had been ignored. Billy Ryan and Michael worked for Cooper and were pretty convinced that her presence was connected to the accusation of arson levelled at their boss that morning. Once she had been bundled into the back, masking tape was used to gag her and bind her hands. A fierce argument had then ensued as to what to do with her.

At first she was terrified, but once it became clear that her elimination was not on the cards, her fear faded somewhat. Instead she felt increasing consternation, as it became apparent that the majority favoured teaching her a lesson, and a thoroughly humiliating one at that. Terri and her boyfriend, the other Billy, argued in favour of merely dropping her off somewhere and leaving her to walk back to London. Dave Symmes agreed with this but thought it would be funny to strip her first. Stacy tried to compromise, saying Susan should be left with at least her panties. At last they all agreed.

They drove out to the dead-end that serviced a large

area of railway sidings. Susan struggled furiously to stop it happening, trying to kick and scratch her laughing captors, but it was useless. Symmes sat on her while her jeans were pulled off and her wrists untaped long enough to get her T-shirt over her head. The girls argued for her being allowed to keep her bra, but it had come off anyway, the men having a good feel of her tits while they got her into position to be hog-tied. This involved rolling her up so her bottom stuck out and her knees were as high as they'd go. Her wrists and ankles were lashed together, and a cord passed under her knees and around her back. The position was not only utterly humiliating, but left her completely unable to move.

Billy Ryan and Dave Symmes had carried her out among the trees and dumped her on the chilly grass. Ryan turned back towards the van, but Symmes stopped him.

'Hang on a bit, Billy,' he said, his voice low and conspiratorial. 'I owe this bitch one, and then some more.'

'Yeah, you could be right.' Billy looked over his shoulder towards the van. All was quiet. 'She made me horny as hell in the pub.'

'I just want to take my belt to her arse.'

Ryan grunted in reply while Dave Symmes unbuckled his thick leather belt and drew it out of the loops on his jeans. Susan shivered at the sight of the powerfully built thug standing over her with the belt in his hands. Her sense of humiliation couldn't have been stronger. She just knew she'd be craving sexual gratification as soon as the leather bit into her vulnerable buttocks.

He rolled her onto her knees and elbows. Her humiliation intensified as he peeled her panties down and fondled the bottom he was about to beat.

Sure enough, from the very first smack she started to feel the intense thrill of punishment. Susan hid her face in the grass and closed her eyes. Her situation was straight from her deepest fantasies, and there was nothing she could do to hide her wanton reaction. The combination of the beating and her utter humiliation was too much. She squirmed and moaned, until the thugs realised she was extremely turned on. Billy Ryan swore and called her a horny bitch, and then quickly freed his erection into the night air.

They took turns with her. At first she tried to deny them by remaining inert, but the effect of the beating and Billy Ryan's cock were simply too much. Abandoning her last shred of dignity, Susan let herself go. Ryan sneered at her reaction and smacked her legs as he squatted and fucked her from behind, Symmes making coarse remarks about her all the while. With her thighs tight together the stimulation of his cock ploughing against her clitoris was too much. It was too much for Ryan too, and he came quickly, deep inside her. Then it was Symmes, bullying his way to a hasty orgasm that left her desperately in need of her own climax.

But there were to be no such considerations.

They tugged her panties back up and unscrewed the lid of the sump oil, for her final humiliation.

Billy Ryan did it. He poured the oil slowly over her. He started with her hair, rubbing it well in, and then worked down to plaster her breasts, and lastly her buttocks, tweaking her panties aside to make sure her pussy got a share of the filthy black slime. Symmes stood watching, laughing heartily.

She had remained still until the sound of the van faded, then begun to struggle, squirming in the dirty oil in the hope of lubricating her bonds sufficiently to free herself. Each tiny movement of her wrists loosened the masking tape and slid the cord a fraction of an inch further down. Her determination increased as the bonds weakened. Okay, what they'd done to her was painfully humiliating, but it hadn't come close to breaking her spirit, and if she could only get free it would spoil at least part of their joke.

The cord slipped over the widest point of Susan's hands. The elation of having achieved freedom was strong, yet she knew there was something she really had to do before releasing herself fully. Slipping a hand into her panties and into the filth between her legs, she started to masturbate.

Chapter Eight

'Nice one, Susan,' Paul Berner said as she emerged from the women's locker room.

She shot him a vicious glare and continued on her way. He laughed quietly to himself, watching her bottom sway sexily under the bathrobe as she walked away down the corridor. What had happened to her not only amused him greatly, but also turned him on, his one regret being that he'd not seen her in the state in which she'd been found. The image of a hog-tied Susan appealed to him immensely. It was better even than what he'd done to her in the burnt-out toilet at de Vergy Fine Wines. If he'd found her, he knew it would have been impossible to resist taking advantage of her vulnerability, just as Ryan and Symmes had done.

As it happened, the operation had been a perfect success, if a little unorthodox. Seven of those involved were already in custody for abduction; Dave Symmes alone having had the sense to make himself scarce. Now they could lean on Cooper's two employees, and perhaps do a bargain for information about the fire – assuming there was any information of course, which Susan still insisted there wasn't; at least not from Cooper or his cronies.

Ted Gage had no such doubts. Unlike Berner, Gage felt guilty and sorry for what had happened to Susan, but he also made no effort to hide his delight at the outcome of the operation. Not, of course, that anybody except Gage, Berner and Reynolds knew what had really happened. As far as other people, and in particular Julia Keeson, were concerned, Susan had gone in entirely on her own and come badly unstuck while trying to gather evidence on Cooper's mob.

Susan was going along with it, something that had surprised Gage but not Berner. He knew Susan's strength of personality and that she'd take what had happened in her stride. He also hoped she might at some time like to re-enact it as a fantasy with him in the role of Billy Ryan.

Susan appeared at the end of the corridor, still clutching the bathrobe protectively round her, but this time sticking her tongue out at him. He smiled; she was clearly in a better mood already.

Susan wearily pushed open the front door of her flat. She was exhausted.

The police had been as helpful as they could be, providing a de-oiling agent intended for seabirds as well as soap and clothes. She had given a statement to Berner, Gage, and their boss, Julia Keeson. Berner had been considerate but obviously amused by what had happened, Gage had shown genuine sympathy, and Julia Keeson had spouted a patronising lecture on not interfering in police matters. Susan had let the words flow over her as she sipped hot tea and nibbled a biscuit. An important reason for leaving the force had been to avoid having to do things the way other people wanted them done, and Susan felt quite capable of living with her own mistakes. Keeson had finished by offering her counselling, which she declined.

Susan also told her story only as far as being dumped in the woods, leaving out the finale with Ryan and Symmes. To mention it would simply have stirred up a whole hornet's nest of interviews and internal inquiries, none of which she wanted to get involved with.

Now her spirits lifted as she saw Paulette was home. The living room floor was scattered with her friend's clothes and she could smell the distinctive scent Paulette favoured. There was also a case and a half of wine on the floor, the box bearing the legend 'Cave Co-Operative de Choray' on its side. Susan smiled, glad that Paulette's trip had apparently not been wasted.

As she closed the door behind her, she was overcome with a sudden desperate need for a cuddle. Peeling off the ill-fitting clothes she had borrowed from the police, she walked naked into Paulette's room, finding her friend curled into a ball on one side of the bed, her arm around an enormous pink teddy bear. Susan climbed in beside her, finding Paulette warm and naked beneath the covers. Snuggling into her friend's body, she closed her eyes and let her mind relax. Paulette sighed and flopped a hand on the arm Susan had slipped around her waist. Moments later, Susan too was asleep.

She awoke to the gentle pressure of Paulette's hand on her shoulder, and accepted a mug of coffee after propping herself up on the pillows. Paulette climbed in beside her, sitting up and not bothering to cover her naked breasts.

'So what happened?' Susan asked after she'd rubbed her eyes and blinked against the light. 'I've had a hell of a time, but you go first.'

'I think I know who killed Alan Sowerby,' Paulette blurted excitedly, and then launched into her description of events in France.

'So we really need to consult a wine expert,' Susan remarked half-an-hour later, when they had exchanged stories. 'Do you know anyone who would help?'

'A few,' Paulette answered, 'but most of them would be annoyed at my having pinched Sowerby's briefcase, and I'd rather not get into that. There's one guy who might be cool about it: Oswald MacNaughton. He knows his stuff, too; he's written lots of books.'

'Great. Give him a call and we'll take the samples round to him.'

'Okay.'

They sat in silence for a while, both sipping coffee. Susan found herself thinking over Paulette's discoveries in France. The co-op manager, Christian Charrier, certainly sounded suspicious, although his behaviour sounded a little too casual. Surely a man who had used Destroying Angel to poison somebody would avoid demonstrating a knowledge of the fungus, even to someone entirely unconnected?

The quality of his sadism didn't convince her, either. Having long sought punishment and humiliation in her sexual encounters, she felt that those who liked to dish it out could be divided roughly into three types. The best were those who were aware of their sexuality and in control of it, like Anderson Croom, who had introduced her to most of the more subtle and refined practices of dominance and submission. Annabella de Vergy fell into that same category.

At the other end of the spectrum were those who just enjoyed it and never questioned whether it was right or not. George and Maria Lyle fell into that category. Both had thought the idea of spanking a white girl's naked bottom both sexy and amusing, George the more so because Susan had been his immediate superior. Once they'd known she liked it, they had just done it when they wanted, even slipping Susan's bikini pants down on the beach on one occasion.

The third sort were those who liked it but got in a stew over it. One boyfriend had given her a fine over-the-knee spanking, fucked her from behind over his sofa, and then spent the rest of the evening in a fit of agonised soul-searching because he'd enjoyed it so much. They were the least satisfying playmates, and she felt Charrier best fitted among their ranks. People who spent a lot of time worrying over their morals seldom became murderers. Nothing, however, could be proved until the wines were analysed, and Paulette's other observations at least looked likely to provide some promising leads.

Jilly Ross sat on her bed feeling thoroughly morose. She held a piece of paper. It bore the number of the police hot line for information about the Fire Ghost attacks. For an hour she had sat wondering whether to ring it or not. Other than Fire Ghost himself and Robin, she was the only person who knew where the next attack was going to be. Unlike Robin, the idea of arson did not excite her – it repelled her. Robin was nice, but he had always resented anybody better off than himself, and she knew it was this resentment that led to his love of destruction.

She was different. Her parents were shopkeepers and had enough trouble keeping their heads above water as it was, without lunatics like Fire Ghost running around. Robin, she knew, would never actually set a fire, but he would certainly go to the warehouse to leave his tag, and that was almost as bad. Leastwise, if the police caught him he'd get much the same treatment as Fire Ghost himself.

Her affection for Robin was genuine. She found a vulnerability in him that was missing in Taz. Currently, she was going out with both of them, neither suspecting the true depth of her feelings for the other. The situation was awkward and added to her depression, although the actual sex was fun. The day she'd screwed with Robin in the shop, she'd also let Taz screw her in the evening. The thrill of knowing that the cock inside her belonged to the closest friend of someone who'd done the same, just hours before, had been lovely. The knowledge that she was doing something naughty definitely added to the thrill. Besides, Taz was always talking about making her have sex with other blokes, and it was half-tempting to tell him about Robin.

But that was just sex. Sex didn't really hurt anyone.

Fire-raising did.

As far as she was concerned, the faster Fire Ghost was locked up the better. But if she split on him and Robin found out, he would never forgive her. There was also the problem of making sure that if she told the police where Fire Ghost was going to strike, they didn't catch Robin at the same time. Still, she reflected with a sigh, the bottom line was that eventually Fire Ghost was going to kill someone, and in the most horrible way imaginable. No, there was nothing for it but to call the police. She'd worry about keeping Robin clear of Merton when the time came.

Jilly went to the telephone, thought better of it, and decided to use the call-box at the end of the road. As she walked she evolved a plan to keep Robin safe. The first step would be to pretend it was she who Fire Ghost had boasted to and that he intended to make the attack alone.

Detective Superintendent Keeson sat behind her desk, eyes sharp and narrow as she appraised her subordinate.

'DI Gage,' she began coldly, 'if I had the slightest evidence that you were in any way involved with last night's fiasco, you would not merely be on suspension, you'd be charged. However, I don't, and Miss MacQuillan claims to have acted entirely independently. Frankly, I have no wish to delve further into the mess. Just be warned.'

'Yes, ma'am,' Gage replied, thanking heaven for Susan's personal strength and discretion.

'Leaving that aside,' Keeson moved on, 'I presume that one or other of those detained might have supplied some information about the fires?'

Her voice had a distinct edge of sarcasm to it, and Gage realised that she knew full well what had been going on. Practicality, he knew, was the virtue upon which Julia Keeson prided herself most of all. As long as she herself was not obliged to take any risks, she would turn a blind eye to his techniques for the sake of results. Unfortunately, there had as yet been no results.

'Not yet, ma'am,' he admitted, 'but we're hoping for something soon.'

'Save that for the press,' she replied. 'In any case, the best we can expect is a result for the last three fires, and we still have nothing on the previous four.'

'No, ma'am,' he answered, conscious of the number of times they'd been over the same ground. 'You know the way it is ma'am, random targets, no rational motive—'

'Yes, I know,' she said, for once with a touch of sympathy in her voice. 'That will be all.'

Gage left with a feeling of intense relief. All it would have taken was for Susan MacQuillan to have lost her head and he would have been out of a job, as would Paul Berner. The thought of Berner put a new spring in his step. After all, it was Berner who'd had the damn fool idea in the first place, and if Keeson could tear a strip off him, then he had much more reason to tear one off Paul Berner. Hoping he was still in the building, he made for the canteen, looking forward to coffee and a sharp word with the Detective Sergeant.

As he passed his own office Sergeant Yates appeared at the top of the stairs.

'There you are, sir,' Yates said, sounding flustered. 'We just had a call on the Fire Ghost line, sir. A tip-off.'

Susan stood looking up at the façade of Oswald MacNaughton's house. A tall narrow structure of brick and stone, it carried an air of reserve and gentility that went with its location towards the top of Hampstead Hill. She found herself facing the coming interview with a degree of trepidation. MacNaughton had readily agreed to see her and Paulette, but his very age and seniority within the wine establishment made her feel uneasy. Presumably he knew Annabella de Vergy, and presumably he had a lot of respect for her. He might well regard

Paulette and herself as merely insolent for suggesting any impropriety within the de Vergy Fine Wines operation and close ranks against them.

Still, the attempt had to be made.

Paulette rang the bell. Susan waited a step below her with the case of samples.

'He's a bit gruff,' Paulette whispered, 'but really quite sweet.'

Susan nodded, as the door opened.

She blushed furiously, and then couldn't suppress a giggle as Oswald MacNaughton, respected writer and patriarch of the wine trade, appeared in the doorway.

Oswald MacNaughton was the owlish voyeur from the car park!

'Hi,' she said cheerfully, 'spied on any cute girls recently?'

'Susan!' Paulette exclaimed.

'Don't worry,' Susan said, ignoring the astonishment on the writer's face. 'Oswald and I have met, in a public car park out along the A40!'

'I, er—' MacNaughton blustered.

'Nice to see you,' she continued, giving him a peck on the cheek and pushing past him into the house. 'I'm glad it's you. It always helps to have met someone socially before consulting them on a professional matter, don't you think?'

'I, er – yes,' MacNaughton blustered again, still looking totally nonplussed. 'Yes, er – come in. The drawing room is perhaps most comfortable.'

He looked up and down the street as though checking to see if anyone had seen the girls enter his house, closed the large front door, and ushered Susan and Paulette into the room. Susan smiled at her friend as she put the case of samples down on the floor.

'I – I understand you have some samples you'd like me to taste?' MacNaughton said, at last gathering his wits and

161

overcoming the shock of meeting Susan again.

'We have,' Susan confirmed. 'In fact, it would really be best if you assessed the wines before we explained what's going on.'

'Ah ha, a blind tasting,' MacNaughton smiled. 'I do enjoy blind tasting. Make yourselves comfortable and I shall obtain a corkscrew and glasses.'

Susan looked around admiringly as she settled into a large brown leather armchair. The room was cluttered with furniture, all of it antique. Rows of books stood in one tall glass-fronted case. Other cases displayed curios: hand-blown wine bottles, a collection of old corkscrews, cut glass decanters. A globe stood in one corner, next to another display case containing stuffed birds. Pulling her attention from the opulence of the room, she exchanged a meaningful look with Paulette. The black girl still had an expression of disbelief on her face.

'Is he really?' Paulette whispered urgently. 'Is he really the one from the car park?'

'He is.'

'And a most enjoyable encounter it was too,' MacNaughton said, having returned without them noticing, his composure seemingly recovered in full. 'The car park in question is, shall we say, generally worth visiting. Though I'd not seen you there before.'

'It was my first time,' Susan admitted.

'But not your last, I trust?' he enquired hopefully.

'Probably not; it was fun,' Susan laughed. 'I'll bring Paulette next time, too.'

'Susan!' Paulette exclaimed again.

MacNaughton laughed and placed the tray of glasses he was carrying on a low table. Sitting in an armchair identical to Susan's, except for being notably more worn, he began to arrange the glasses.

'Let us see, then,' he said. 'Paulette, my dear, perhaps you would do the honours? But do sit down.'

Paulette made herself comfortable on the settee close to the case of samples. Using the corkscrew offered by MacNaughton, she opened the first of the bottles. He steepled his fingers and gazed out of the window as she poured a glass of pale white wine.

MacNaughton took the glass as soon as Paulette had returned the bottle to the case. Holding it up to the light he admired its colour, then swirled it gently in the glass and held it beneath his nose. Humming and tutting he again looked at the colour, took a sip, assessed it, and then swallowed.

'Sauvignon, of course,' he pronounced with absolute confidence. 'Not, I think, New Zealand, although it is hard to tell nowadays. Nor is it Bordeaux. No, unless it is a rather poor Sancerre or from one of the neighbouring communes, I would say it's from the plateau of the eastern Touraine, possibly Oisly or Sassay?'

'Choray,' Paulette corrected.

'Only one village out then,' MacNaughton smiled, evidently well pleased with himself for the accuracy of his assessment. 'Not bad for an old man.'

Susan sat back, impressed by his ability. Paulette passed her a glass of the Sauvignon. She sipped it and wondered what factors in the flavour allowed MacNaughton to be so precise.

The tasting continued, MacNaughton pronouncing on each and declaring the wines to be of moderate quality at best but typical of the region. Only when Paulette poured him a glass of the mature Côt did he show real enthusiasm.

'Ah ha!' he declared, favouring his glass with an expression of satisfaction not unlike the one Susan had seen when they first met. 'Here we have an example of what a region is truly capable of. Only in the best years, of course, and then only from the best sites, but I think you will agree the difference is remarkable. It's Côt, isn't it my dear, and almost certainly an '89 or a '90?'

Paulette nodded.

''89,' she confirmed, 'from the private estate of a grower called Christian Charrier.'

'I regret that I have never met the gentleman,' MacNaughton said. 'Still, there are too many growers to meet them all, even in great Burgundy, never mind the eastern Touraine. Are these all his wines?'

'The rest are from the co-op he manages,' Paulette told him. 'The Cave Co-Operative de Choray. I expect you've heard of it.'

'I know Choray,' MacNaughton said pensively, 'but only vaguely. If I remember rightly, the co-op is to the south of the village, but I've never tasted there. The wines are adequate, it is true, and I dare say cheap, but frankly one can only taste so much and I prefer to stick to private estates when visiting a region.'

'De Vergy Fine Wines import them,' Susan added.

'De Vergy Fine Wines?'

'Annabella de Vergy's outfit. Surely you know her?'

'I'm afraid I haven't had the pleasure,' MacNaughton answered. 'There are so many small merchants these days, you know.'

'But I thought you knew everybody?' Paulette said.

MacNaughton spread his hands in a gesture of resignation. 'The wine trade is somewhat exclusive,' he said, 'and I fear I am perhaps not as objective as I might be. Still, it is impossible to have a comprehensive knowledge of the trade and, as I say, one can only taste so much. Also, if these are typical of their wines, then they are clearly a rather straightforward commercial operation. Do they supply mainly to the restaurant trade or to private clients?'

'I'm afraid I don't know,' Paulette admitted.

'No matter. What did you want to ask then?'

'Actually, we thought they might be adulterated,' Paulette said. 'Not the Côt, the others.'

'Adulterated?' MacNaughton was clearly surprised.

'They may be involved in some sort of scandal,' Paulette explained.

'I'm a private investigator by trade,' Susan added. 'Paulette asked me to help with the investigation.'

'Are you, by Jove?'

'Yes, and by the way, the man I was with the other night is a Detective Sergeant attached to the area crime squad.'

'Good God!' MacNaughton gasped. 'You weren't... what's the phrase... on a stake out, were you?'

'No, that was just for fun,' Susan assured him. 'Anyway, do you think they might be adulterated?'

MacNaughton eyed her carefully for a few moments, and then seemed to accept her word that his reputation was not in any danger. 'Not at all,' he eventually said. 'Indeed, I can't imagine why anyone would want to adulterate such wines.'

'Why not?' Paulette asked, a little crestfallen.

'It could scarcely be worth the risk,' MacNaughton explained. 'Such wines are cheap, and adulteration would at best marginally increase their profitability. Meanwhile, they would almost certainly be caught when the wines were analysed by the authorities. French Appellation laws are quite strict these days, you know.'

'Oh,' Paulette said.

'No,' MacNaughton continued. 'Adulteration is only worthwhile if it makes a cheap wine appear expensive. Take the diethylene glycol scandal of a few years ago. The anti-freeze was added to make cheap mass-produced wine appear to be of a higher quality than it really was. Profit margins were therefore greatly increased. It could hardly be so in this case.'

'That's true I suppose,' Paulette said, 'but some things struck me as odd in the winery as well. Perhaps you could explain them to us?'

'If I can, I shall.'

'Three things,' Paulette started. 'One: other than a few specialities, they only do the four main wines and bring two more in from the south, all of which you've tasted, yet they have sixteen tanks. Two: the slates on the tanks were marked with annotations that appeared to indicate sulphuric acid levels. Three: there were lots of blackcurrant bushes planted among the vineyards.'

MacNaughton laughed, taking a sip of his Côt before replying. 'All perfectly ordinary, I fear,' he said, shaking his head. 'The tanks will hold wines from different vineyards and different years. A winery always needs plenty of capacity, and getting enough storage space is always an important consideration. The sulphuric acid annotation is merely a convenient way of expressing the natural, and highly complex, acidity levels within a wine by comparing it with a standard solution of sulphuric acid. The blackcurrants are for making cassis. Who knows, a few bunches may end up in among the cabernet grapes now and then, but really that is no bad thing. After all, we accept the flavour of oak in wine, even when added in the form of powder. I try not to drink such horrors, but I understand it to be common practice in America. If artificial oak, then why not good honest blackcurrants?'

Paulette shrugged, looking deeply disappointed.

'I'm sorry not to be more positive, my dear,' MacNaughton concluded, 'but I fear that if you have unearthed a scandal, then it does not involve adulteration by the co-op at Choray. Still, I would be prepared to send what's left of these samples for a detailed laboratory analysis, if you like?'

'That would be very kind.' Paulette managed a smile. 'Thank you.'

'A pleasure to be of assistance. But you must tell me the background to your suspicions. I confess to fascination.'

Paulette sighed and glanced at Susan. Susan responded

with a shrug. MacNaughton seemed well disposed towards them and there was nothing to be gained by obfuscation. 'Do you remember Alan Sowerby?' Paulette began.

'Certainly,' MacNaughton confirmed, 'poor old Alan. I knew him well, and was astonished that he was foolish enough to consume Destroying Angel.'

'We don't think he was foolish, we think he was murdered,' Susan put in.

'Good heavens!' MacNaughton exclaimed, 'But the police—'

'Have no evidence and never even opened a case,' Susan interrupted. 'The coroner's verdict was accidental death. Paulette, however, discovered that Alan had been on the track of what he considered a major wine scandal when he died. The only lead we had was that it involved de Vergy Fine Wines in some way.'

MacNaughton nodded pensively. 'Hence your suspicions of adulteration.'

'Exactly.' Susan explained the case, Paulette adding the occasional remark and Oswald MacNaughton frequently putting in questions.

'I must admit your reasoning appears a trifle speculative,' he said, when Susan had finished. 'Yet you clearly have a better grasp of the mathematics of probability than I. So you suspect this man Charrier?'

'He seems the most likely suspect,' Susan answered. 'We were assuming that he and Philip Ruddock were working together to bring in bad wine and splitting the profit. Sowerby found out and they poisoned him. If the wines are clean, though, it rather wrecks our reasoning. I need to think out a new theory.'

'Have another glass of Côt,' MacNaughton offered. 'It'll lubricate your thought processes.'

Susan accepted the wine and sat back in her chair, thinking deeply. If de Vergy Fine Wines were importing an honest product from the Choray co-op, then Charrier had nothing to gain and so was probably innocent. Yet he had shown Paulette the Destroying Angel growing in local woods, which added yet another low probability event to a long chain of them. Something was wrong, but what?

Of course, Charrier might well make a habit of showing customers around the area, particularly pretty female customers. Annabella was a customer, a good one in fact, and certainly fell into the categories of pretty and female. Could Annabella – or Ruddock, for that matter – have picked up the Destroying Angel in the woods around Choray? Another suspicion was forming in her mind.

'Getting back to de Vergy Fine Wines,' she said, interrupting the conversation between Paulette and Oswald MacNaughton. 'You say you've never heard of them, but Annabella de Vergy makes herself out to be pretty well known in the trade. She's certainly successful, anyway. She owns a house in Little Venice.'

'Oh.' MacNaughton looked a little thoughtful. 'Well, yes – to be honest, I would expect to know her, or at least to recognise the name. I fear I must be getting past my prime.'

'Not at all. I think there's a very different reason why you've not heard of them.'

'Oh yes?' Paulette asked. 'What's that?'

'Have patience,' Susan told her. 'I'll explain when I've thought it through.'

'I'd be delighted to know the outcome,' Oswald MacNaughton said, 'and I shall certainly send these wines for analysis. I won't hear of payment, either: Alan Sowerby was, after all, an old friend of mine. And if there's any more information you need, don't hesitate to ask.'

'Thank you,' the two girls echoed.

'You might, however, grant an old man a small favour and enliven what will otherwise be a solitary and dull dinner,' MacNaughton continued. 'This Côt is excellent, yet in such warm weather a white might be more

168

appropriate. By chance I have some Chablis in the fridge; a Premier Cru Fourchaume, '85, a truly wonderful wine.'

Susan relaxed, letting the heady red wine wash away the stresses of the past twenty-four hours. The comfort and refinement of Oswald MacNaughton's drawing room seemed a world away from the noise and smoke of the Bell, his gentility in even greater contrast to the personalities of the likes of Billy Ryan and Dave Symmes. Sitting in a leather armchair in a Hampstead drawing room was definitely therapeutic, especially when faced with the prospect of fine wines and food. After that...

MacNaughton's behaviour in the car park had suggested a taste in sex as hedonistic as his taste in wine, and something might well be in order after dinner. It would be very easy to submit to him, not just because she was slightly drunk but because, after the episode in the car park, there could be no embarrassment in discussing sex with him. A slow, gentle spanking might be nice, followed by a long period paying court to his cock. Susan exchanged a look with Paulette, finding similar thoughts mirrored in her friend's face.

The hour before dinner passed in light conversation. MacNaughton then produced an impressive feast from his larder and more fine wines from his cellar. They ended up back in the drawing room, thoroughly relaxed and sipping Cognac. Susan had abandoned the armchair in favour of lying on the sofa with her head in Paulette's lap. She watched MacNaughton idly as he enlarged on the qualities of the Cognac they were drinking.

Sitting back with his jacket open over an impressive spread of fancy waistcoat, he looked fatter and more extravagant than ever. His suit was of a deep green velvet, the waistcoat of a similar green but with patterns of gold and black. An ivory silk shirt and a bow tie of black velvet completed an image that made Susan feel distinctly underdressed in her simple frock of red cotton. Paulette

169

had insisted they wear frocks, choosing white herself. MacNaughton's whole image seemed calculated to make her feel like a naughty girl, and the idea of being spanked by him was even more appealing than it had been earlier.

'Do you visit the car park in Greenford often?' she asked, when a suitable lull occurred in the conversation.

'When the mood takes me,' he replied, now without the slightest embarrassment. 'I freely confess to a passion for the delights of voyeurism, and it is among the best sites. There are several regulars, and an unspoken agreement that we may look if we don't actually interfere. It is surprising how many men like to show their ladies off, and how many ladies enjoy such attention. For all that, the night you were there was exceptional.'

'Tell us about some other good ones,' Susan urged.

'Certainly, if Paulette has no objection to such a discussion.'

'None at all,' Paulette smiled. 'Go on.'

Susan settled her head more comfortably onto Paulette's lap as their host chose his story.

'From the point of view of that particular car park,' MacNaughton began, 'your own little adventure was, in truth, the best. One other event does spring to mind though, a fine evening while I was still an undergraduate at Oxford, in the mid-sixties.'

He paused a while and smiled dreamily as he reminisced.

'It was mid-summer, and myself and a friend had taken a punt up as far as Islip,' MacNaughton went on, resting his head against the back of his chair. 'North of the town, the Cherwell runs through open fields with willows on the banks and patches of reed – quite beautiful. It was a warm evening not unlike this one, and we hadn't seen a soul for an hour or more, when we rounded a bend to find the most entrancing sight. A group of girls were bathing in the river, five in all, some quite naked, some in their panties. They seemed to find our appearance amusing, if anything, and made little effort to protect their modesty. I particularly remember one fine young thing pulling herself up out of the water onto a willow trunk. She had very pale skin and a sweet figure, with her wet panties clinging tight to quite the roundest little bottom. I was entranced, of course, and slowed the punt to watch…'

He drifted away again with his memories.

'Anyway,' he suddenly seemed to remember the two girls listening to his tale, 'as we drew level the girls began to taunt us, not nastily, but so as to suggest that we shouldn't be looking, even while they were quite clearly showing off. My friend was somewhat bashful and wanted to continue, but one of them noticed we had some bottled beer in the punt and swam out to us. She pulled herself up on the side with her breasts just above the water and asked quite boldly if she could have a beer. My friend said no, rather gruffly in fact, but I told him not to be an ass and gave the girl a bottle. She thanked me and asked if we were enjoying watching them, still in the same cheeky manner that suggested we were somehow guilty of peeping at them, despite their having chosen to bathe naked on their own accord. I admitted I was and, to my amazement, she brazenly offered to masturbate me in return for another beer.'

'That's nice,' Susan broke in dreamily. 'Why not get your cock out now?'

'For the simple reason that I intend to spank you both, and that it is highly undignified for a gentleman to have his genitalia hanging out while he chastises a girl.'

Paulette giggled, and Susan made a face of mock disappointment as MacNaughton continued.

'My friend was something of a prude and was quite horrified, but even at the tender age of nineteen I was not one to turn down such an opportunity. A rather hot discussion followed, which ended with me standing on the bank with the beer while my friend disappeared down

171

the river with his nose in the air. The girl was very businesslike, suggesting a comfortable spot to sit and taking my penis out for me. It was a delicious experience; her sitting beside me quite naked and stroking and cajoling me to an erection.

'The others were keen to watch and emerged from the river with much giggling. The cheekiest of them started to pose for me as I became fully erect, holding her breasts and sticking her bottom out in a delightfully rude manner. All three of the others still had wet panties on, and the girl masturbating me suggested they take them down. Two did without any fuss, showing me their pussies. The last one was shy and wouldn't strip, so her friends grabbed her and pulled them down. They made her bend over and showed me her delightful bottom. It was too much for me. I ejaculated, my semen coating the fingers that pumped my penis so delightfully. My orgasm caused a final burst of giggles from the pretty group.

We had no more sex, but I stayed with them for an hour or so before setting off back to Oxford. I didn't get back until after dark.'

'I wish I'd been there,' Susan remarked. 'I'll bet your friend was jealous.'

'Not at all,' MacNaughton replied. 'He was something of a prude, and very probably gay to boot. He's something terribly senior in the civil service these days, so I won't mention his name. It was an exquisitely erotic experience and gave me not only a lasting taste for voyeurism, but confirmed me in the opinion that, at heart, women are as rude as men.'

'Ruder,' Paulette suggested.

'Possibly, possibly; at least, my young friend of the river bank seemed to think nothing of masturbating a complete stranger in return for a couple of bottles of beer. Nor was she concerned with what her friends thought. Since then, I have found that rivers, and particularly canals, are

172

excellent sites for the voyeur. Girls frequently bathe naked in the more remote spots, and there are always plenty of bikinis, tight shorts, little dresses and so on. Beaches are good, too. I recall a pretty redhead in a lonely cove in Cornwall. I was on the cliff top and watched her strip—'

'I think it's about time you dealt with us,' Susan encouraged, stretching sexily and squirming a little. 'Your story's made me feel really horny.'

'Excellent,' MacNaughton enthused. 'Do you have any little preferences I should know about?'

'I like to be humiliated,' Susan drooled.

'And I like to feel I'm being punished,' Paulette put in, 'but be a little gentle – I was birched the other day.'

'Well, I dare say you deserved it,' MacNaughton said, getting ponderously to his feet. 'Now come on, let's have the pair of you kneeling on the sofa, and we'll have those plump bottoms warm in no time.'

Susan twisted up onto her knees, already trembling with excitement at the thought of her coming punishment. Pressing her cheek into the warm leather sofa, she stuck her bottom up as far as it would go. Next to her, Paulette assumed a similar position, looking into Susan's face with wide excited eyes.

'Dresses up, first, and then we'll see about your panties,' MacNaughton announced.

Susan sighed as he held the hem of her frock and lifted it. She imagined she could feel his lecherous eyes on her, first admiring her thighs and then her panties. She knew they'd be stretched taut across her full bottom, white and tight with a little damp patch over her pussy.

'Very pretty,' MacNaughton adjudged as he settled the material onto her back. 'Loosen your belt. I see no reason to leave those lovely breasts covered.'

She did as she was told, reaching behind her to loosen the knot that held the dress around her waist. He slipped it up further, bunching the material around her shoulders and then taking a soft breast in each hand. His belly pressed against her panty-clad bottom. He was in no hurry, taking his time to fondle her. Susan closed her eyes and enjoyed the pleasurable stroking and pinching.

'Splendid,' MacNaughton said, his cultured voice quavering just a little. 'You are very beautiful, Susan; as is little Paulette.'

Susan opened her eyes and watched Paulette's frock being lifted. MacNaughton had a good feel of her smooth dark flesh, and then stepped back.

'Now, let me see...' he said. 'Punishment for Paulette, humiliation for Susan, but bare bottoms for both of you. Susan first, I think.'

Susan shivered as his hands went to her underwear.

'Pull your back in,' MacNaughton ordered as he took a firm hold on the waistband. 'Let's see those cheeks tensed.'

She could feel his fingers inside the elastic, the fingernails hard against her skin. She obeyed his instruction as he began to draw her panties down slowly over her buttocks.

'Plump, but well formed,' he remarked. 'A nice high cleft and full cheeks. Very spankable.'

Susan trembled with pleasure at the feel of her panties being eased down and the humiliation of what he was saying.

Once the flimsy garment was around her knees he prised her buttocks apart. 'And such a pretty anus, too,' he commented. 'Nice and tight. It would be such a delight to bugger you. Is it virgin?'

'No,' Susan admitted, her humiliation so intense that tears burst from her tightly closed eyes.

'Shame,' MacNaughton said, but didn't dwell on the matter. 'And your cunt is as pretty and tempting as your anus. You really are a delightful creature.'

His hands left her and she peered back over her shoulder.

'Now,' he said, 'I think we'll have your friend's panties

down, too.'

Susan watched as he lowered Paulette's panties, settling them around her friend's knees just as her own were.

'Beautiful,' MacNaughton announced. 'Chocolate and cream, two plump little ladies awaiting their spankings. Dresses up, pants down, just as it should be. Titties dangling, behinds stuck up, pussies and bottom-holes on show; perfect.'

MacNaughton began to spank Paulette without further ado. He held the black girl around the waist and applied his hand to her bottom. Paulette took it well, only squealing a little as her buttocks warmed. Her large breasts swung with the smacks, tempting Susan to reach out and squeeze one and pinch the nipple. Paulette opened her mouth and put her tongue out for a kiss. Susan responded, finding her friend's mouth and melting into a kiss as she fondled Paulette's breasts. She could feel the gentle smacks through her friend's body, a delicious feeling amplified by the sure knowledge that it would soon be her turn.

Susan tensed as he finished Paulette off with a salvo of harder smacks, leaving the girl breathing hard against Susan's face. MacNaughton's arm then curled around her waist, lifting her a little. A hand touched her bottom, cupping a cheek and then lifting. A sudden smack made Susan jump. Her lips lost contact with Paulette's. Her friend moved closer and put an arm around Susan's shoulders, and stroked her hanging breasts in return.

'Do it hard,' Paulette urged.

'Hey!' Susan squeaked as the gentle smacks immediately increased in force. She heard Paulette giggle, and did her best to remain composed. With his bulk, MacNaughton was impossible to move, and she could do nothing but squirm and squeal as he spanked her. She started to cry again and pounded the sofa with her fists.

'I, for all my experience, have never seen such a fuss,' MacNaughton panted, tightening his grip on Susan's waist and starting on the backs of her thighs.

The smacks stung even more on her legs. Susan bucked and struggled as the tears streamed down her cheeks. Finally she could take no more and begged him to let her go. MacNaughton added a last few hard smacks across the fattest part of her bottom before complying.

'Back in position, Paulette,' MacNaughton ordered.

Paulette scrambled back into the submissive kneeling position in which she'd too been spanked. Susan was whimpering into the sofa, knees wide apart, panties stretched taut between them.

'You may both masturbate,' he said. 'I shall enjoy watching you do it in that position, but only after I have completed Paulette's punishment. Susan, hold her down.'

Susan sighed from the discomfort as she obeyed. She held her friend tightly around the waist and lifted her bottom. MacNaughton moved away, but quickly returned with a long brown cane. Paulette squeaked in alarm at the sight of it.

'Oh please, not my bum,' she protested, 'it's too bruised!'

'I wouldn't dream of such a thing!' MacNaughton declared. 'To cane a girl so soon after a birching would be the act of a sadist. No my dear, I intend to cane your thighs.'

Paulette gulped as Oswald MacNaughton raised the cane above her unprotected legs. Susan's grip was firm about her waist. Her own knickers felt tight around her thighs. She knew it was going to hurt – indeed, she wanted it to hurt – but the waiting was still agony.

The cane struck without warning, biting into her soft flesh. She yelped and bucked, only to be pushed back into place by Susan's surprising strength. Another cut landed and she squealed again, her whole body shaking. The two lines were already burning on her skin when the third stroke came, landing just above her stretched panties. She howled and dug her fingers into the sofa.

A fourth stroke landed and suddenly it was too much.

Her hands burrowed between her legs to find the wet valley between her sex-lips. She was vaguely aware of Susan touching herself too. It felt utterly shameless and utterly delicious; knowing that MacNaughton was watching them play with themselves. He'd always seemed so respectable, so aloof, and now he was watching them both masturbate.

He'd be watching their fingers work on their clits, their pussies swollen and moist. He'd be looking at their anuses, watching the little rings pulse and pout in their ecstasy. The four cane-stripes on her thighs were burning, a much sharper pain than the warm glow of her freshly spanked bottom. Susan would be the same, buttocks as red as cherry skins, bottom tingling from her spanking. It had been lovely holding Susan while she blubbered and squealed in her spanking tantrum, but it was she who'd been caned…

'Beat me,' she begged as she started to come.

The cane landed immediately. Paulette shrieked in ecstasy as a line of fire cut across her thighs.

'My bum!' she managed, rubbing frantically at her clit, her back arching as the cane cut hard across her naked bottom. She screamed her emotion. Her orgasm exploded in her head; once, twice, and then she slumped onto the sofa, blissfully exhausted.

Susan cuddled her and Paulette swooned in her friends embrace. She was vaguely aware of Oswald MacNaughton sinking into his armchair.

'Come on,' Susan whispered.

Paulette slipped wearily to the floor and crawled to where he sat. His large cock was sticking up from his open trousers. Susan cradled his balls while Paulette curled her fingers around the rigid stem and leant forward to lick the bulbous tip. It was impressively large in girth and length; a great pillar of male flesh. As she pumped her fist she lowered her head and tightened her lips around him. She felt him shudder and heard a soft groan. His generous dimensions quickly had her jaw aching.

'Perfect…' MacNaughton croaked. 'Make me come in your mouth, my dear.'

A hand fumbled with her breasts as she began to suck and toss him avidly. She knew he was about to ejaculate, and sucked all the harder.

Susan knew too: 'Let me share it,' Paulette heard her friend implore.

An instant later his cock spasmed and her mouth filled with his salty seed. She skilfully rode his jerking hips until he gradually stilled and she was sure he was fully spent, and then she turned to Susan. They kissed hungrily, equally overcome with passion as Paulette fed his offering into her friend's voracious mouth.

'Port is ideal after an erotic encounter,' MacNaughton said as he studied his glass against the light. 'And a truly excellent encounter that was, too. My thanks to you both.'

'Not at all,' Susan smiled. 'I loved it.'

'Me too,' Paulette concurred sleepily.

'Tell me something, though, Susan,' MacNaughton continued. 'Do you always cry like that?'

'Only when I'm having fun,' she said. 'I—'

'Just yesterday,' Paulette broke in, 'an operation went wrong and she ended up being stripped, tied, dumped by a railway yard, shagged, and covered in filthy oil. And all she needed after that was a cuddle!'

'Somehow you don't surprise me,' MacNaughton replied. 'I've often found that it's the most submissive females who are ultimately the strongest inside. I enjoyed your tears though, Susan, I freely confess it.'

Susan accepted his words as a compliment. 'Thank you,' she said.

Chapter Nine

'So if Ruddock or Annabella did it, then they must have been in France recently,' Susan stated.

'I simply cannot believe it of Annabella,' Paulette responded. 'Not murder, anyway.'

'At the very least she's a fraud and an accessory to arson,' Susan insisted. 'She's a good actress, too. Keep an open mind.'

'But if Ruddock burnt the warehouse?' Paulette said.

'Then he's probably the murderer,' Susan admitted, 'but all Paul says is that Ruddock owns a river cruiser, nothing more.'

'Still—'

'Okay,' Susan interrupted, 'so Ruddock's our prime suspect. Look at it like this, though. It is highly improbable that the murderer kept a store of dried Destroying Angel just in case they needed to poison someone. It does occur in England, but it's rare, whereas the related Death Cap, *Amanita Phalloides*, is much more common, grows in the same habitat and is even more deadly. All that argues for prior knowledge of a Destroying Angel site. It can't have been collected before Sowerby told Annabella he thought that de Vergy Fine Wines were being ripped off, and we know that that was July the fifteenth, from his diary.'

Susan paused, pushing the guide to poisonous fungi aside and reaching for Alan Sowerby's diary. She lay on her front on her bed, surrounded by books and papers. Paulette sat cross-legged on the floor. Among the papers was a note Paul Berner had left the previous night. It stated two important things: that the police had received a tip-

179

off that another Fire Ghost attack would happen that night, and that Philip Ruddock owned a river cruiser. There had also been a veiled apology for his part in the previous night's debacle.

'And he died on August the twenty-fourth,' Paulette added.

'Exactly. And, given the time Destroying Angel takes to act, that puts his poisoning some time in the second week of August. So if we are right in assuming the fungus was collected from France, then Annabella or Ruddock would have to have visited France between the sixteenth of July and, say, the twelfth of August. They surely wouldn't have visited their main supplier when the manager was in England, so when was Charrier over here?'

'He said he visited some sort of trade fair,' Paulette replied. 'Look in Sowerby's trade calendar: it's that thin one with grapes on the front.'

Susan reached for the slim book Paulette indicated, flicking over several pages before speaking again. 'There was some sort of combined co-operative show in a hotel in Victoria in mid-August,' she said. 'Nothing else seems likely, so that's probably it, and if so it clears Charrier, unless he arrived nearly a week early. No, what we want to know is whether Annabella or Ruddock visited France over the relevant period. If either did, it makes them pretty well certain. Both of them seem to have had dinner with Sowerby at that time, so if we just knew about their trips we could probably work it out. Unfortunately their work diaries will have gone up with the warehouse. Still—'

'What struck me,' Paulette interrupted, 'is what Oswald said about it only being worth adulterating wine if you can make it look much more expensive than it really is. It was wines that tasted a lot poorer than the bottles looked that made Sowerby suspicious in the first place. I think we should go to the restaurant he tasted them at and see if they've still got any left.'

'I agree,' said Susan. 'After all, if whatever was going on happened actually in the warehouse, then any wines still around will be different from our samples from France. It wasn't obvious what it did, and it was too small to have been a bottling plant or anything, but after what Oswald said, I suspect I know what's going on. Let's find this restaurant.'

Susan flicked through the pages of Alan Sowerby's diary once more, discovering that the restaurant in which he had first become suspicious of a wine scandal was called Chez Emil and located in Golders Green.

'We'll have lunch there,' Susan stated decisively, snapping the book shut.

Paulette looked around the interior of Chez Emil, her mind automatically considering how she would word a review of the establishment. 'Pretentious rather than impressive' was a phrase that came to mind, not that she'd ever have actually reviewed the place as it completely lacked the young, fashionable atmosphere on which she concentrated her reports. She was surprised Alan Sowerby condescended to review it. The menu was entirely in French, yet had less variety than that of the tiny hotel in Choray. The patron, presumably Emil himself, was a small, greasy man who smelt of garlic and all too obviously had an unjustifiably elevated opinion of himself.

The decor was stereotypically French, the prices high and the entire place pervaded by an air of snobbery. Oswald MacNaughton, she imagined, would have been horrified; Christian Charrier hardly less so. Both men certainly would have had something to say about the wine list. It was exclusively French and predictable in the extreme. It also included no wines from the Choray co-op at all, a fact which was evidently puzzling Susan as she scanned the list.

'Champagne, Chablis, Vouvray, Sancerre, Châteauneuf-du-Pape, St. Emilion, Beaujolais...' she read out. 'Just as I suspected. Order the Sancerre, will you?'

'What's just as you suspected?'

'Nothing.'

'Susan!' Paulette objected.

'Just shut up and order the Sancerre,' Susan whispered. 'I'll explain later.'

'You'll explain now, or I'll put you over my knee!' Paulette whispered back. 'With your knickers down! In front of the creepy Frenchman!'

'Mmm, yes please!' Susan chuckled cheekily, before becoming serious again. 'Look, I think I know how the scam operates, but it's possible Emil over there is in on it, so for God's sake don't mention de Vergy Fine Wines.'

'Okay,' Paulette agreed, looking nervously at the owner of the restaurant. He was seated at the bar, holding forth with some piece of supposedly deep philosophy to a couple of cronies.

Susan thought again. 'Actually, order the house white. We ought to sample all these wines, except the Champagne.'

'If we sample all the wines we'll be as pissed as newts, not to mention broke,' Paulette protested. 'Have you seen the prices?'

'Yes,' Susan answered, 'and I wasn't suggesting we pay for them. We need to take the bottles away, so we'll pinch some.'

'Susan!' Paulette hissed.

'Relax, I'll do the risky part. All you've got to do is distract Emil.'

'How?' Paulette demanded. 'And what about the waiter and the barmaid, not to mention the customers?'

'Relax,' Susan repeated. 'Just follow my lead. I think I'll try the goat's cheese salad.'

Paulette began to study the menu, feeling rather exasperated. Susan's casual attitude to theft alarmed her, as did her equally casual assumption that it would be easy. A range of bottles was stored behind the bar, in easy reach but impossible to take without being seen.

She ordered the house wine and salad, then ate slowly. Susan chatted of this and that with total unconcern. Around two o'clock the restaurant began to empty of the local businessmen and women who had come in for lunch. Susan ordered crème brûlée for both of them and then cognac. Emil and his two friends had more than once turned lecherous eyes to the two English girls. At last all the customers had left, and Susan leant forward over the table.

'Just go with me,' she whispered. 'I'm going to pretend we've got no money and offer to do the washing up. If he refuses and threatens to call the police, I'll suddenly find a credit card. Otherwise, continue washing until the staff and those other two have left, then pretend to get fed up and offer Emil a little fun instead—'

'Oh no!' Paulette objected. 'I'm not doing anything with that greasy little man!'

'You have to,' Susan hissed.

'No! You do it. You're the one who likes to feel humiliated.'

'I need to nick the wine and get a look at the files. You've got to get him out of the way. I'll act outraged and refuse to go along with it or even be in the same room. He'll have to take you down into the cellar or you'll be visible from the street. Come on, Paulette, don't let me down!'

'Couldn't you just bash him over the head with a bottle?'

'Don't be ridiculous. This isn't the movies!'

'Oh, I suppose so – I just can't bear the thought of him touching me!'

'Come on, Paulette. It's the only way.'

'Oh God… okay, but I'll expect maid service for a week!'

'Anything you want – just make sure you take your time

with him.'

Paulette groaned inwardly as Susan began to go through the motions of pretending to have no money. The plan worked smoothly, failing only in that Emil's two mates showed no signs of leaving. Paulette and Susan washed and tidied as slowly as they could, but when Emil sent his staff home and opened yet another bottle and poured three glasses, it became apparent that his two friends would not go before the girls' chores were done.

'You'll just have to do them all,' Susan whispered. 'It'll be easy; the little bald guy can't keep his eyes off our tits.'

'Susan MacQuillan,' Paulette snorted, 'when I've finished with you, your bottom will be *so* sore you won't want to sit down for a month!'

'Promises, promises,' Susan teased as Paulette threw the dishcloth into the sink and walked towards the three men with a sexy wiggle.

'You have not finished,' Emil said in an arrogant drawl as she approached.

'Yes, I have,' Paulette responded. 'I'm finished with being your skivvy. Look, I'll put this straight. I'll be nice to you – you know what I mean – if I can leave afterwards.'

The sudden silence was deafening. The bald man's glass of wine stopped and hovered halfway to his mouth, and his big red-haired companion turned to stare at her.

'Well?' Paulette asked, keeping her voice deliberately aggressive.

'Go for it, Emil,' the bald man encouraged, licking his rubbery lips and blatantly ogling her cleavage.

'What about your friend?' Emil asked.

'She's a prude – she won't go for it,' Paulette answered. 'Come on, I'm supposed to be back at work.'

Emil blew his cheeks out and looked at his companions. The bald man nodded enthusiastically.

'Hey, hey, hey,' the big one interrupted as Emil was about to accept her offer. 'You guys have no idea. A little negotiation is required here. Let the expert handle it.'

Paulette sighed inwardly, cursing the fact that not only did she have three men to handle instead of one, but that one of them was a complete jerk.

'This is the deal,' the man said to her. 'Now, it's not like you're not going to enjoy it, we both know that.'

Paulette managed a smile, despite her real feelings.

'So,' he continued, 'how about a nice leisurely fuck; three on one?'

'No way!' Paulette shook her head, silently cursing Susan for getting her into this.

'Not got the balls for it, huh?' the man sneered. 'Okay, if you're shy, then one at a time.'

'You are not going to fuck me,' Paulette insisted.

'Blow-jobs, then,' the loathsome man persisted. 'With you topless.'

'Look, let's get out of sight of the street and I'll let you do it between my tits, but that's it.'

'Like I said,' he grinned arrogantly, 'negotiation.'

Emil unlocked the cellar door, switched on the dim light, and they led a reluctant Paulette down the rickety steps. It was a little chilly down there, making her nipples stiffen, but Paulette sat on the wine cases Emil indicated and pulled her top off. As the three lecherous men stared at her breasts, encased in the snug bra that squeezed and lifted them together, she noticed the cases were marked 'de Vergy Fine Wines'.

'Well, now,' said the big man, rubbing his hands together, his eyes still glued to the silky dark slopes of her breasts, 'this is your lucky day.'

I wouldn't say so, thought Paulette bitterly.

'I think,' said Emil, 'as restaurant owner, I should go first.'

Paulette slipped her bra off, and three pairs of eyes bulged as her firm breasts spilled forth. Despite the unsavoury predicament, their mutterings of homage ignited

185

a proud spark of arousal in her tummy.

Emil shuffled forward. Paulette sat quietly and let him cup her breasts. His clammy fingers kneaded her flesh as though he was making dough in his kitchen as he treated himself to a lengthy grope. Paulette did nothing to interrupt the molestation, reasoning that the more time Susan had alone upstairs, the better.

He finally released the luscious globes and feverishly undid his trousers. Paulette watched quietly as he dropped them and his pants to display a thin erection peeping out from under his shirt-tails. Paulette sighed resignedly, and moulded her breasts together to make a deep, warm valley for him.

He needed no further invitation, and slid his cock up into the soft cleavage. Paulette adjusted her position until the purple tip protruded from where the pulsing shaft nestled comfortably. Breathing hoarsely, he placed his hands against the wall above her head, leant over her, and pressed his corpulent belly against her face as he began to jerk with little finesse. His bulbous helmet nudged her chin each time he shoved. Paulette prayed he wouldn't take too long, but he kept pumping and grunting, and muttering to himself in French.

At last he did come, ejaculating copiously against her throat, and then taking himself in hand to drain his cock and spatter her breasts with the last of his sperm.

'Oh, I do love the sight of a girl wearing a pearl necklace,' the big man chuckled as Emil staggered back. 'Now is when the real fun begins, girlie.' Without consulting the bald man, he replaced Emil, opened his trousers, and held his semi-erect penis before Paulette's face. She knew exactly what he wanted, and although it had not been part of the original deal, she peeled her lips apart and allowed him to feed it into her mouth, reasoning that it was best not to upset these men and risk Susan's mission upstairs.

'Oh yeah,' he croaked as his cock stiffened under her

expert ministrations. 'I knew the horny bitch would give good head.'

Paulette correctly judged he was overexcited and braced herself as he curled his fingers into her hair and held her still, his cock fully embedded in her mouth and his humid groin pressed against her face. He tensed, and then his cock jerked and erupted into her throat. Paulette gagged and swallowed. He spurted again and held her in place, ignoring her efforts to push him away until he had spent fully and their breathing had slowed.

'That wasn't part of the deal,' she complained as he pulled back.

'No,' he said weakly, 'but you loved it.'

That, Paulette could not deny, although she would never let the arrogant pig know.

Before she could gather her wits the chubby balding bloke moved in, his trousers and pants already around his ankles. Paulette sat wearily as he squeezed her breasts together and ground his feeble erection between them. He squealed strangely as he thrust against her, and then at the last moment he gripped her head, stuffed his cock into her mouth, and with an erratic flurry of jerks and bucks he anointed her tongue and throat with yet more semen.

Paulette found some tissues and cleaned herself as the three men congratulated each other with much backslapping. She hoped Susan had got away with the evidence, and now she had to make her own hasty exit before the men went back up and noticed the missing wine and possibly that the files had been touched. They were straightening their clothing. 'Wait—' she blurted. 'Let me go and get my friend.'

'But you said she's a prude,' said Emil.

'But I've enjoyed myself with you *so* much,' she lied in her most sexy voice. 'I'm sure I can convince her to come down, and then we can have some *real* fun.'

The men looked at each other, their eyes sparkling.

187

'Would the two of you give us a show?' asked the red-haired man, his husky tone betraying his returning lust.

'Mmm…' drooled Paulette, 'that would be nice. We love it with each other.'

'Blimey,' panted the bald man. He dabbed his large forehead with his sleeve. 'Blimey.'

'I'll go and get her, then?'

The three men nodded dumbly. She put her bra and top back on, explaining that she didn't want to be seen topless from the street, and dashed back up the wooden steps. As she glanced down, just before closing the cellar door, the morons were lowering their trousers again in readiness for the delights to come.

Jilly pouted at Robin. They sat together on a car blanket belonging to her parents, on the floor of a square concrete room, featureless but for doors and a great cluster of rusting cables that protruded from one wall. Once it had housed switchgear for a major substation, but now it was given over to the elements. She had taken him there with the promise of sex, choosing the abandoned substation as somewhere Taz was not likely to turn up unexpectedly, and somewhere she could keep Robin indefinitely. She had then insisted on a long heart-to-heart, ignoring his protests that time was short, on the grounds that their fledgling relationship was more important than getting away to meet the Fire Ghost.

'I've got to go soon, Jilly,' he protested, glancing at his watch yet again. 'I'm meeting him in Merton. I can't let him down. He's relying on me to tag the warehouse.'

'But I thought you wanted to be with me?' she sulked.

'I do, Jilly, but…'

'He can wait a little while, can't he?' she coaxed softly. 'I—'

'Robin,' she pouted, 'I'm here, ready for you. If you leave me now I swear I'll never so much as kiss you again.'

'But—'

'Robin...' she flashed him her most seductive look, with fluttering eyelashes, 'what would you like me to do to you?'

'I... I...' his brain churned slowly. 'What do you mean?'

'Well, what would you like? You know, something sexy.'

'Blimey! I'm not sure really.'

'Shall I tell you what I'd like to do?'

Robin nodded dumbly, his mouth dry.

'I'd like to tie you up, and then do all sorts of naughty things to you.'

'B-blimey!' he stammered again, not wanting to admit that she'd just hit on one of his favourite fantasies.

'Would you like that?

'I—' he blushed as his cock lifted the front of his jeans and Jilly saw it. She grinned mischievously at the answer bulging clearly in his lap.

'I think you would... wouldn't you?'

Robin nodded again, too excited to speak.

Before her chance could be lost, Jilly undid his belt and pulled it free from his waist. Upon her order Robin crossed his wrists and she cinched the belt as tightly as she could around them.

'Careful!' he whined. 'That bloody hurts!'

'Shhh... It's supposed too – just a little,' she assured him, not really knowing if it was supposed to hurt or not. 'It all adds to the excitement.'

Robin remained quiet after that, and allowed her to push him onto his back. He blushed again when he saw the denim tent pressing up from his groin.

Jilly gave him a teasing kiss, and then found a length of old cable. She wrapped and tied that around his ankles, and he was quickly bound and immobilised. Apart from making sure Robin was safe from the arsonist, she was also pleasantly surprised to discover an immense satisfaction in taking the dominant role and having him at her mercy. She took a hanky from inside her bra and stuffed it into Robin's mouth, and mentally patted herself on the back for doing such a good job of stopping him from getting into trouble. She wouldn't release him until much later, and by then the police would have their man.

She gazed down at him. He looked extremely appetising: trussed and gagged.

'Now,' she whispered sexily, as a finger and thumb found his straining zip and the heat from within the bulging denim warmed her palm. 'Let's see what we have here then...'

Susan lay back in her bath, her mind turning over the details of the case. It was coming together nicely. Once they had the evidence properly together and the formal support of Oswald MacNaughton and maybe even Christian Charrier, they would be able to present a solid case to the police. Ruddock and de Vergy would be charged with fraud and doubtless the details of the arson would come out in the course of the police investigation. Sowerby's murder could then be investigated at leisure, although it was entirely conceivable that it would prove impossible to put a solid case together on that score. Still, if Ruddock or de Vergy had been in France...

'Paulette?' Susan called, an idea suddenly coming to her. 'Have you got the number of the hotel in Choray?'

'Somewhere,' Paulette called back from the kitchen. 'Why?'

'Give them a ring and find out if either Annabella de Vergy or Philip Ruddock stayed there in late July or early August,' she called. 'Tell them you're Ruddock's secretary and ask for a receipt for their most recent stay. If there was one, you should be able to get the right dates.'

'Okay.'

Susan began soaping herself as she listened to Paulette attempting to speak French on the phone. Eventually the stilted conversation ended and she heard the receiver click back into place.

'Well?' she asked.

'Got him!' Paulette beamed as she hurried into the bathroom. 'Annabella was there in August and came back on the thirteenth. Ruddock was there from July the twenty-third to the twenty-ninth. That makes it Ruddock, doesn't it?'

'Probably...'

'Oh, come on,' Paulette said, unable to hide her frustration. 'You say he was poisoned in the second week of August. To get him, Annabella would have had to make the lethal pâté and invite him to dinner to poison him in quick succession. Remember, he used to review restaurants. That means he had to dine out just about every night of the week. He wasn't the sort of person you could just ring up on the off chance and ask over to dinner; he'd need weeks of notice...'

'She could have planned it in advance,' Susan countered. 'It's a shame his diary is inconclusive.'

'Hold on,' Paulette said, disappearing again.

She returned a moment later with Alan Sowerby's diary, flicking through the pages to find the point where his entries ceased. 'Let's see,' she said. 'Here we are. He left it in the Pipe of Port on the tenth, when Annabella was in France. He's got reminders for dinners after that, but not with Annabella, so there was no arrangement. How's that for logic?'

'Fair,' Susan admitted. 'She could have called him from France after the tenth, or he could have cancelled a date for the sake of his beloved Annabella. But I do concede it's less likely. Did he have dinner with Ruddock after the twenty-ninth of July?'

'Hang on,' Paulette said as she turned the pages back. 'Yes, on the eighth, after Annabella left for France!'

'Well, it looks like we might have him,' Susan concluded, with not a little pang of triumphant pleasure.

'So let's go and see Paul Berner.'

'No. This is the point where we take things carefully. Before we present the case to the police, we need every loose end tied up. For instance, we need Oswald's support for the wine analysis, maybe Charrier's, too. We need to know why Sowerby didn't realise he'd been poisoned deliberately and accuse Ruddock. We need to know what happened between his dinner with Ruddock and his death. What was he supposed to be doing on the evenings from the ninth to the thirteenth?'

'Let's see,' Paulette responded. 'Attending a tasting in Guildford on the ninth... nothing on the tenth... reviewing somewhere called Jacob's Barn on the eleventh, in Chelmsford... another tasting on the twelfth, and also the thirteenth.'

'According to the poisonous fungi book, he'd have been suffering agonising stomach cramps on those days,' said Susan. 'We can probably find out if he reviewed Jacob's Barn easily enough; the tastings might be harder. Basically, the question is: was he ill on those days?'

Ted Gage surveyed the narrow approach road. A tall fence on either side held back straggly brambles and sycamore trees, and a single streetlight illuminated fifty yards or so of the gravel track. It was the most obvious approach to the trading estate on which he and his men were concealed, watching for the fire-raiser to make his eighth strike. At the main entrance a night-watchman and plenty of illumination made an approach unlikely. Here, at the rear, there was a much better chance of catching the man. That was why he had chosen the station for himself, leaving a constable to guard the front.

The tip-off had come from a worried girl who wouldn't leave her name, nor the name of the man who had boasted to her that he intended to set fire to a DIY warehouse in Merton. She had sounded genuinely scared, but after three

192

hours of waiting in the upper story of an empty industrial unit, Gage was beginning to wonder if it might not have been a hoax. The seven fires had attracted a fair bit of publicity, and it was inevitable that sooner or later the cranks, jokers and attention seekers would crawl out of the woodwork.

Another nagging, though minor, doubt came from Susan MacQuillan's theory about canals. The Merton estate had no canal bordering it. Still, at the end of the day, only three of the seven fires had been close to proper canals and he remained fairly certain that MacQuillan's ideas were nothing more than over-elaborate hot air.

A slight movement at the far end of the approach road caught his attention, instantly causing a rush of adrenaline. He raised his radio to his lips and whispered a message to control.

As two shadowy figures ambled closer and passed under the light his pulse returned to normal. They were a couple, teenagers, presumably intent on using the deserted estate for a little hanky panky. He watched as they approached, giggling, occasionally swigging from a bottle.

The girl looked quite pretty, blonde, and dressed in a light frock that showed plenty of shapely leg and clung to a pair of pert breasts. The boy was tall and also fair-haired. Gage wet his lips, experiencing a not unwelcome pleasure in spying on them – and also a touch of jealousy.

He watched as they stopped in the lee of a clump of brambles that had worked its way through the fence. The girl glanced up the track as her boyfriend folded her in his arms, one hand still clutching the bottle, the other fumbling at her bottom. They kissed, and her skirt was edged up to reveal brief white knickers stretched tight across a rounded teenage bottom. Gage found his hand inching to his crotch and he was unable to resist squeezing his cock through his trousers. The youth lowered her knickers, revealing a little of her pale buttocks.

Gage felt his jealousy rising with his lust as he squinted and strained to see as much of her as he could. He envied the scrawny youth, and yearned to have those soft buttocks in his own hands. How was it even an inexperienced and undeserving teenager should have more fun than him?

Suddenly the couple froze. Gage felt his pulse quicken as he tried to see what had startled them. All seemed normal, but the girl quickly straightened her knickers and they hurried back into the inky shadows beyond the range of the light.

Gage watched intently. Something had startled them, something he couldn't see. The scene remained absolutely still for a long moment and then a shadow detached itself from the shade of a clump of sycamores. Once more Gage's pulse began to race and he raised the radio to his lips. It was a man: thin, tall and with a pinched face, alone and moving with a caution that Gage considered definitely suspicious. He was also carrying a plastic bag, clearly containing something heavy. Gage relayed the man's presence to control, relying on them to spread it to the other officers on the widely dispersed team. As he spoke, the suspect approached the gate, carefully avoiding the area within the sweep of the estate's closed-circuit cameras.

Now came the critical period. Arresting him was one thing, but getting a successful prosecution quite another. It had always been Gage's policy to risk property, if not human injury, in return for firm evidence. He had seen too many cases slip away because the police had moved in to make an arrest before the suspect had actually committed a crime. This time, he had no intention of giving the scum such an easy escape route.

Suddenly the figure slipped out of sight through a gap in the fence, suggesting he was moving in the direction of the DIY warehouse. Hastily relaying instructions to his men, Gage left his post and made for the ground.

He smiled to himself as he left the unit and moved cautiously towards the gate. He had anticipated the fire-raiser's move, realising he would almost certainly strike from outside the perimeter fence, thus avoiding the problem of getting in and out of the industrial estate. The majority of his men were stationed in a wide ring that surrounded the area, with only himself and three others actually inside the estate. Even now they would be moving to cut off the man's escape, waiting only for his signal to move in. In fact, he had correctly anticipated the fire-raiser's entire plan of action, a piece of judgement that would look good on his record.

The padlock that held the chain on the rear gates clicked open under his key. Gage slipped through and moved to the gap in the fence through which the man had disappeared. He made his way carefully through the dense undergrowth. Beyond the undergrowth was a stretch of uneven wasteland, across which the suspect would have to move to get within range of his target.

A torch flicked on ahead of Gage. He ducked quickly, but then realised the beam was directed at the ground, barely visible but enough to guide the figure forward. Gage continued to follow, staying low and alert for a change in pattern of the beam's movements that would tell him he'd been detected.

The figure eventually stopped, and stooped to perform some action on the ground. Gage stopped too, watching carefully and judging his moment. To his right, the wall of the warehouse reared up, dull against the black/orange sky, the windows reflecting the distant lights from the road. To the left and front the small trees and mounds of the wasteland created a jagged horizon. Somewhere out there, other policemen would be closing in on their man, waiting for Gage to decide when there was adequate proof of criminal intent.

Nothing happened for a minute, then the torch went out

and the figure rose. There was a rapid motion and an instant later the crash of broken glass as one of the warehouse windows shattered.

Gage was shouting into the radio and calling to the figure to stop even as he scrambled to his feet. There was a cry of surprise and a flicker of flame, then a burst of yellow light. Gage saw the man clearly, illuminated by the flickering wick of a crude petrol bomb, then it was hurtling towards him, the flame trailing back in the air.

'Jesus!' Gage swore as he hurled himself to one side. The bomb exploded behind him with a roar and a flash. Something scolded his leg and, for a moment, he had the awful vision of being set alight by the burning petrol. Rolling frantically to the side he slapped at his trousers, but quickly realised he had only been struck by a piece of hot flying glass. He stopped to draw breath. 'I'll make the bastard pay for that!' he cursed savagely.

His radio crackled into life. It was Berner, reporting the successful apprehension of a youth trying to flee the area.

Chapter Ten

'Yeah, it was me,' gloated the cocky arsehole across the desk from Ted Gage. 'All seven of 'em.'

Gage suppressed the rage that had been simmering since the start of the interview. The Fire Ghost had turned out to be a Paul Eady, an unemployed loner in his early twenties. He was making no attempt to deny his crimes, and was clearly enjoying the notoriety. What infuriated Gage was his casual attitude to what he had done; the destruction of property and the flagrant risk to life. Gage also disliked having petrol bombs thrown in his general direction by useless layabouts who weren't fit to scrape the dog shit from his...

'Do you realise how much damage you've caused?' he asked, his fury threatening to boil over.

'Get real,' Eady answered. 'It's all insured. Anyway, you rich sods have always got cash when you need it.'

'I—' Gage began, and then quelled the verbal and physical response that would only get him into a great deal of trouble... 'So you're prepared to sign a statement to the effect that you were solely responsible for all seven arson attacks attributed to the Fire Ghost?'

'You are under no obligation to do so,' the wet duty solicitor interjected.

'No problem,' Eady grinned. 'I wouldn't want to disappoint my public, now would I?'

'Very well,' said Gage. 'For the benefit of the tape, Sergeant Yates is now passing Paul Eady a pen and paper with which to write his statement.'

Gage sat back wearily as Eady began to scrawl. True,

Eady was an annoying little shit and, from the first moment he'd set eyes on him, he'd had a strong desire to punch him. But there was, at least, a satisfaction to counter his anger. He had caught the little prick and was about to get a signed admission to all seven fires, and it also meant he could abandon the line of enquiry that had so nearly cost him his job; the Cooper theory.

Susan MacQuillan annoyed him because she had insisted the last three fires had not been Fire Ghost attacks, yet his feelings toward her were tempered by the way she had declined to drop him in it after being put into a dangerous situation with Cooper's boys. They were still charging all seven of them with assault, there being no reason not to as long as Berner, Reynolds and MacQuillan held their peace.

Now Julia Keeson would be all smiles and the press would take a very different attitude towards him, now that the Fire Ghost was caught. Now he'd be the hero who'd managed to crack a difficult case against the odds. The fact that he'd only succeeded because of a timely tip-off would be played down. He'd done it and that was what mattered.

Susan put the phone down and inhaled sharply. The morning had not been going well. Paulette was still at Companies' House, retrieving data on de Vergy Fine Wines, and hopefully would come back with what they needed. Other than that, everything possible had gone wrong. None of the people she'd called had been able to provide any useful information on Alan Sowerby's movements before he died. Most simply didn't know, as was the case with the various companies whose tastings he was supposed to have attended. All of them said he might or might not have been there, and the receptionists had been unwilling to let her talk to anybody who might remember. Jacob's Barn had been nearly as bad; a waitress trying to be helpful but failing completely.

Worse had been the call from Paul Berner to say they had caught the Fire Ghost and that he had admitted to all seven fires. Susan's protestations that the man was obviously psychotic, and his word could not be relied on, had fallen on deaf ears. They had a confession and that was that. Not that Berner had been unsympathetic. In fact, he had sorely wished Susan had been right, mainly because he would then have avoided a severe dressing-down from DI Gage. He had even agreed to come over the next day and talk to Susan about the case, although she suspected it was more in the hope of boosting his own tarnished reputation than of helping her.

Susan knew she was right, yet proving it was not going to be as easy a task as she had anticipated. At least they had the samples from Chez Emil, with which it should be possible to prove that de Vergy Fine Wines had been involved in fraud. Paulette would then have her wine scandal, which was something. But Susan wanted Ruddock for murder and arson, and was not prepared to back down until she had him.

The morning's frustrations left her feeling distinctly insecure and in need of a cuddle from Paulette. But at least there was the prospect of lunch with Oswald MacNaughton, whose impeccable taste in food and wine couldn't fail to improve her mood.

Paulette watched as Susan filled Oswald MacNaughton's glass. He went through the ritual of tasting the pale yellow wine, before finally setting the glass down with a slightly puzzled expression.

'Is it not the same Sauvignon de Touraine you showed me before?' he asked. 'Because if it is not, it is certainly very similar.'

Susan held up a finger for patience and extracted a second bottle from the case by her side. As with the first, it was wrapped in brown paper, the label hidden. She poured, and MacNaughton declared it to be the Chenin they had tasted on their previous visit. The third white wine he identified as the Choray co-op's southern French Chardonnay, the three reds that followed as their Gamay, Cabernet and southern French blend.

'I confess to bafflement,' he declared as he set the last glass down. 'These are the same wines as we tasted before.'

'Not according to the labels,' Paulette said as Susan removed the paper sheath from the first bottle. 'What you have just tasted are de Vergy Fine Wines' selection of French classics: Sancerre, Vouvray, Chablis, Beaujolais, St. Emilion and Châteauneuf-du-Pape respectively.'

'Good God,' MacNaughton replied, picking up the supposed St. Emilion bottle and looking at it as if disinclined to accept its existence.

'And there we have the scam,' Susan said. 'They were importing a range of cheap French wines, relabelling them as classics, and selling them at prices that would have been close to impossible, had they been the real things. They knew they could always undercut their competitors.'

'So they sold to restaurants that were only interested in getting the famous names at the lowest prices,' Paulette took over. 'Which means most of them, in my experience. Their profit margins were huge and they were safe, as long as they kept their books in good order. De Vergy Fine Wines' VAT and tax returns are immaculate, and the authorities are happy as long as the paperwork looks good.'

'Good God,' MacNaughton repeated. 'Well, I suppose at least they made their fakes true to the original grape varieties, but still.'

'It also explains why they were so keen to avoid becoming well known in the wine establishment,' Susan continued. 'Presumably you'd have spotted these as fakes immediately.'

'Well, to be honest, no,' MacNaughton admitted. 'You see, the wines are made from the right grapes, so they do taste vaguely right. If I came across them at a tasting, I'd simply have taken a couple of sniffs and returned the glass politely to the table. In fact, they're not that bad. The reds are palatable; I've tasted worse Sancerre and Vouvray; and it's only the supposed Chablis that's really poor. It's a brave man indeed who stands up and denounces somebody as a fraud in the middle of a tasting. It's far simpler to just pass on to something else, and that's what would have happened if any experts tasted these wines.'

'Except Alan Sowerby,' Paulette put in.

'Except poor old Alan,' MacNaughton agreed, 'but again, even though he was sure the wines weren't what they said they were, he assumed they'd been made on the cheap and that it was de Vergy Fine Wines who were being cheated, not that they were the cheats themselves.'

'He was also infatuated with Annabella de Vergy,' Susan added, 'and he got on very well with Philip Ruddock.'

'Annabella is wonderful,' Paulette put in, 'but you should see what he wrote about her in his diary.'

'So,' Susan continued, 'they were bringing the wines into the warehouse, changing the capsules and labels with their machine and sending them out as these fake classics. When Sowerby started to investigate, they must have realised he would eventually get to the truth. So, knowing his taste for exotic food, they made up a fancy pâté with Destroying Angel and poisoned him. The initial symptoms are identical to those of ordinary food poisoning, which anybody who ate like he did had to get now and then. The symptoms then wear off for a day or two, only to come back with a vengeance. By the time he got to the liver and kidney failure stage, it was presumably too late.'

'Good God,' MacNaughton said once more, looking doubtfully at the block of Foie Gras he had put out on the table.

'Their list,' Susan continued, passing the copy she had stolen from Chez Emil to MacNaughton, 'does not include brandy, and Annabella told us they only imported from France. Yet when the fire happened they had a pallet of cheap Greek brandy by the office. Therefore, they must have decided to wrap up the scam before Paulette and I visited Annabella. The run of Fire Ghost attacks provided an excellent opportunity to destroy the evidence and collect on the insurance, allowing them to either call it a day or set up again once things had quietened down. We also know this because the World of Pine furniture warehouse burnt down before we visited Annabella—'

'You're losing me a bit,' MacNaughton halted her.

'Sorry.' Susan paused, allowing him time to catch up with her. 'You see, Ruddock needed the fire to look like another Fire Ghost attack, and there hadn't been one for a while. He may also have wanted to get some practice and ensure that the details of his own warehouse fire didn't stand out from those of the other attacks. Therefore he burnt down the World of Pine first, throwing the petrol bomb from his boat on the Lee Valley canal. They then bought the brandy and were ready to do their own warehouse when Paulette and I went to Annabella. Our visit may have spooked them – or they may have been intending to burn the warehouse that night, anyway.

'In any case, they moved the pallet of brandy that Sunday, and Ruddock attacked that night, using the same petrol bomb technique from the Grand Union Canal. The canal is too wide for a bomb to be thrown accurately from the far side, which made me think a boat must have been used. The boat also allowed Ruddock to retreat without being seen. It struck me that the genuine Fire Ghost was unlikely to be able to afford a boat, nor to do his attacks in such quick succession. The police psychologist, Dr Potheroe, agreed with me. They then burnt Crazy Joe's Carpet Madhouse to complete the sequence of fires in such a way that their own didn't stand out.'

'But you say the man they've arrested confessed to all seven fires?' MacNaughton queried.

'He's an inadequate, psychotic, pyromaniac, attention-seeking little prat,' Susan answered. 'He's proud of what he's done. If he can take credit for three fires he didn't start then all the better. In fact, he probably sees Ruddock as a rival. Not that he knows it's Ruddock, of course.'

'Well, my dear,' MacNaughton said, shaking his head as if to clear it from Susan's barrage of logic. 'You can certainly count on the backing of my expert opinion, for what it's worth. Once the scandal is out I expect the rest of it will become plain soon enough.'

'Thank you,' Susan smiled. 'May I have a glass of something that doesn't come from de Vergy Fines Wines now, please? My throat is a little dry.'

'With pleasure. I thought we might try a late-harvested Tokay with this Foie Gras, which I sincerely believe to be free of Destroying Angel or any other impurities.'

'I sincerely hope so,' Susan said wryly.

Paulette waited while Oswald MacNaughton served lunch, joining the toast to the imminent imprisonment of de Vergy and Ruddock, but without the same enthusiasm as the others. Philip Ruddock, as far as Paulette was concerned, could be locked away for good. Annabella de Vergy was a different matter. From the way Susan was presenting the case, it looked as if Annabella would be charged with fraud and also as an accessory to arson and murder. She was guilty of fraud, but had hurt only the likes of Emil and his obnoxious friends, and that only in a rather abstract sense. Emil she despised, Annabella she idolised. Punishment from her had been an exquisite experience, delivered with a skill and understanding that was in total contrast to the coarse, selfish sexuality of Emil and his loathsome friends...

'Tell Oswald about our little adventure at Chez Emil,

Paulette,' Susan said, breaking into her thoughts.

'I – pardon?'

'Tell Oswald what we did.'

'Oh… okay.' Paulette began, launching into a description that deliberately painted Susan as a wicked, manipulative villain who had forced her to submit to a degrading sexual experience in order to steal the wine and the list. Susan protested occasionally, which only increased Paulette's determination to denounce her. MacNaughton chuckled now and then, obviously enjoying the story.

'I trust Susan will not be allowed to get away with this dastardly act of delegation?' MacNaughton said dramatically when Paulette had finished.

'She's my maid every evening for the next week,' Paulette confirmed. 'She has to serve me naked and she gets spanked if she's not up to scratch.'

Susan lowered her eyes and blushed. Watching her friend's reaction, Paulette felt a sadistic glee.

'Actually,' she continued, turning the screw, 'I think she deserves a punishment more in keeping with her crime.'

'And I think I would agree with you, my dear,' MacNaughton said casually, slipping into Paulette's game without difficulty.

Susan hung her head submissively and pouted.

'And what would you like to do to her?'

'I think, my dear Paulette,' mused MacNaughton, 'I would like to sample that rather delectable bottom of hers.'

Susan looked up and shook her head. Even Paulette wondered whether it would be wise to expect her to accommodate a thing of such proportions in her rear passage.

'In my younger days I always found butter to be a most effective aid,' he continued, answering their unasked question. 'I have always taken a particular pleasure in the penetration of a pretty female's bottom, though I freely confess that none have permitted me such delights for quite some years.'

'I can quite understand that,' said Paulette.

'Indeed, being favourably endowed does have its drawbacks,' he admitted matter-of-factly. 'Still, by Susan's own admission she is no virgin there. I'm sure, with a sufficiency of butter, we'll manage beautifully.'

MacNaughton smiled at them both, and then poured more wine and helped himself to bread and pâté. The sexual tension was maintained as he ate lunch; Paulette had suddenly lost her appetite because of the tantalising prospect of watching her friend being fucked in the arse by such a splendid weapon, and Susan losing hers through uncertain anticipation.

When MacNaughton had finished eating and drinking Susan rose and meekly asked to use the bathroom.

'Of course, my dear,' he said, smiling warmly and dabbing his lips with a napkin. 'You know where it is.'

'I would imagine she needs to be spanked first?' he asked Paulette, as Susan's footsteps faded up the stairs.

'Oh, definitely,' Paulette replied. 'Catch her unawares and slipper her over your knee. She'll love that!'

'An excellent suggestion,' MacNaughton nodded thoughtfully, with the air of one discussing important wine issues with a colleague. 'Perhaps we should adjourn to the study.'

He picked up the butter dish and Paulette followed him, already imagining MacNaughton's oversized cock plunging between Susan's reddened buttocks. They entered the study, an impressive book-lined room. It overlooked the garden, a riot of late summer flowers and assorted trees and shrubs, and beyond, was itself overlooked by the rear windows of neighbouring houses.

'Oh,' Paulette clapped her hands together beneath her chin, 'she'll love this! It's just the sort of atmosphere she adores: homely yet severe, like a headmaster's study.'

'Indeed,' MacNaughton agreed. 'Then I shall fetch a

slipper.'

He left the room, leaving Paulette to admire the view from the window. If she knew Susan, the possibility of being seen by someone else would excite her immensely, although it was hardly fair to expect MacNaughton to risk his reputation with the neighbours.

'I'm ready,' she heard Susan's voice, and turned to find her standing in the doorway. She looked pretty and coy in her long summer skirt and white blouse, the picture of an innocent English rose. She was eyeing the butter dish with evident apprehension.

Oswald MacNaughton reappeared behind her. He held a worn bedroom slipper in one hand and an expression of pompous severity on his owl-like face. Without further ado he gripped Susan's arm and pulled her towards a chair.

'Hey!' she protested as he sat down and pulled her over his knees. 'Hey, no one said anything about this!'

'It's no more than you deserve, my dear,' MacNaughton told her.

Paulette watched with delight as he folded Susan's skirt up, exposing white panties stretched tight over her mouthwatering bottom. He twisted an arm into the small of her back and tucked the light material beneath it. Then he pulled her panties down, baring her plump white buttocks. She instinctively sighed and raised her hips as the panties reached her knees.

'Go on,' Paulette urged as he held the chosen instrument of punishment aloft.

He brought the slipper down across Susan's behind with a resonant smack. His victim squealed as her bottom bounced under the impact, trying to get her free hand back to protect herself as the second smack fell. She squeaked again and moved her hand to cover where the slipper had fallen, only for the next strike to fall lower and on the other cheek. Paulette relished Susan's attempts to protect herself.

For a while MacNaughton played the game of dodging her flailing last line of defence, but suddenly he grabbed and held it into the small of her back, his large hand easily able to clamp both her wrists together, rendering her completely unable to do anything about the spanking. He then began to use the slipper with a will, raining smacks onto Susan's naked and defenceless rump.

Paulette watched her friend's cheeks bounce and wobble, occasionally opening to give a glimpse of her pussy or hint at the ruder secrets hidden between her full cheeks. Susan kicked in vain. Her bottom was very red. MacNaughton released her arms and caught her around the waist, raising her bottom into an even more revealing position. He laughed triumphantly as Susan began to beat her fists on his leg and the carpet.

'What a fuss!' he declared, a little out of breath. 'I really have never known a girl make such a fuss over a little spanking. Now, if I took you over my knee in public, I could understand the tantrum. Maybe I should. Maybe I should take you to the High Street and pull your panties down in front of everyone. That would teach you what *real* humiliation is.

'Or perhaps I should have your skirt up on the Heath. It'll be very crowded. Imagine how you'll feel when I take your panties down and spank you in front of everyone.'

'Oh… yes please,' Susan purred.

He smiled ruefully and shook his head. 'Alas, I fear we would attract the attention of your ex-colleagues. And besides, I can wait no longer for my *special* treat.'

'Oh, God,' Susan moaned anxiously as MacNaughton slid her to the floor.

He stood up, told her to kneel, and then made her lean over the seat of his vacated chair, dip her back, and lift her hips. 'Perfection,' he muttered. 'Absolute perfection.' He loosened his tie. 'Put your hands behind your back,

Susan my dear.'

She obeyed, crossing her wrists, and he used his tie to bind them together so there would be no significant struggling while he enjoyed himself. Susan sank lower and rested her flushed cheek on the warm leather seat.

'Just say if it's too uncomfortable, my dear,' MacNaughton said, 'but I doubt it will be, as I have no intention of rushing such a rare treat.'

Paulette took the butter and knelt beside her friend, almost unable to believe just how gloriously submissive she looked; kneeling in readiness with her eyes closed, he moist lips slightly apart, her wrists bound behind her back, and her raised bottom pink and blotchy from the expertly administered spanking.

Paulette applied a knob of butter, smearing it between Susan's buttocks. She found Susan's tight rear entrance, and felt it yield to the gentle pressure of her fingertip. She watched her straightened digit sink slowly inside. Susan moaned a moan of sheer bliss that encouraged Paulette to draw her finger in and out.

Oswald MacNaughton watched with absolute fascination. He could deny himself no longer, and eagerly unbutton his trousers. Paulette gazed hungrily upon his huge erection again as it sprang free. She could not resist it, and without asking permission she knelt up, opened her mouth wide, and sucked the awesome stalk in while continuing to frig Susan's clutching bottom. Her lips stretched uncomfortably – but she loved it!

'Enough, my dear,' MacNaughton said as he gently extricated his cock from her warm wet mouth. 'Too much more of that and I fear I shall disappoint our little plaything.' He knelt between Susan's spread legs and aimed his shaft at her wet pussy. Paulette curled her fingers around its immense girth and guided it in until his belly rested against Susan's red buttocks.

Susan groaned and bravely dipped her back and pushed

back as she was stretched and filled. MacNaughton squeezed his hands between her and the chair, tugged up her top, and gripped her naked breasts as he started to fuck her.

Feverishly shoving a hand between her own thighs to stroke her pussy through the taut cotton of her trousers, Paulette watched Susan being fucked with utter fascination. She looked tiny beneath MacNaughton's great bulk, a curvaceous nymph, near-naked as she was mounted by a grossly overweight satyr. His hips stabbed with uncompromising shoves, somehow made more deliciously rude because Paulette couldn't see the actual juncture between cock and vagina. But she knew he was deeply embedded within her friend, and that delicious knowledge fueled her own arousal.

He suddenly pulled back, his erection glistening with Susan's juices. With fingers and thumbs he prised her buttocks apart. Paulette followed his unspoken directions and pressed the huge purple helmet against Susan's exposed and lubricated rear entrance. He pushed. Susan moaned as her anus began to dilate. Paulette watched the ring open and stretch, then heard Susan's grunt as the knob popped in.

'Slowly,' Susan gasped between gritted teeth. 'Gently, gently... oooh, that feels *so* nice.'

Paulette watched the mighty shaft disappear until MacNaughton's belly curved snugly around Susan's tender buttocks. He started to rut against her, and Susan grunted in unison with the creaking chair and each aggressive shunt of his broad hips.

Wrenching her trousers open, Paulette got onto her back and squirmed beneath the couple. She pulled her damp knickers aside and masturbated while watching her delicious friend being sodomised. Just above her face his dangling balls slapped against Susan's vacant pussy. She spread her own pussy-lips and rubbed her clitoris. She lifted her head and managed to kiss his balls, her nose pressed against Susan's pussy, the scent rich and intensely feminine. Transferring her attention to her friend, she began to lick. Both Susan and Oswald were grunting and moaning above her.

'I'm going to come…!' Susan squealed.

'As I am!' panted MacNaughton, suddenly thrusting even harder.

Paulette felt Susan's thighs tighten around her head, signalling the onset of orgasm. The balls buffeting her face suddenly jerked and MacNaughton groaned loudly.

Paulette felt her own orgasm coming as MacNaughton slowly pulled his cock out of Susan's bottom. It emerged inch by inch, slippery with butter and sperm. Paulette's eyes locked onto the wondrous sight as her fingers worked in her pussy. At last the full glory of his penis emerged, still impressive despite losing some of its rigidity. Unable to resist the temptation, Paulette dreamily raised herself and wormed her tongue into Susan's empty anus. She came too, with her friend's gorgeous soft bottom grinding back onto her perspiring face.

'That's it,' Susan said, laying down her pen. 'The figures show clearly that the volumes coming into de Vergy Fine Wines from the co-op at Choray account for all their sales. It looks innocent until you see the actual wines. With Oswald's back-up we should have a clear case, although I'd still like some better proof on the dates for Sowerby's poisoning.'

'Don't worry, they'll come,' Paulette replied, a little distractedly. 'Look, Susan…'

'What's up?'

'Look… I mean, I know she's guilty of fraud and everything, but do we have to involve Annabella?'

Susan looked at her friend, a little disappointedly. She knew Paulette had a soft spot for Annabella de Vergy, but that didn't detract from the woman's involvement in a serious crime. She looked down at Paulette, who was sitting cross-legged on the floor, looking undeniably dejected.

'Yes, Paulette, we do,' Susan asserted. 'I know Ruddock's the real villain, but she must know about both the murder and the arson.'

'Maybe. But even if she does she's probably only keeping quiet—'

'To save her own skin,' Susan broke in, 'which is inexcusable. I'm sorry, but she has to be reported too.'

'Okay,' Paulette sighed, 'I suppose you're right.' She rose elegantly and stretched. 'Now I need a long soak, and you can be my maid, in accordance with our deal.'

Susan was happy to make a fuss of her friend and take her mind off the scandal for a while. She ran the bath, and then when Paulette followed her into the bathroom she took great pleasure in undressing her. She was still a little excited in the aftermath of their afternoon encounter, and her fingers trembled slightly as she unbutton Paulette's blouse and they touched the firm swell of her breasts beneath the soft material. When both naked, they kissed and cuddled for a while, and then shared a hot bath, with Susan gleefully enacting the role of subservient maid throughout.

Once scrubbed and dried, Paulette left Susan in her fluffy bathrobe to tidy up and rinse the tub. Having done as she was ordered, Susan padded through to the bedroom and found Paulette looking deliciously sexy in a short skirt that left most of her shapely legs bare, and a top that clearly struggled to contain her breasts. She was toying with Susan's handcuffs.

'Take your robe off,' she ordered curtly. 'I want you naked.'

Susan willingly did as she was told.

'Wrists.'

Susan obediently held her arms out and Paulette snapped the cuffs into place. She was then told to get on the bed and curl up, tucking her knees to her chin. As she complied she wondered what mischievous things Paulette would do to her once she was completely helpless.

Paulette gave no indications of her intent, verbal or otherwise, but fixed Susan into tight bondage with a workmanlike thoroughness. Susan's legs were tied with a belt so firmly that she could do no more than squirm uselessly where she lay.

Paulette rummaged in the linen basket until she found a pair of red panties. These she stuffed into Susan's mouth and tied in place with a scarf. Susan could taste Paulette on them, something she found especially humiliating. The final touch was a linen shoe-bag pulled down over her head and tied beneath her chin. Unable to move, talk or see, Susan waited for Paulette to begin whatever torment she had in mind.

'There we are,' she heard her friend say. 'You do look inviting. Anyway, I'm going out now, so be a good girl and don't wet the bed.'

A moment later Susan heard the front door slam and realised she really had been left alone. What on earth was Paulette playing at? They'd certainly never played a game like this before.

Paulette ran down the stairs, her eyes brimming with tears of guilt. The door-latch failed to catch behind her, but she didn't notice. Susan would be furious, she knew, but in the end she simply couldn't let Annabella go to prison. Annabella was refined and elegant, subtle and sensitive. Prison would destroy her. All she had done was sell ordinary wine to people fool enough to think more of what it said on a label than what their palate told them. It might warrant a fine, but not imprisonment, which was what Annabella would get – if only because of her association with the far more wicked Philip Ruddock.

212

Susan would forgive her eventually, she was sure. Her friend would be unable to resist her method of apology.

Realising she didn't have Susan's car keys, Paulette hesitated. She stood indecisively for a moment, then hurried in the direction of the tube station, unable to face returning to the flat for them.

Twenty minutes later she was in Little Venice, ringing Annabella de Vergy's doorbell.

'Paulette Richards?' Annabella said, clearly surprised as she opened the door.

'Can I come in?' Paulette blurted. 'It's very important.'

'Of course,' Annabella replied, moving aside. 'Come through to the kitchen. Whatever is the matter?'

'You – you've got to get out of the country,' Paulette stammered.

'I'm sorry?' Annabella responded, sounding amused and astonished.

'I'm serious. We know all about the fake wines and the relabelling and the brandy—'

'Slow down, slow down – you're babbling,' Annabella interrupted. 'Whatever are you talking about?'

'You know,' Paulette sighed. 'Your wine operation. You import from the co-op at Choray, relabel the bottles as classics and sell them cheap to undercut your competitors. We know everything; Susan's worked it out to the last detail. We know about the fire, too, and what Philip Ruddock did to Alan Sowerby.'

'I don't believe what I'm hearing!' Annabella snapped angrily. 'This is utter nonsense!'

'It's not, and you know it,' Paulette retorted, exasperated by the woman's refusal to admit to the deception.

'You really believe all this poppycock you're saying, don't you?' Annabella said with convincing incredulity.

'It isn't poppycock, it's true!'

Annabella didn't respond any further, but went and sat rather heavily.

'It's true – you know it's true,' Paulette repeated.

'I think you may have got slightly the wrong idea about my position at de Vergy Fine Wines,' Annabella said at last. 'Look, if you didn't sound so sincere I wouldn't believe what you're saying, but I'm just the figurehead for the company. All this – the house, the company, everything – came from my father. He was a major shareholder in one of the independent French aero-engineering companies. When they were bought out he was left with a vast sum. I bankroll de Vergy Fine Wines, that's all. I swear, if Philip's been doing something underhand, it's nothing to do with me.'

Annabella looked upset, but not as upset as she should have looked upon hearing such accusations. But what she said might be the truth. Nothing Paulette could think of gave it the lie. Even Annabella's presence at the warehouse on the day of the fire might be explicable. Ruddock had left last, while Annabella might not have known about the brandy.

'And what about Alan Sowerby?' Paulette eventually asked.

'Alan died of food poisoning. That's all there is to it. Philip wouldn't murder him.'

'But I'm afraid he probably did.'

'No—' Annabella started, then checked herself.

'There's a lot of evidence,' Paulette said gently. 'Susan's pretty good at what she does, and I've seen Destroying Angel growing in the woods around Choray.'

'You've been to Choray?' Annabella asked, looking up sharply at Paulette.

'We've been everywhere,' Paulette confirmed. 'Susan's been through the warehouse debris. I've been to Choray and spoken to Christian Charrier. We've taken samples both from the co-op and from Chez Emil, who you used to supply. Oswald MacNaughton has tasted them and sent them for analysis. Believe me, Annabella, we've been thorough.'

'So, why are you telling me all this?'

Paulette took a deep breath. 'Because... because I couldn't bear to think of you in prison,' she stuttered, blushing just a little. 'When we played together you were so skilled, so sensitive to my needs... I just didn't want you...' Paulette fell silent, smiling awkwardly in her growing embarrassment.

Annabella looked into her eyes, her expression suddenly tender. For a long moment neither female spoke.

'I promise, I know nothing about this business,' Annabella eventually said, 'but I can hardly ignore all the evidence you seem to have discovered. Look, sit down and we'll talk. I badly need a drink.'

Paulette accepted one too, but for all her infatuation with the beautiful, dominant Annabella, she made very sure that the woman took the first sip of wine.

Chapter Eleven

Susan struggled futilely in her bonds. Paulette had made a thorough job of tying her, using the combination of handcuffs and belt to ensure she could do nothing more than squirm slowly along on her side. The fact that her head had been bagged added to her problems, making it impossible to see what she was doing. At first she tried her best to get free, wriggling and writhing, but to no avail. Then she lay pondering her predicament for a long while.

It was obvious Paulette had gone to warn Annabella of her impending arrest, leaving Susan in helpless bondage until Annabella was away. Although furious with Paulette, she was also worried for her safety. It was possible, if unlikely, that Annabella would harm Paulette. More likely was that she would tell Ruddock that they were about to be arrested. Ruddock, already in the frame for murder, might well decide to silence Paulette. If the news reached Ruddock that the police had accepted Fire Ghost's confession, then he might still think he could get clean away if he could get rid of both of them. True, Oswald MacNaughton might still bring the case down on Ruddock's head, but that would be little consolation for her and Paulette.

Fired by this unpleasant possibility, Susan began to squirm again in earnest, this time not in an attempt to get free, but in the hope of reaching the phone which was on the living room floor.

She had managed to fall off the end of the bed and crawl as far as the lounge door when the phone rang. She stopped, unable to do more than listen to the answering machine.

'Good evening,' a well-modulated voice said after Paulette's cheeky message of welcome, 'this is Lydia Torrington at Jacob's Barn. You called earlier to ask if Alan Sowerby visited us last month. The waitress who answered your call has been a little concerned that she wasn't very helpful, so I'm just ringing to confirm that he did, on the eleventh of August... er... that's it, really.'

The machine clicked off, leaving the flat in silence and Susan in a cold sweat. If Sowerby had been well enough to visit a restaurant in Chelmsford on the eleventh of August, then he very definitely had not been poisoned with Destroying Angel on the eighth. She had read the description of the lethal toadstool's effects often enough to be sure that, three days after ingestion, Sowerby should have been suffering what appeared to be severe food poisoning as the cocktail of toxins which the horrible thing contained worked on his system. Instead, he'd driven to Chelmsford and devoured an expensive meal. It could only mean that he'd been poisoned *after* the eleventh, which in turn probably meant immediately after Annabella de Vergy's return from France.

Susan renewed her struggles, squirming inch by inch across the floor until her head bumped against the telephone. After more contortions she managed to get her fingers to the thing, remove the receiver, and feel out Paul Berner's number on the buttons. Wriggling frantically, she managed to turn until the receiver was near her head. For a moment she heard Berner demanding to know who was ringing, then the line went dead. She tried again, this time using the tip of her nose to re-establish the connection. Again she heard his questioning voice. Unable to do more than mumble, she prayed Berner would have the sense to realise something was wrong and find out who was trying to call him. Five times she repeated the procedure, only then rolling to the side to lie exhausted on the carpet.

Paul Berner replaced the receiver and reached for his jacket. The quick check told him the calls were coming from Susan's number, and could only mean that she was in some sort of trouble. Biting off more than she could chew seemed to be something she was good at, yet he felt a definite sense of obligation towards her, following the foul-up with Joe Cooper's boys.

A fast drive took him to Susan's flat. He got out of his car and looked and listened cautiously for anything unusual. There was nothing obviously wrong, so he made his way carefully up the stairs to her door. It was closed but not locked. Nor did it show any signs of having been forced. Puzzled, he pushed it open and peered inside. Nothing appeared to be amiss and there were no unusual sounds. He went in, and then stopped short as he looked into the living room.

Susan was lying on the floor, naked and in tight bondage. Her wrists were strapped into the small of her back and immobilised by handcuffs, and her thighs were pulled up tight to her chest and strapped in place. A linen bag covered her head. She appeared to be totally helpless.

He paused, wondering what the hell was going on. The phone was near her head and off the hook. Other than that the room was as it should be. He wondered if she'd been attacked and left tied up, but there was no sign of a struggle. It actually appeared to be bondage of an erotic nature, and it gradually dawned on him that it must be a very elaborate sex-game intended for his participation and pleasure.

Susan's flatmate had obviously put her in the bondage and left her for him – certainly, there was no way she could have put herself in such a position. The apparently desperate phone calls were clearly intended to increase Susan's own fantasy and heighten the enjoyment of the game. And the open door provided the conclusive proof.

Well, if sex in bondage was what she wanted, then sex

in bondage she was what she would get!

Berner surmised he was supposed to be the white knight come to rescue her, only to get turned on by her naked vulnerability and take advantage of it before letting her go. It was a role he had no difficulty in falling into, and he intended to take full advantage of the situation before untying her.

'Kinky bitch,' he muttered as he started to undo his trousers.

The flatmate would probably be out all night, but if she did return he'd be more than happy to involve her in the little game. He undressed slowly, admiring Susan's nude body. She squirmed and mumbled throughout, obviously enjoying her helplessness.

When naked, Berner knelt and laid a hand on the silky sweep of her hip, the sudden contact making her writhe and moan all the more. 'My, my, you are turned on, Susie. I'll have to make sure I don't disappoint you, not that I've ever disappointed a lady before.' He grinned smugly at the thought of his own immense sexual prowess and surveyed the length of her tightly trussed body. 'I must say this is a very nice treat, Susie. A little thank you for all my help?'

Her squirming became more pronounced. Still, there was no need to hurry; the more turned on she got the better. And the novelty of the hood made his cock throb powerfully; no need to remove that while he enjoyed himself. He began to explore her body with one hand, while nursing his bursting erection with the other. Her position accentuated the swell of her hips and thrust her bottom out in smooth curves of creamy white flesh. He stroked and pinched, and then remembered her predilection for spanking and began to smack her. The flesh reddened quickly, bouncing and quivering under his slaps. He started with his fingertips, then used a cupped hand to cover more of her unprotected flesh and produce a satisfying retort as he spanked her.

By the time her whole bottom was an even warm pink, he could resist the temptation no longer. He crouched over her, and Susan tensed as he rubbed the bulbous helmet against her juicy opening, and then pushed until he sank smoothly in to the hilt. Susan's pussy was warm and tight, encasing his cock beautifully in a gripping sheath. He took his weight on straightened arms and began to fuck her, moving with long, slow strokes.

Their position soon became uncomfortable, and so he rolled her onto her knees without interrupting his steady rhythm. Susan squirmed so much she almost dislodged him, and her muffled expletives grew in volume until he was sure the neighbours would hear, but her unreserved passion merely increased his own and drove him on to screw her harder and faster.

'Bloody hell, but you're a wild one!' he panted, his exertions causing the sweat to sting his eyes.

After a frantic effort Susan suddenly fell limp beneath him, and lay breathing deeply and sighing inside the hood. Her hips twisted and her buttocks ground back against him, and he knew she was close to coming. He was relieved for the respite, and settled down to a steady pumping rhythm, savouring the sight of her spread bottom and his glistening cock sliding in and out of her. As Susan began to shudder in the throes of a powerful orgasm, he gripped her hips, pulled her tight against his groin, and ejaculated deep inside her vagina. His release was so powerful he slumped onto her back, and they rolled, exhausted, onto the carpet.

Ted Gage sat at his desk, watching the sun set over London. He held Paul Eady's confession, and he was sure there was something wrong with it. The descriptions of the first four fires were accurate to his own memory and read like a story from a children's adventure book. Eady was evidently proud of what he had done and the way he had managed to elude the police.

The fifth and sixth fires, however, were described in much less detail, particularly the fifth. The seventh was better, but still a far cry from the first four. Possibly he had got bored with writing – but then why make the last one more detailed? Eady had also described his eighth attempt in great detail, even saying he'd had an accomplice who'd got cold feet and failed to show up. Of course, the three fires that had been described less well were also the ones Susan MacQuillan had insisted were someone else's work. Indeed, she still did, or so Paul Berner said.

It was the description of the fifth fire that really bothered Gage. He cast his mind back to the events at the World of Pine furniture warehouse. The petrol bomb had been thrown across the Lee canal, a fairly impressive throw and one of the things that had made him think Susan MacQuillan's theory about canal boats might be correct. Gage flicked back the pages and re-read Eady's description.

I threw the bomb at the window and it went right in. It went up like a rocket and I had to step back smartish...

The description made no sense. On the far side of the canal Eady would have been completely safe. Gage remembered the fishermen he had seen the next morning. There had been no debris or scorch-marks on the bank opposite the warehouse. Eady was lying.

With his temper already beginning to boil, he marched out of his office. Downstairs, the station was moderately quiet. Gage made straight for the cells. With a nod to the duty sergeant, he took the keys and went into Eady's cell.

Paul Eady was asleep, curled up on the cell bed. He looked dejected, a lot of his cocky attitude worn away by his time in the cell. This time, there was no duty solicitor and no tape. Gage decided to handle Eady the way he felt the dangerous little bastard ought to be handled.

He shook the little arsehole awake. Eady shrank back and cowered against the wall beneath Gage's furious and unexpected renewal of questioning.

'All right, all right!' he sputtered, putting his hands up to protect his face from the Inspector's raised fist. 'I did four, all right! I just said I done the last three!'

'You wanker!' Gage snarled. 'I'm going to throw the fucking book at you! Are you sure you're telling the fucking truth now?!'

'Yeah! Yeah, I swear! I wasn't even there for the fifth one! I ain't never been there! I just said I done it to look good!'

Gage let go of Eady's collar and stepped back a pace. He had to cool his temper or he risked getting himself into trouble. 'You little wanker,' he spat again as he took some deep breaths and gradually calmed down.

Eady looked up at him sheepishly. 'I – I tell you what though,' he offered cautiously, 'I reckon I saw the bloke what did the last one at that carpet place.'

'Oh yeah?'

'Yeah. That's near where I live, which is why I never did one around there. I heard the fire engines and saw the flames. I wanted a look, so I ran along the canal. You see, I knew I was all right if I didn't go on the roads. Anyway, there was this boat, right, going along the canal. It must have been two in the morning. There was a bloke in it, on his own. I reckon he's got to be the one who done it.'

'Can you describe him?'

'I only saw him for a second, and it was dark. There was a little light on the boat, though, and I reckon he had red hair and a really red face.'

'Ruddock!' Gage snarled. Of all the irate victims of arson, Ruddock had been the rudest shit he'd ever had to deal with. Arresting Ruddock would be an absolute pleasure, and he had no intention of waiting until morning to enjoy that pleasure.

'Paul! You moron!' Susan yelled the instant she managed to spit the red panties out of her mouth. 'I'm not tied here for your perverted benefit, you idiot! Paulette's in danger! We have to get to her!'

'Eh?' Berner responded blankly, the conceited leer vanishing immediately as he realised he might just have been very foolish. He suddenly felt incredibly stupid, squatting naked with a bag and a scarf in his hands, and his shrivelled penis hanging uselessly between his thighs.

'Untie me,' she snapped. 'Jesus, Paul, talk about having your brain in your backside.'

They dressed hurriedly as Susan blurted out what she now knew. With every breathless word Berner became increasingly frightened that his stupidity and his ego might have unthinkable consequences for Paulette. If anything happened to her as a result of his actions – or lack of them…

Within minutes they were in his car and speeding towards Annabella de Vergy's house.

Ted Gage hammered on Philip Ruddock's front door. Sergeant Yates stood behind him, a warrant card in his hand. The door opened and Ruddock stood there, his expression a cocktail of concern and belligerence.

'Philip Ruddock,' Gage stated with relish, 'I am arresting you on suspicion of…'

Ruddock's whole demeanour quickly became one of weary resignation as Gage read him his rights.

'Okay,' he said once Gage had finished, his voice betraying a tiredness and strain that Gage had not expected. 'I burnt the warehouse, and the other two as well. You can book me for fraud as well, but not murder. That wasn't me. I had nothing to do with it.'

'The murder of Alan Sowerby?' Gage asked curiously, remembering Susan MacQuillan's suspicions.

'Yes,' Ruddock sighed, 'but it's not me you want, and I can prove it.'

'Who then?'

'Miss Annabella bloody de Vergy.'

'Look,' Annabella said, 'we had better sort this out. We'll drive over to Susan's and untie the poor girl, and then we'd better call the police. Then my innocence can be quickly proven and this nonsense settled once and for all. Just let me fetch a few things and we'll go.'

She and Paulette had discussed every detail of the investigation and the girl was totally convinced that Annabella knew absolutely nothing of any of it. She had never been more than a figurehead at de Vergy Fine Wines, supplying the money to back it and appearing at the more public functions. Philip Ruddock had done everything else, and whatever charges there were to answer to would be laid at his door. Paulette felt a great sense of relief that her faith in Annabella had been justified.

They took Annabella's Jaguar, making the trip to Susan's flat in minutes. Paulette climbed the stairs and unlocked the door, calling Susan's name as she went through to the bedroom, although she didn't expect a coherent response from her friend.

Susan wasn't there.

'That's very odd,' Paulette said over her shoulder to Annabella, who had followed and now stood close behind her. 'She must have managed to get free. It can't have been easy.'

'Never mind,' Annabella said, her tone suddenly hardening. 'I'm sure she'll be back soon, and then we can finally conclude this little problem.'

Paulette felt an icy chill run down her spine, but as she turned something solid caught her a glancing blow across the temple, and she slumped to the floor as the room went black and her legs folded beneath her.

Berner stood back from the front of Annabella de Vergy's brooding house. 'Nobody here,' he decided, looking up at the dark and sinister windows.

'But we've got to get in there,' Susan insisted. 'Paulette could be in real trouble!'

'It's not that simple,' Berner said. 'We can't just go around breaking into people's homes. We're not in—'

'You owe her, Paul,' she cut him off. 'And if anything happens to her I'll do all I can to see you pay!'

The squad car he'd requested only five minutes earlier pulled up just then. Two uniformed constables got out, one of them following Berner's order and fetching the ram from the boot.

The door gave way on the third blow, bursting inwards in a shower of splinters. As they entered the house, DI Gage and Sergeant Yates arrived.

Gage and Berner compared notes and updated each other on the latest developments while Susan, Yates, and the constables searched the building.

Nobody was there.

Something made Susan linger in the kitchen. A pleasant but faint smell was just discernible, and she immediately recognised it as the scent of the powder she had used to dry Paulette after her bath.

She rushed through to where Berner and Gage were still talking. 'They were here!' she exclaimed. 'And not so long ago!'

'Just a minute please,' Gage snapped impatiently. 'We've important matters to discuss here.'

Susan hopped agitatedly from one foot to the other. 'But Paulette was here, I know she was!'

'I asked you to be quiet!' Gage turned on her again.

She looked from him to Berner, who gave her a sheepish shrug of apology and then returned his attention to his boss.

'I don't believe you two!' she shrieked, and then dashed

out of the house to Berner's car, knowing he had left the keys in the ignition.

'I am genuinely sorry to have to do this Paulette,' Annabella de Vergy said as her trussed victim struggled on the floor. 'You really are rather sweet, but you must understand that I simply can't have people running around the country who know as much as you do.'

Paulette's head throbbed abominably, and she couldn't speak. She was bound and gagged on the floor with the same handcuffs and belt as she had used on Susan.

Annabella sat down, placed her leather bag on the coffee-table, and took a bottle of over-strength vodka from it. She was wearing a pair of pretty gloves, the significance of which were all too ominous.

'Don't worry, my dear, it won't hurt too much,' she continued. 'I imagine you'll just go quietly to sleep in a drunken stupor. It's quite appropriate, I suppose, that you and your friend Susan should die in a particularly mucky sex accident. These things happen for real, you know. I don't suppose the police will look too closely, especially when they discover what you and Susan got up to together.'

Paulette squirmed in terror as Annabella produced a large syringe from her bag.

'Of course, with Sowerby it had to be food,' de Vergy said, as casual as ever despite her murderous intentions. 'Mark you, he was an annoying little man and deserved to die in pain. He was always pestering me with pompous little love poems and absurd protestations about how pure his feelings for me were. I tried to get rid of him gently, but he wouldn't take the hint, so he had to go. You were right about me picking up the Destroying Angel in Choray. Christian Charrier showed me where it grows in a wood he owns. Now there's a man worth sleeping with, although not my personal taste. I bet he liked you, though. Did you let him get you over his barrel? Yes, I would imagine you

226

did.'

Annabella had filled the syringe with vodka, leaving the bottle nearly half-empty. 'I'm sorry, my dear Paulette, but I have to do this...'

Susan left the car still running in the middle of the street and ran up the stairs to her flat. She fumbled with the key in the lock, burst into the living room, and stopped dead. Paulette was lying on the floor, bound and helpless. Annabella de Vergy stood over her, an enormous syringe in one gloved hand. A half-empty bottle of vodka stood on the coffee-table.

'Ah, so you've come back,' she said. 'Excellent... it will look so much more convincing if you are dealt with at the same time. You won't escape, Susan, so you may as well make it easy for yourself and submit. I promise it won't hurt.'

Annabella de Vergy stepped forward, tall, lithe and commanding. She reached out as Susan edged back, and then she doubled up with shock and agony etched on her face as Susan's fist sunk into her solar plexus. Her head snapped back and she crumpled as Susan's second sweeping blow caught her on the chin. Never allowing her opponent a second to recover, Susan twisted, snatched up the vodka bottle, and drove it down as hard as she could on the vile woman's head.

Annabella de Vergy slumped to the floor, unconscious. Susan turned to Paulette, breathing heavily, and then turned back at the sound of footsteps running up the stairs. Berner and Gage burst into the room. Susan dropped the shattered vodka bottle and managed a weak smile as they stared open-mouthed at the incredible scene before them.

227

More exciting titles available from Chimera

1-901388-09-3*	Net Asset	*Pope*
1-901388-18-2*	Hall of Infamy	*Virosa*
1-901388-21-2*	Dr Casswell's Student	*Fisher*
1-901388-28-X*	Assignment for Alison	*Pope*
1-901388-39-5*	Susie Learns the Hard Way	*Quine*
1-901388-42-5*	Sophie & the Circle of Slavery	*Culber*
1-901388-41-7*	Bride of the Revolution	*Amber*
1-901388-44-1*	Vesta – Painworld	*Pope*
1-901388-45-X*	The Slaves of New York	*Hughes*
1-901388-46-8*	Rough Justice	*Hastings*
1-901388-47-6*	Perfect Slave Abroad	*Bell*
1-901388-48-4*	Whip Hands	*Hazel*
1-901388-50-6*	Slave of Darkness	*Lewis*
1-901388-51-4*	Savage Bonds	*Beaufort*
1-901388-52-2*	Darkest Fantasies	*Raines*
1-901388-53-0*	Wages of Sin	*Benedict*
1-901388-55-7*	Slave to Cabal	*McLachlan*
1-901388-56-5*	Susie Follows Orders	*Quine*
1-901388-57-3*	Forbidden Fantasies	*Gerrard*
1-901388-58-1*	Chain Reaction	*Pope*
1-901388-61-1*	Moonspawn	*McLachlan*
1-901388-59-X*	The Bridle Path	*Eden*
1-901388-65-4*	The Collector	*Steel*
1-901388-66-2*	Prisoners of Passion	*Dere*
1-901388-67-0*	Sweet Submission	*Anderssen*
1-901388-69-7*	Rachael's Training	*Ward*
1-901388-71-9*	Learning to Crawl	*Argus*
1-901388-36-0*	Out of Her Depth	*Challis*
1-901388-68-9*	Moonslave	*McLachlan*
1-901388-72-7*	Nordic Bound	*Morgan*
1-901388-80-8*	Cauldron of Fear	*Pope*
1-901388-73-5*	Managing Mrs Burton	*Aspen*
1-901388-77-8*	The Piano Teacher	*Elliot*
1-901388-25-5*	Afghan Bound	*Morgan*
1-901388-76-X*	Sinful Seduction	*Benedict*
1-901388-70-0*	Babala's Correction	*Amber*
1-901388-06-9*	Schooling Sylvia	*Beaufort*
1-901388-78-6*	Thorns	*Scott*

All **Chimera** titles are available from your local bookshop or newsagent, or direct from our mail order department. Please send your order with your credit card details, a cheque or postal order (made payable to *Chimera Publishing Ltd*) to: **Chimera Publishing Ltd., Readers' Services, PO Box 152, Waterlooville, Hants, PO8 9FS**. Or call our **24 hour telephone/fax credit card hotline: +44 (0)23 92 646062** (Visa, Mastercard, Switch, JCB and Solo only).

UK & BFPO - Aimed delivery within three working days.
·   A delivery charge of £3.00.
·   A charge of £0.20 per item, up to a maximum of five items.
For example, a customer ordering two books for delivery within the UK will be charged £3.00 delivery + £0.40 items charge, totalling a delivery charge of £3.40. The maximum delivery cost for a UK customer is £4.00. Therefore if you order more than five items for delivery within the UK you will not be charged more than a total of £4.00 postage.

Western Europe - Aimed delivery within five to ten working days.
·   A delivery charge of £3.00.
·   A charge of £1.25 per item.
For example, a customer ordering two books for delivery to W. Europe will be charged £3.00 delivery + £2.50 items charge, totalling a delivery charge of £5.50.

USA - Aimed delivery within twelve to fifteen working days.
·   A delivery charge of £3.00.
·   A charge of £2.00 per item.
For example, a customer ordering two books for delivery to the USA will be charged £3.00 delivery + £4.00 item charge, totalling a delivery charge of £7.00.

Rest of the World - Aimed delivery within fifteen to twenty-two working days.
·   A delivery charge of £3.00.
·   A charge of £2.75 per item.
For example, a customer ordering two books for delivery to the ROW will be charged £3.00 delivery + £5.50 item charge, totalling a delivery charge of £8.50.

For a copy of our free catalogue please write to

Chimera Publishing Ltd
Readers' Services
PO Box 152
Waterlooville
Hants
PO8 9FS

or email us at
info@chimerabooks.co.uk

or purchase from our range of superbly erotic titles at
www.chimerabooks.co.uk

*Titles £5.99. **£7.99. **All others £6.99**

Another sizzling story by the author of
Destroying Angel

Rough Justice
by
Sam Hastings

Detective Constable Susan MacQuillan achieves promotion to her dream post – Inspector in the Carapine Islands. On arrival reality proves very far from what she had imagined. The locals treat her with a friendly contempt that quickly leads to a bare-bottomed spanking over the local matriarch's knee. Nor do the local criminals – a drug cartel – treat her with any more respect, viewing her body as a toy and her determination to bring them to justice as a joke. Only when she destroys one of their boats do they begin to take her seriously, and things take on a much darker complexion.

1-901388-46-8 ● £5.99

Chimera Publishing Ltd

PO Box 152
Waterlooville
Hants
PO8 9FS

www.chimerabooks.co.uk

info@chimerabooks.co.uk

www.chimera-freedating.com

***

Sales and Distribution in the USA and Canada

Client Distribution Services, Inc
193 Edwards Drive
Jackson
TN 38301
USA

***

Sales and Distribution in Australia

Dennis Jones & Associates Pty Ltd
19a Michellan Ct
Bayswater
Victoria
Australia 3153